BOUND

The *Catalytic* Rose

ARIANA KEDDIE

Bound – The Catalytic Rose

Book 2 (Bound by Infidelity trilogy)

Published by Ilomilo Press 2020

ISBN: 9780648836711 (eBook Edition)

ISBN: 9780648836728 (Paperback Edition)

Ariana Keddie asserts her right to be identified as the author.

This book is a work of fiction derived from the imagination of the author. For the sake of realism certain locales, business names, events and places have been used, but have been done so in a fictitious manner. Any resemblance to a true event or business is purely coincidental. Any character or name resembling a person, alive or dead, is also purely coincidental.

The contents here within are explicit and adult in nature. Some scenes or themes may affect sensitive readers. Reader discretion is advised.

Draft edit – Chelsea Kuhel MS Editing Services

Final edit – Marni MacRae and Julia Davies

Final proof read – Amber Kleesh and Joanne Thompson

Cover design by David Prendergast @ Reedsy. Photo complements of Pixabay

1

———

YOUTH

I'm covered in perspiration. My joggers have caused blisters and my heart is striking so hard against my ribs, I'm surprised it hasn't given up on me entirely. Stripping off my running clothes to my underwear, I plunge into the freezing pool. This gives my body even more to deal with, but also makes it's impossible to cry. Last night's fight with Gerard had brought up memories of a past I'd successfully buried. All night I'd tossed and turned. Then every time I started to drift off to sleep, the memory of Gerard's forceful act jolted me awake. Although he seemed remorseful, I'm sure it was a deliberate act to traumatize me to my senses. His cruel behavior and malevolent words, a reminder—I am beneath him, and his love is something I should be grateful for.

I stay submerged until my lungs burn, and even then, once I break the surface, I only snatch a quick gulp of air before going under again. Exhaling, I sink to the bottom of the pool. For an indulgent second, I wonder what Gerard would do. How he'd react if he found me dead on the tiled floor, my body blue and lifeless but my eyes wide and haunting. A huge part of me wants to punish him with my death. But now I'm questioning, would he even care?

Even immersed in frigid water I can't get Gerard's voice out of my head. "I needed to pay Alex to have sex with you again, Paige. That's right—don't look so surprised. Do I need to remind you, you were a revenge fuck to begin with?"

I groan into the wet and curl into a fetal position before what's left of my rational mind slaps me into action. Springing from the bottom of the pool I burst through the water to suck in air so I can let out the trapped anguish via a sob.

"Don't you see it? You're getting yourself attached to a man who is not only a thief and a player, but he's also unscrupulous. Do you honestly think he's a good catch? He's got nothing, Paige. For Christ's sake, the man's been in prison. Is that who you want to spend your life with? A lowlife who will never love you or give you what I have. In some sick way, I think Alex must remind you of Carlos or something."

I dunk my head and scream into the water to stifle the noise. Gerard never really forgave me. He's punishing me. That's what this is. How dare he even say Carlos and Alex in the same sentence? The thought of me being attracted to Alex because of Carlos, makes me want to scrub myself. To stop the relentless chatter and flashbacks, I do laps until my arms are screaming and my heart gives off shooting pain. Exhausted, I roll onto my back and float, staring into the early morning sky. For a moment, I forget about the disgusting truth and just let my mind go numb.

~

Hours later, Gerard finds me sitting on the edge of the pool, dangling my feet in the water with nothing on but my underwear. I must look like a wax figure, given my blood is near frozen in my veins. Plastered all over my shoulders, my hair is like a dripping shawl and I'm staring off into space.

When Gerard sees me, he grabs a towel and puts it around my shivering body before pulling me to my feet.

"Paige, honey, what are you doing?"

"I have a headache," I whisper.

"So, you thought you'd go for a swim?" He cups my face with his warm hands then pulls me into a hug and rubs my back vigorously. I stand lifeless in his arms. "Come inside, you need a shower, you're freezing."

"I don't want a shower. I need to figure it out first. It needs to make sense." I don't even try stopping the tears anymore. Warm, they slide down my cheeks and land on my lips.

"What, what do you need to figure out? How long have you been out here? Come inside." He looks about the yard, most likely concerned the neighbors might see.

"I can't work out what's worse. What you did to me last night, or that you needed to pay someone to sleep with me, or maybe even that Alex took the money, or—or that you've just been pretending to love me because my past disgusts you. You're punishing me, and now there's someone else, isn't there? Why manipulate me into a threesome if... No. I know. You want me to be jealous. That's part of the punishment too. Isn't it?"

"I beg your pardon?" He falls away and steps back, his hands going on his hips. Dressed in his boxers and tee from last night, I figure it must still be relatively early. "Is that why you've been sitting out here, you think I have someone else in my life, that I manipulated the three-way to even some score?"

"Well, did you? Is there another woman? And is she the

reason you turned my romp with Alex into a sordid… sordid —I don't even know what to call it… Sexcapade?"

"Look, Paige." He comes closer and takes hold of my arms, but I shrug him off.

"Are you seeing someone else?" I demand.

"Don't be ridiculous. I love you. Christ, I just wanted to see you—enjoy yourself, that's why I paid him."

"But what you did last night—what were you trying to do? Why were you saying all that stuff? You think I'm a whore," I scream, not caring if the neighbors hear. "You promised you wouldn't hold it against me but you do."

"I just wanted us to have an understanding, that's all." Gerard grits his teeth. "Now get inside and have a goddamn shower and discuss this like a fucking adult." He doubles up his insult by grabbing my arm like I'm a child. I pull away and storm off ahead of him.

Twenty minutes later, I come back downstairs in jogging gear again, still seething and intent on running away from my muddled thoughts—and Gerard. He's sitting at the dining table babbling on his phone about a stupid client and looking concerned. There's a breakfast of French toast and juice spread out for us, but the smell just makes me want to puke.

"Well, that's not what he told me." Gerard, hunched over his phone on loud speaker, glances up when I enter. When I go for the door he shakes his head, so I wait.

"I need to go. I'm having breakfast with my gorgeous wife." He smiles but I don't smile back. Gerard ends his call and places the phone on the table. "Feel better?" He picks up his cutlery and gestures for me to sit.

"Not really."

"Please, sit down. Have some breakfast with me and we'll talk."

"I'm not hungry. I'm just going to run."

"No. You'll have breakfast with me, now sit down." His tone is a little firmer, but I still don't make the move to sit down.

"I'm—not—hungry."

"Sit, fucking, down," he snaps.

Stunned, I stare at him for a moment. Who is this man?

Using his knife, he tears into the toast looking like a demented med student dissecting a cadaver. Realizing I'm making things worse, or he might even turn the knife on me, I sit. I miss Gerard's genuine smile, his electric eyes. I miss my husband and want him back. But he's gone. And really, it's me who's to blame.

"I'm sorry I told you about Alex, but you needed to know the truth, Paige."

"Most people pay a lover to get out the way. Why did you need to pay Alex to join in on the threesome?"

"Because he wouldn't agree." He raises his eyebrows looking nonchalant then takes a mouthful of French toast with maple syrup and strawberries. Trickles of fruit pulp escape, leaving a mess on his lips before he licks it away. I can't understand how he can even eat. Watching him makes me feel putrid inside.

"But why wouldn't he want to do it?" My disappointment is audible. Gerard knits his brow and jabs his fork at my plate, wanting me to eat. "I thought..."

"What?" he snaps. "That he was in love with you? Oh, come on, Paige, seriously? How many times do I have to tell you? He's a player. He had sex with you in the first place because he's a spiteful, jealous little shit who wanted to get back at me. And some men just don't go back for seconds.

I'm sorry, but it's true." Gerard shrugs. "So, I had to pay him. It's no big deal and it was certainly worth it."

Shaking my head, I pick up my fork and stab at a strawberry, trying to make sense of what Gerard is saying because in the back of my mind, I'm reliving the private moments Alex and I had shared, making it difficult to know whether Gerard is playing mind games with me or Alex is toying with me, period.

"The way I see it…" Gerard continues,

"The way you see it? No! The way I see it is that I made a mistake and then you…"

"Shut up." Gerard callously cuts me off. "Yes, you made a mistake, you fucked a man who is a player. He was always out to use you. I simply took advantage of that, so sue me for wanting to see you fucking come. When are you going to understand how ridiculous this is? It's just sex for God's sake."

"Just sex?"

"Honestly, Paige." He pauses and shakes his head slightly for maximum intimidation. "I had hoped you'd be more open-minded about this. Christ, I didn't think you'd get attached. Were you honestly thinking of trading this for him?" He gestures around the room with his cutlery, looking mystified, then chuckles.

"I didn't say that. All I want, is for things to go back to normal." I place down my fork with the strawberry still attached.

"Normal is boring. Most women would jump at the opportunity of having their cake and eating it too."

"Having too much cake makes you fat and unattractive to your husband, eventually."

"Is that what you're afraid of? That I will discard you?" Gerard asks, leaving the table to pick up the newspaper he has spotted outside the French doors.

"I know you will. After a while, it will gnaw at you. You'll see me as a slut. You already do. Sex should be special. A one-on-one loving experience."

"Well, you changed all that when you cheated on me, didn't you?" Gerard glosses over the front page of the paper. I can't believe how matter-of-fact he is. It's like he's detached himself.

"What's that supposed to mean?"

"It means our relationship has become something more complex now. And come to think of it, I don't know why you're angry at me. I'm the one who should be upset. You admitted last night you have strong feelings for my brother. How do you think that makes me feel?"

"Stepbrother," I mumble.

He gives me a sarcastic look. He's right though. If the situation were reversed, I know I'd have trouble looking at Gerard again, let alone forgive him.

"And as far as discarding you." Gerard smiles, his muscles making the movement but there is no warmth in the gesture. "Not a chance. We made vows. Now, all I need is your willingness to grow up and accept the changes."

"What changes? And what do you mean grow up? This has got nothing to do with maturity. What happened was stupidity. I hate myself for being so easy and giving in now."

Gerard drops the newspaper on the table and glowers at me. "We both know you wanted to sleep with Alex again. So, you can stop the charade."

"I knew you'd end up holding this against me."

"I'm not holding anything against you. I'm just speaking the truth."

"Okay, great, fine. If that's how you want it. Set up another date with Alex. Pay him for all I care. You can watch, I'll be the dirty little girl you want me to be. Let's do it every night. Ask him to move in. Whatever. I don't care."

"Now you're sounding vindictive. You need time to cool down. I understand you're hurt about Alex, disappointed he doesn't care like you hoped. Now please, eat. It will make you feel better, and maybe it's best we keep Alex out of it then. We'll find someone else." His phone rings again. "I need to take this, Paige, I'm already late." Assuming he gets the last say in all this, Gerard gets to his feet. But like hell there'll be anyone else.

"Who's Jolene?"

"Excuse me?" He takes a step back stunned then rolls his eyes at the ceiling. "That prick is trying to ruin me."

"Who is she?"

He glares at me with his phone still ringing in his hand and without answering it or me, he slaps his cell on the table and walks straight out the French doors, mumbling to himself. I don't know what to do. Should I follow or leave him alone? Standing, I see he is heading for the gazebo. He must feel my gaze because he turns and looks back.

After a few moments of questioning whether I should push the issue of Jolene, I zip up my jacket and follow him outside, tucking my hands under my armpits to stop them from shaking. When I'm close, I survey the dewy ground before settling my gaze on Gerard who is now sitting. He shakes his head and draws in a heavy breath.

"It was Alex who told you, wasn't it? Is that what you talk about while you work? Do you even work on the house or do you just fuck and then talk about me?"

I try swallowing, but I have no saliva.

"No, it's not, and yes we work. You can see for yourself, and I told you, I haven't had sex with Alex since the hotel." Which—is the truth.

"But you'd like to."

Ignoring him, I confess I overheard him and Alex the morning after Jenna's party.

He huffs loudly. "You were eavesdropping? Typical childish behavior."

I don't even need to nod because my flushed face is enough acknowledgment.

"How much did you hear?"

"Enough to know you didn't want me finding out about her."

Gerard keeps his eyes locked on me, his jaw balling at the edges before he clears his throat and looks away. "That's correct. Because you of all people should know I hate discussing my past." Clasping his hands, he rests his elbows on his knee and stares at the ground. "Alex shouldn't have even brought her up. The past belongs where it is. We've talked about that."

I slip onto the bench opposite him. "So, you're not seeing anyone? You're not living a double life?"

Gerard snaps his head up. "No, I'm not living a double life. Honestly, Paige. Where do you come up with such stupid ideas? She's of no relevance to us, that's why I didn't tell you."

"But who was she?"

Stalling again, he looks over the yard with a passive expression. I join him and realize how unkempt it appears. It's not just the fact that the weather has changed, and leaves are littered everywhere, but there are weeds in the gardens too, and I've been so preoccupied I haven't even cared.

"I suppose I need to hire a new gardener," Gerard says offhandedly, I'm sure out of spite. It's my punishment, but it's Alex who will suffer. When will I ever learn to keep my mouth shut? But then, he's just as much to blame, so why should I be concerned about him, anyway.

"You'll miss him."

"Not anymore," I reply.

"I think you're lying, but whatever."

"Are you going to tell me about Jolene?" I pester, because he's trying to distract me.

Gerard takes a deep breath then stands. Smiling or smirking, I can't tell, but he takes my chin in his hand and looks down into my face. "She is an ex-girlfriend who…"

"You mean the one you stole from Alex?"

Gerard huffs. "So you're taking Alex's word on this are you? She damn well came willingly, Paige. Then she claimed the baby was mine."

My mouth falls open. I twist my face out of his hand that feels more foreign than ever. "You have a child together?" I get to my feet, a hundred questions going through my mind. "Oh my God, you *are* living a double life." I'm so shocked, I shove him. Gerard stumbles backward then grabs my readying fists. I just want to punch him.

"A double life? The child is six years old, Paige."

"But you told me we wouldn't have children." How is that fair? I rip myself free from his vice-like grip.

"I told Jolene the same thing, and the stupid girl got herself pregnant, anyway."

My eyes spring wide open. "You abandoned her when she became pregnant?"

Gerard points a finger in my face. "Don't you dare judge me. She knew I didn't want children; she was trying to trap me." He turns on his heels and marches away, back toward the house. My mind is calculating the timing. They must have broken up just before we got together. Was I the cause? Is that why Alex has been messing with me?

"Why did you abandon them? Was it because of me?" I ask, chasing after him. Feeling so sick, my chest hurts. Please tell me it wasn't because of me. Not again.

Stopping, he faces me. "Because it turned out the child wasn't mine. Seems I attract sluts, doesn't it? Besides children are a nuisance."

"Children aren't a nuisance." Wait. Not his?

"Is that right, is it? Weren't you a nuisance to your father? Don't you ever stop to think that's why he left?"

Gerard may as well have physically punched me in the solar plexus because his comment winds me, forcing me to grab onto him. "That was a such a low blow, Gerard." My eyes burn, but I refuse to cry.

"I'm just stating that some adults find children a problem. I am one of those people. Now, I need to get ready for work." He sweeps his eyes around the yard again then lets his gaze fall on me, his brows raised. "Are we done here?" He tugs his arm free and stomps away.

"Gerard," I snap, making him stop in his tracks. "After all these years, why wouldn't you tell me about this?"

Gerard marches back and grabs me by the arm, starts pulling me along. "Jolene and her little girl are part of my life from a mistake I made with a stupid young woman. This," he waves a hand around our property then gestures to the house, "is us. Why would I burden you with that mess?"

"So why is Alex still in contact with her?"

"Gee, I don't know, Paige. Maybe he's still fucking in love with her. Look." He grits his teeth. "I was trying to make amends with Alex by giving him work. I thought I was doing the right thing. If you hadn't had sex with him in the first place, then we wouldn't even be having this stupid conversation. So, I think it's fair to say you're to blame that this is becoming so damn ridiculous."

"Did Jolene let you watch? Did you do that with her?"

"Why are you asking such moronic questions? No, I did not."

"You didn't." My voice waivers slightly.

"You and Jolene are—different."

"Or is it you were different with her?"

"Don't try to psychoanalyze me. It won't work. I love you, not Jolene, and that's all that matters."

"All that matters! Is that all you can say about it?"

"I need to get ready for work. I've been late enough these last few weeks, this bullshit needs to stop. Do you understand? You're my wife and I need you to work with me, not against me." Gerard yanks the door open and pushes me inside, the warmth is welcoming against the cold hard reality that I know nothing anymore.

Dismayed, I pull out a chair and sit down, watch as he walks away then climbs the stairs and I don't move the entire time it takes Gerard to get ready. Before I know it, he's standing in front of the French doors in his suit, his hand poised on the doorknob looking at me. For a moment we just stare at each other, my lips trembling and tears resting on my eyelids, just waiting until he leaves.

Putting down his briefcase, he marches out the room and moments later he returns with a piece of paper in his hand. He places it on the table then slides it in front of me. It's a signed check. My focus dart to him, searching for answers in his furrowed face.

"What's this for?"

"If you're so in love with Alex, I'd rather you leave. I mean, you're not the only fish in the sea, are you?"

"You want me to leave?"

"I didn't say that. I love you, I want you to stay, but if you're going to become intolerable, like screw men behind my back without an invitation for me, or regurgitate my mistakes to punish me, then you should leave."

So now I've become disposable. He explains nothing else, just walks away, shaking his head and mumbling to himself. Then he's straight onto his phone again as if the last twenty-four hours' revelations, change nothing at all.

2

HURT SOMEBODY

The second Gerard's car is out of sight, I'm sprinting down our drive and onto the road. By the time I reach Jenna's house, I'm out of breath and clutching onto my knees. Banging on the front door, I glance around the immaculate garden with its bordered edges and random outdoor art, wondering who their gardener is but hoping it's not Alex. Knowing Jenna, however, it's likely she's also proficient at gardening, making me sigh. I give the green-eyed monster in my head a good shaking down. This is not the time.

It seems to take forever for Jenna to answer the door but when she does she looks gorgeous, and instantly she annoys me. No wonder Alex had sex with her. I've no clue how a woman can get herself preened to perfection at this early hour of the morning. Jamie and Erica come to stand beside their mother at the door, looking equally charming in their school uniforms. How does she do it?

Concerned that I'm lost in my thoughts and ogling her children Jenna shoos them away. "Paige are you right?" she

13

asks, holding the door wider and I cop a whiff of what I think to be warm waffles and syrup. "Come in."

"No, I won't bother you for long. I was just wondering... Do you..." I peek over her shoulder. "Do you have Alex's phone number by any chance?"

Jenna's looks over her shoulder then comes onto the porch, pulling the door partially closed behind her, her brow creasing. "Why would you think I have Alex's number?"

I knew she was too drunk the other night to remember her admission. When I lean in closer, her perfume invades my senses. Something soft and delicate like talcum powder with a hint of floral. "You told me about the two of you at the party."

"What! I did?" A hand goes to her mouth before she pulls the door closed completely and folds her arms over her chest. She looks at the ground nodding, her tongue playing with her teeth.

"So, have you seen him lately?" I ask, curious if it's an ongoing fling.

"No, I haven't seen him since the dinner party, actually. Paige, I swear it's not something I normally do. I can't believe I told you. My God, was anyone else around at the time? I'm having trouble remembering anything from that night, except Nadal disappearing with that silly Jamison fellow, and we all thought they'd drowned themselves in the pool after challenging who was the better swimmer."

When she adds nothing more, she leaves me wondering where they did disappear to, if not to the pool.

"So, do you have Alex's number or not?" I ask, jiggling on the spot and throwing my eyes around as if any second Gerard will pull up in their driveway.

"Yes. You don't?"

"No, Gerard has it. I've never needed it."

"Oh." She looks confused and maybe a touch smug. When

I don't offer an explanation why I don't just ask Gerard, or why I don't have the number of a man I've been intimate with, she asks if I want it.

"If you don't mind, that would be super." Like duh. Come on, woman, hurry.

"Not at all. It's not like he's answering me. Maybe you can ask him to call me if you get ahold of him."

I swear, Paige, it's not something I normally do. Liar. I wonder if she realizes she's contradicting herself. Obviously, he's ignoring her calls.

She leaves me by the door to get her phone. Coming back onto the porch, she has her head down looking at her screen, presumably searching her contact list.

"Jenna," Nadal calls out from inside.

"I'm just at the door with Paige. Can you ask the children to pack their bags? I'll be with them in a minute," she shouts out behind her.

"Nadal's home? I'm sorry Jenna, I thought he'd be at work."

"The flu. Now he's stuck at home, and we'll be playing tag at the restaurant because I guarantee, I'll be next." She sounds overly cranky and I think about her rule and Annabel missing out on the dinner party because of it. Jenna might need to revise her scope and exclude friends of friends with colds because thinking about it, I was most likely the carrier. I shouldn't smirk, but I do.

She keeps scrolling, "Golly gosh, only happens when you're in a hurry. Ahh, here it is."

With my phone in hand, my finger poised, she is just about to tell me, when Nadal comes to the door.

"Ah Paige. You are out today early. How is your day?" he asks. Along with his congestion, his American translation sounds peculiar.

"I'm fine. Sorry to disturb everyone this early. I was just

after the phone number of Jenna's yoga instructors. I'm thinking of joining."

Nadal puts an arm around his wife and looks down at her phone. Both Jenna and I follow his gaze. The screen has gone blank. Thank God.

"Oh. All right. I will see the children to get ready for school." He kisses Jenna's temple. "Adiós, Paige."

"Thank you, Nadal darling." Jenna pulls the door closed after he goes.

"I'm sorry, Jenna. I don't want to get you in trouble." And I didn't. Despite my feelings, I'm not the malicious type.

"Don't worry about it. Like I said, I've got plenty of ammunition should he find out about Alex. Right, here it is," she announces, and again I'm wondering if she hears herself. Trying one minute to convince me she doesn't remember telling me about Alex, but it was in the same conversations she told me about Nadal. Jenna, Jenna tsk tsk, you're so full of lies. But then it would seem, aren't we all.

After reassuring her I would mention her to Alex, I get on my way. At the end of our road where there is a shady spot under a cluster of gigantic bamboo grass, I make my call to Alex. He answers on the third ring.

"Yo, Alex here."

"Hi, it's me."

"Ah, Princess, at last I have your number and you are where, when I'm expecting you here?"

"I'm not coming to help anymore, Alex. You were right yesterday—I need to catch up on my own work from now on." I swipe at the flies that keep trying to stick to my face. When there's no answer, I glance down at the screen, concerned we've been disconnected. "Are you there?" I ask, checking if he's still on the line.

"Yes. But I'm just wondering what's going on. Where are you?"

"Jogging."

"Paige? Is everything all right? You sound weird."

"Everything is fine. I just didn't get time to do my work last night after we finished so late, and I realize I don't have the spare time to help you anymore. I've got too many commitments as it is."

"Why are you lying? Has something happened with Gerard?" The annoyance in his tone surprises me.

I kick at a small ant hill and send hundreds of insects on the hunt.

"I'm not." Why does he have to be so damn astute? It's like he has a hidden camera on me or something. For a moment, I think about the game Sheree and I used to play, sending mind waves to each other, she from her room, and me in her dad's shed, testing if we were clairvoyant or telepathic. But that only ever seemed to work on her dad, and suddenly, I'm getting paranoid that Gerard knows exactly what I'm doing because he's there with Alex, making sure he sticks to the story he wants me to believe.

"Paige?"

"Have you spoken with him this morning?"

"No, should I have? What's going on?"

"Nothing, I was just wondering. Anyway, I just wanted to let you know, so you weren't waiting on me. I've got to go."

"Don't you dare hang up. Tell me what's going on."

"Gerard and I had an argument that blew out of proportion, that's all. But we sorted it out. I think we just got too drunk last night." I don't know if I should go into any more details. Alex was reluctant to talk about Jolene when I asked him, and I'm still questioning whether he and Gerard are playing me somehow.

Alex stays quiet on the other end, making me so crazy I can't help but get narky.

"You know, I needed to resort to getting your number

from Jenna this morning, which was embarrassing." My tone is deliberately tight. "It's odd really, that I don't have it, considering we had sex and all. And well, I had a guess you'd give it to *her*." I pause for a moment letting that sink in. When there's no response from him, I add, "Jenna said to say hello, and she hoped you had a good time the other night. She also said she'd love to hear from you, again."

"Did she?"

I wait in the uncomfortable silence for what seems like an eternity.

"I know about the two of you, and this time I am being selfish, because I need you to know that I know, so we can all stop pretending."

Still, he doesn't respond.

"Why did you have to tell her about us, Alex? You know I felt ashamed, and God knows who she'll tell."

Alex stays silent.

"Aren't you going to say anything?" I raise my voice.

"I don't know what to say. For one, I'm fucking stunned. I told Jenna jack shit about us, and two, I'm pissed she told you about me and her. That's not something you needed to know about. Christ, that neighborhood of yours, it's like, man!..." He leaves the rest unsaid.

"Anyway, I've got to go. I felt I owed you an explanation, that's all."

"No, you didn't. You wanted to confront me, and you have. Good for fucking you. Stop beating around the bush. Mean what you say and say what you mean. At least that way I'll know where I fuckin' stand."

"Gee, Alex, and that coming from you. How about you tell me what's really going on then? Who else are you having sex with and do you charge everyone or just my husband?"

Alex snorts. "Un-fucking believable. I'm not sure what Gerard told you, but it wasn't like that."

I hate that he sounds so sincere because not only am I questioning myself but I'm tearing up, and I'm sick of crying. I desperately want to believe I mean more to him than a business transaction. I kick at the ant hill, keeping quiet. Just listening to his silence through my AirPod, that is strangely comforting now.

"Paige, Jenna was just a quick fuck. She put it on me one morning when you were out, asked if I'd be interested in working for them, and then she was all over me, saying shit I couldn't ignore." He clears his throat. "I didn't know she was a close friend. I thought…"

"She's not, really, and I guess it shouldn't even matter. Like you said, you're a free agent. But it shocked me that Gerard had to pay you. I only agreed because I had feelings for you, and I thought… Even you said… Oh, I don't know what I thought or what I'm saying. It's just, Gerard needing to pay you to have sex with me after that first time, well—that's deflating," I mutter.

"Honestly, it's not how you think. You must know I care about you, and I had a good reason for taking the money."

"Yeah, well, it just means I've got a lot of thinking to do, that's all. Gerard's gone psycho on me. Look, I've got to go. I need to run to clear my head, then I'll be fine. Bye, Alex."

"Doing the six?" he asks, making me pause from disconnecting.

"Yes, doing the six, and then I've got some serious brown-nosing to do."

"Sounds interesting, can I watch?"

"Hilarious. Don't you start." I grumble. I'm thankful though, that he's at least trying to make me laugh. "Yesterday was the angriest I've ever heard Donnie and losing my job right now is the last thing I need."

"Are you sure you don't want to help out here anymore? It seemed like you were enjoying yourself."

"I was, but I don't think I can. I've pushed Gerard too far. The house is a mess. Not that I care, but I'm sure it's half the reason he was so irate last night," I say, absentmindedly.

"Irate, hey?"

"You know what I mean. Anyway, I need to go. There's a suspicious car doing its third pass. They're either planning an abduction or casing a house along this road, so I should keep moving. I'll see you around, I guess." I kick at a new patch of dirt.

"Be careful. Call the cops if you're worried."

Despite how I'm feeling I chuckle to reassure him. "No, I'm exaggerating. I'm sure they're just lost—Bye." I disconnect abruptly because I realize I started digging a new hole for myself by mentioning Gerard was irate last night. I glance down the road at the silver vehicle that has slowed and reeks of suspicion.

Taking off at a sprint, I put as much distance between me and the car before whoever is driving has time to turn around. When I reach the walker's track that runs through park lands before coming out at the partially developed new housing estate, I slow down to a walk. I shouldn't have even come out again. The blisters I incurred earlier feel to be bleeding. Oddly, the pain is a good distraction from my internal anguish, even if it was short-lived. Before I know it, I'm analyzing everything again as I amble along, wincing in pain.

I should have asked Alex more questions. Was Gerard telling the truth when he said the kid wasn't his? I think back to the conversation Gerard and I had about children, just before we married. He wanted to make sure I was okay with the decision, and I was at the time. But armed with this latest information, I feel the anger rise, and I break into a jog, thinking over how Gerard addressed the issue. Was it, "We will never have children?" Or was it, "I hope you're okay with not having children?" No, it was something more like, "I want you to understand there will never be any children with me." That's how he'd said it. Adamant that he never wanted children. I'd agreed then because I felt we had a perfect life ahead of us without children. I adored Gerard—he was all I needed, or so I thought.

Then a flashback from last night rises to haunt me, followed by a huge wave of nausea. He was going to rape me to teach me a lesson. What sort of husband does that? Gerard has never been so… unpredictable. I picture the check he handed me that I left on the table. I'm not sure if I'm insulted that mentioning Jolene was enough for him to want me gone or relieved that at least I wouldn't be out on my ass with nothing. My stomach churns with the confirmation that Gerard would let me go.

I should be feeling sorry for him. He was in love with Jolene and then… just like me she cheated on him. I groan aloud. No wonder he got so angry. It's history repeating itself. And not only did Jolene cheat, but she got pregnant.

Suddenly I'm thinking about Sheree, wondering if I should call and get all of this off my chest. Which only compounds everything, making me feel worse because I know I can't drag her into this mess. My head feels like it's going to explode. Even Annabel feels out of reach because she and Stuart were friends with Gerard before me. I can't expose our dirty laundry. They might shun us or worse still, talk and ruin Gerard's reputation. No, I've got to keep this to myself.

When I reach the end of the path, I turn left, which leads back to Rye Court. Once I cross Carnegie's Creek, it's another three miles. With my AirPods in, I try jogging along the main road with my back to the traffic, but my blisters, and now tears, get the better of me.

Was it really so wrong that he criticized the shorts I was

wearing? He's right. I have a cupboard full of beautiful clothes that he provides for me. Haven't I always known he has high standards? He expects his wife to have class and manners. Is that so wrong? Was I slouching? Had I changed being around Alex? Was that what he was implying and worried about? Had I taken it the wrong way? Suddenly, Jolene becomes a real threat. "An ex-model," Alex had said. Maybe Gerard is lying, and he's still in love with her and because she's had a child to another man, he's bitter and angry and he's stuck with me.

Unconsciously, I pull myself taller and stride out, tucking in my stomach and giving myself a vigorous workout, breaking into a decent sweat and fighting my growing insecurity. I'm still the same woman you married, Gerard.

I start stressing over stupid clothing and what to cook for my husband tonight. When my thoughts drifts to Alex again, I remind myself that Gerard had to pay him to have sex with me. That I don't really mean anything to Alex at all. Gerard has always been my stable. The man I can trust and be grateful for.

Stopping in my tracks, I'm suddenly sickened that I keep glossing over who I've become. Someone flagrant and disrespectful. Gerard terrorizing me last night was to remind me of what he'd rescued me from. I fold over, my hands going to my knees to keep me upright and I need to stifle the urge to vomit. What am I thinking? I need to go home, rip up that check and start behaving like a married woman who appreciates what she has. I spin around intending to turn back, when from out of nowhere, a truck swerves around me and pulls up. I scream. My thoughts scattering as I jump out the way.

Clutching at my chest, I stare at the rear of Alex's pickup truck then pull out my Airpods and move closer to the passenger-side window that Alex winds down.

"Alex, what are you doing here?" I peer up and down the road as though expecting he has an entourage, or maybe just looking for Gerard.

"I got worried, get in," he demands.

I look up the road to where I intended going. "You drove half an hour because you're worried? Alex, I'm fine. I just need to finish my run, well, walk," I mumble.

"Paige, get in, I want to talk." He refuses to let me brush him off.

"Alex, I need to be on my own. Everything that's happened is just too weird."

"I know." He nods. "But still, get in the truck."

When I don't move, he reaches over and shoves the door open.

"No, you don't know, Alex." I take hold of the door. "I thought you cared about me. I thought—well I thought you felt the same way as me. But, Christ! Gerard had to pay you? And what the hell! Why Jenna? Like I know we're not in a relationship, but shit. Everything feels so cheap now. You've just been playing with my feelings. I liked you, Alex. A lot." I slam the door and stride away. It's only a second before Alex's truck is crawling along beside me because I can't move at any decent speed.

"Paige, please get in."

I throw him a glare before stopping, making him slam on the brakes then bend to look through the open window. "No. Because this is how bad it's gotten. I confronted Gerard about Jolene and you know what he did? He handed me a check. Basically, telling me he doesn't care anymore. How's that for a major fuck-up? And now you want me to get in the truck with you. You're part of the problem, Alex. You need to leave me alone."

"No, maybe you need to fucking leave Gerard. If he's given you money, take it."

"And go where?" I yell. "And ten thousand dollars will not get me very far."

"Go any-fucking-where. And ten grand. I'd sure as shit be able to get out of town with that kind of money. Besides that, you're entitled to alimony. Take him for everything you can and get out. Seriously, I don't think you understand who he is."

"Believe me, Alex. I know him better than you do. And it's easy for you to say just go, because you haven't got a life here. And the fact that my husband had to pay you to be with me means I'm delusional thinking you cared. That I could trust you."

With my elbows resting on the open window, I cradle my head and look down at the asphalt, realizing I've just gone on a tangent and revealed more than I wanted to. When I look back at him, I know I must have puppy-dog eyes, because even though I don't want to, everything I feel for him comes oozing out. I just want him to go so I don't feel so torn. But then, Gerard's warning is clouding my judgment again. Is Alex who I think he is, or am I just getting lost in the fantasy of him?

"You can trust me, Paige. And sure as shit I care about you —a lot…" His hand falls on my arm as though preparing me for what's coming. The dreaded B word.

"But, it's more complicated than that. I've just gotten out of prison and there's shit I need to sort out. Look, will you just get in the truck? It's stupid talking like this." Alex smiles reassuringly.

I hesitate long enough for my feet to remind me how irrational I've been behaving. Sighing, I get in his truck. Then Alex is pulling out onto the road before I even have time to fasten my seat belt.

Even though the inside of his vehicle is tidy, it smells like dirt. He has a cap hooked on the headrest of the passenger seat and I notice the peeling stickers on the rear window that hint of a rodeo long gone. With my window still open, the breeze whips two air fresheners, that are hanging on the rearview mirror, into action. The windshield is still a cemetery to hundreds of bugs I noticed last week when we were picking up supplies. Finally, I settle in and look at Alex again.

"Sorry. It's not the Lexus." His smile seems a little strained.

"You know I'm not like that, Alex. I'm just looking." I clip my belt. "You're taking me home, I hope?" I study him all over until I realize I'm actually checking him out for all the wrong reasons. He's wearing shorts today. Old board shorts that end midway down his thighs, allowing me a decent look at his solid, tanned legs again. "Did you play football?" Instantly I'm turning away, embarrassed by the random inquiry and lack of restraint.

"Were you ever a cheerleader?"

"Don't answer a question with a question," I banter and smile back.

"Then yes, and you?"

"Runner." I gesture to myself and my clothing.

When we get to the end of the road Alex takes a left turn and, within seconds we're entering the highway en route to Malibu.

"Um, this is not the way home."

"I'm taking you for coffee."

"What? Alex, no," I whine. "I need to get some work done. I wasn't lying. Donnie will fire my ass if I don't get my shit together. Besides, after last night, I don't think I can risk Gerard seeing me out with you. He's seriously not impressed with me."

"I think you can spare an hour, and we'll go to the beach house then. Nothing wrong with the owner being in her own home, right?" His smile broadens as he looks back to the road. Just then, a silver car flashes past, overtaking us.

"Hey, I think that's the same car I saw earlier."

He puts a hand briefly on my knee and squeezes. "See, better safe than sorry. Now tell me, what did Gerard tell you about Jolene? Why did he get angry?"

"Don't worry about it. It's my problem to sort out. You don't need to rescue me."

"Sure about that? Seems to me you need rescuing from yourself. What the hell happened last night that you suddenly can't come and work on your own freakin' house anymore? Tell me."

"Why, when I know you're just going to say how stupid I am and all I supposedly need to do is leave him." I shift in my seat. I'm feeling way too many conflicting emotions. "Please take me home, Alex. I can't do this anymore—you'll drive me insane. Just being around you makes my head go all crazy."

Alex keeps looking from me to the road, concerned. He doesn't respond or change the direction we are going, so I stare out my window.

"What made Gerard *irate*, Paige? Was it something to do with me? Obviously, it was if he told you about the money. The cunning bastard."

I face him but stay quiet for some time. Unsure if I can bear a lecture.

"Paige?"

"He asked if we'd slept together again. I said, 'What if we have, what then?'"

"Why the hell would you say that?"

"In my defense, he was being an ass, picking on what I was wearing and criticizing how I was eating." I rush, trying to explain my response.

"Jesus, Paige!"

"Don't worry, I know, and I paid the price. So, now I'm moving on. That's why it's better if I leave the renovations up to you. I hope we can still be—you know, friendly in-laws though?" A horrible feeling rises and heats my cheeks. I'm aware now that I essentially used Alex. How could I have not taken into consideration the repercussions my lie might have on him?

"What do you mean you paid the price? You mean the check?" he asks, ignoring my grand finale speech and making me explain.

"No. And why does it matter now, anyway?" I let my head fall against the side window. The magnitude of sorting it all out in my head is taking its toll, and a tiredness overwhelms me.

"What happened?" Alex demands, impatient with my evasive responses. He grabs my upper arm. "What happened, Paige? Just fucking tell me and stop playing games, will you?"

"Put it this way. It wasn't how I expected him to react."

He squeezes my arm harder. "Keep going."

"It wasn't so much what he said." I shrug his hand off. "Although he said things that made me understand exactly how he feels, but it was more what he did that scared me."

Alex's expression turns grim. "What did he do?"

"He tied my hands together and was rough," I blurt quickly, hoping the speed in which I say it will carry less weight. I'm wrong. Alex's green eyes darken, and he clenches his jaw.

"What a stupid, fucking, cocksucker," he cusses loudly, hitting his palm on the steering wheel. "You do the man a service, and he fucks things up. What a fucking dip shit," Alex grumbles, looking straight-ahead.

"It was my fault, Alex. When I told him nothing

happened, he stopped, and then he was sorry. I should never have tested him like that."

"No, you shouldn't have, you shouldn't fuck with people's emotions, you seem to be getting good at that," he balks.

"Me! Why did Gerard have to pay you then, Alex? I thought you liked me. How do you think finding out my husband paid you to have sex with me felt?"

Alex accelerates until I'm sure we are speeding.

"You don't get it, Paige. I've got no money. I live hand to fucking mouth. The money Gerard was paying me for gardening was fuck all. I owe people, and since getting out of prison, it's been tough," he confesses.

This is *not* how I expected Alex to respond, and my expression must show my surprise. He twists his hands around the steering wheel and quickly looks away.

"Paige, I needed money. I still need money." He glances at me then back at the road. "There's... fuck, you don't get it. There's more people involved here than just you and me. What did Gerard tell you about Jolene?"

I'm stumped and still staring at him. Not sure how to react, what to think. Is he asking me for money now? Has he been pretending to like me, to care about me so he can somehow extort money?

"Are you asking me for money?"

"No. Fuck, no. I'm trying to explain why I took the money."

"Well, explain it properly then."

He keeps silent while watching the traffic, looking at me occasionally. Finally, he says,

"Don't hate me but I was hoping to help Jolene out."

Internally, I implode. Every organ seems to fold in on itself, pulling fiercely on my heart. It's not Gerard who's in love with Jolene, it's Alex.

Alex keeps switching his attention between me and the

road, looking for a response before going on to explain. But I'm crushed into speechlessness. Everything Gerard said is true. But I don't want Gerard to be right. I want Alex to be the truth.

"When Gerard rang, I told him I wasn't interested in a three-way anymore."

"So, it was because of her then. You're still in love with her? Oh God, Alex." I slump forward and catch my face in my hands. Press firmly onto my eye sockets so I don't give him the satisfaction of seeing me tear apart. "Are you seeing her? Does she know about us and what happened?"

"Hell no. I'm not fucking in love with her. That fuckin' ship sailed the second she fell for Gerard's crap. I said no because it felt wrong after what you said about trust and love. But he kept offering more and then I started thinking of Jolene and how I was just taking what was rightful anyway. But look, I wouldn't have gone through with it if you weren't comfortable with it. I did try and give you an out."

"I know, I remember, but maybe if you'd added the little detail you were hired to perform, I may have changed my mind."

"It wasn't like that. I swear. It's just the money was too good to knock back."

"Why wouldn't he just loan you the money? Why make you earn it by having sex with me?" I groan and hug myself.

"Because he's kinky, he likes to watch. And as far as just giving me money, why should he? It's not his job to bail me out of the shit I'm in."

It takes a moment for me to accept the truth. Gerard didn't just pay Alex, he bribed him so he could watch. He manipulated me, then used Alex, pressured him, instead of helping him unconditionally. He put the squeeze on him. What a self-centered asshole.

I feel like I'm tailspinning. Deceit and lies. Manipulation, corruption, sex, money, power. I can't quite sift through it all. There's a barrage of people's faces closing in around me, and I remember I haven't taken my contraception pill yet this morning, like it's suddenly the most important thing I must remember, and then I remember something else.

It was my fifteenth birthday. I'd gone into the kitchen to look in the fridge, hoping and praying that by some miracle, there was a cake in there for me, big and beautiful from the bakery. That my dad was back, and he'd brought a cake. But there was no cake, just my overweight mother sitting at the table smoking and counting money. Then she handed me a bag. It was from the chemist. I felt a slight flutter that she might have bought me a new pair of earrings or maybe sunglasses. "Happy Birthday, baby girl," she said, shoving it at me. I smiled and took the bag, but when I looked in, all I found was a packet of contraception pills. My smile must have slid away because she snapped, "Well, say thank you. They're not cheap you know, and from now on, you better start taking it cause you're gonna need the protection." I must have looked confused because she added, "You know, sex." She crudely poked her index finger through the circle she'd formed with her finger and thumb.

"Paige?"

"What?" I come back from wherever I was and stare at Alex, feeling dazed.

"Are you okay?"

I look down at his hand rubbing my leg then look at him again.

"Yeah. I was just thinking. How much do you need, you know, money?"

"Fuck off." He screws up his face. "That's not why I told you all that, I don't want your money."

I take his hand off my leg. "I didn't say *I* would give you money, Alex."

He watches as I weave our fingers together and then looks up to meet my gaze. "I want Gerard to give you money," I say, smiling. "If his kink is making him so desperate he'd coerce you and pay for it—then let's make him pay."

3

MY WAY

Taking one step at a time, I follow Alex up the stairs to the beach house, marking off the red flags I ignored about Gerard's subtle controlling nature. One: "Do you have any family apart from your mother who would object to us marrying?" Two: "I hope you're not the type of woman who needs to hang off her friends and join in on everything they do." Three: "I'd like you to dress nicely for me and to stay slim." Four: "I like routine. Please don't change things I have set in place. I find it disrespectful." Five: "When I go to bed, I'd like you to join me."

Then I'm remembering the psychiatrist's words when I told her Gerard preferred me to work from home. So I was there to care for him.

"When people allow themselves to be controlled by others, there is a strange sense of belonging. They feel—seen. The fact is, in most cases the controlled has his or her own issues. Both become co-dependent on one another. The controller has a desire to stay in control, so they feel secure. They know what's happening next because they strive to orchestrate the situation. In my experience, most people with abandonment issues suffer in either of these ways. They feel important when being controlled or, if they are the dominant, they feel powerful, therefore safe controlling others."

She'd nailed that.

"Coffee?" Alex asks, allowing me to go ahead of him before closing the door with a decent shove. Instantly, I'm hit by paint and wood-shaving smells. Still a construction zone, the furniture Alex has moved in to make it somewhat homely, sits amongst surfaces covered in either canvas or plastic tarps.

"Got anything stronger?"

"Christ, I shouldn't have told you." He throws down his keys and wallet on the kitchen counter and moves over to the kettle, which is the only thing on the bench apart from a toaster and an electric frying pan.

"You didn't, you just clarified it. I'll have tea if you have it. Thanks." I place my cell phone on the coffee table and head toward the back deck.

Through the glass sliding doors, on the slim rectangle table setting we've been lunching on all week, are several empty beer bottles and a few wine glasses indicating he's had company overnight. I hug myself as though I'm cold and eye the two large potted plants left by the previous owner that look like they could use a drink. Then I spot the surfboard I never noticed before.

"Do you surf?" I ask, trying to avoid my own mental analysis.

Alex nods then opens the kitchen window a little. "I went out this morning actually."

"Wow, who would have thought," I say more to myself than him, opening the glass doors just a crack. When a strong breeze whistles through, I change my mind about going out and close it abruptly. Instead, I lean against the counter, watching Alex mess with the coffee machine before filling a pot with water to put on the stove. Now I feel bad asking for tea.

"Alex, what was Gerard's dad like?" Even though Gerard has told me a little about his childhood, I'm curious what Alex thought of him.

"An asshole," he replies pointedly and shocking me.

"Really? I got the impression from Gerard he was nice. That he admired him."

"Only if you call abusing women and children a nice sort." He pulls open an overhead cupboard and pulls out tea and coffee canisters.

"That's odd, Gerard's never said anything negative about him."

"Well, I've got no problem saying how it was. He was a violent drunk. My mom caught him backhanding me just months after they married. I've got this scar to prove it." Alex brushes his hand over his neck. "First chance she got, she headed out with me. I always felt sorry for Gerard. That my mom had to leave him behind. She cared about him. He was a nice kid, and smart. Someone I looked up to. There was the odd time he became an asshole, I guess. I thought he was just lashing out. Now I'm thinking it's in his DNA."

After last night, I'm worried Alex is right. "It's true his mom died in a car accident—isn't it?" I'm hoping not everything is a lie.

"Yeah, when he was a teenager. I suspect it's why his dad, Eric, started drinking and why his sister moved in with an aunt."

"Huh. I'd forgotten about Cassandra." I gather together odd bits of paper laying about the counter, stacking them into a pile. "You know, Gerard never talks about her. It's like she doesn't exist."

"I think it pissed him off she got to leave. Eric was always trying to cut Gerard down to size. Making him feel like shit on the end of his shiny fuckin' shoe. Can't blame him for leaving home so young. It's lucky he is where he is, I guess. You know self-made millionaire."

"How is it I have to find out all these things from you?" I huff out a sigh, feeling uneasy that Gerard's childhood was so bad, and he's been keeping more secrets than I ever believed possible.

"Have you ever asked him?" Alex asks.

"I suppose not. I guess, I avoid asking about his family because he doesn't like me talking about mine."

"And why is that?"

I shrug. "My dad left, and my mom was a drunk. You connect the dots."

"Sounds like the average American nightmare."

"It was. Where is everyone today?" I ask, referring to the few random tradesmen that were here earlier in the week, trying to steer the conversation elsewhere.

"They've mostly finished their part. Max and his guys only needed a few days to knock down the downstairs walls and install the new lighting and fire alarms." His eyes dart up to the ceiling, and with a nod, he indicates the newly installed fixtures. "They finished installing your flashy lights downstairs."

"I wish I could say I'm still excited about the gallery, but Gerard's behavior last night makes me question his motive."

"Just Gerard's behavior? What about you? I hope that doesn't mean you were serious before, you know, in the truck, about making Gerard pay."

"Wouldn't we all be getting what we want? You need money. Gerard likes to watch, and well... I suppose you were right. I want more of you," I confess, brushing my hand over the counter, leaving a trail in the dust as I maneuver around toward Alex.

Squinting his eyes as I inch closer, Alex puts a hand on his hip and rubs the back of his neck, his mouth becoming a tight line until I stop advancing.

"Nah, you don't want me." He suddenly looks amused. He turns away and readies the mugs. "You're just bored with Gerard and that pretentious life you're living." Still smiling, he flicks me a sheepish look, then notices I'm deadpan. "What? You're serious!" He pauses at untangling a tea bag. Now he looks uncomfortable. "Shit. Don't go falling in love with me, Paige. That wouldn't be your smartest move, would it?" He turns away and hovers over the stovetop, waiting silently for the water to boil.

Deflated, I move back out into the lounging area and find a spot on the worn overstuffed brown couch that should be covered in a tarp by the amount of dust that billows when I sit down.

"You—do remember what I said at the hotel, that this is complicated?" He waves a finger between the two of us, and I nod. "Well, I wasn't joking. Gerard's my stepbrother. I admit, he's got issues that don't sit right with either of us, that's for sure. But I think the best thing you could do is leave him, but hell no, not for me. What have I got to offer? You or anyone," he adds with a dry chuckle.

"Leave him for what then?"

Alex pulls back his head and screws up his face. "What do you mean for what? To fucking get in amongst the living, Paige. You don't belong there, and you know it."

"Oh, and where do I belong then? Back in a trailer, is that what you mean?"

"If that's where you need to go to find yourself, then sure." His sincerity makes it clear he has no idea about my past.

Stalling until the heat leaves me, my gaze fall to the coffee table and the pile of books he has there. One on landscaping, another about unsolved mysteries by the looks, and a paperback classic I remember reading in school, *The Clash of Civilizations.* Then I spot a book depicting a man holding a gun to his head, the title ironically reads, *Love Yourself Like Your Life Depends On It.* Picking it up, I read the blurb on the back cover, then study the front again before opening it to the first page. Spotting a handwritten inscription, I glance up to see if Alex thinks I'm intruding. With his back turned at the fridge getting milk, I quickly scan over the words before he notices.

"To my beautiful son, Alexander. Inside a broken heart, pearls of wisdom are waiting to be found. Love Mom x"

Doubting the truth in that statement, I huff then toss the book back on the table. Then I remember how Alex introduced himself to me as Alexander when we first met and I understand his reasoning. My eyes sting and when I look up, Alex is staring at me.

"She gave it to me just before she died." He rubs his nose and gazes at the mugs, still jiggling away at a tea. Again, my face heats. I pick up another book not knowing what to say except that "I'm sorry."

"Cancer's a bitch, but if she were here, she'd say different." Alex gathers up the mugs.

"What do you mean?"

"She reckoned it was a gift. Said it made her realize where she went wrong in this life. She was into all that kind of stuff —you know alternative medicine, meditation, and shit. Didn't stop her from dying though." There's a hint of bitterness in his tone which he shakes off. "Anyway, she's gone now." Obviously not wanting to talk about his mother, he drops the subject and comes from around the bench. "Want anything to eat?"

I ignore his question. "Alex, why did you bring me here?" I put down the book I wasn't interested in anyway.

Alex halts in his tracks, his eyes darting about like he's

searching for the right way to start. But the deep frown that furrows his face tells me all I need to know.

"I should go. It's obvious you want to tell me how stupid I am when I already know. I'll get a cab." Standing, I grab my phone.

"No, that's not it. It's about why I took the money," he says, halting me and placing the mugs on the coffee table. "There's a lot more to it than what I said, so will you sit down, at least let me try to explain?"

I take a seat again and after a moment, I reach for my mug. "It sounded to me like a straightforward transaction. Gerard pays you money so he can watch you fuck me," I say, blowing steam away. Instead of sitting next to me on the couch, Alex chooses a worn canvas studio chair opposite and runs a hand through his hair. "Except I didn't fuck you in front of him, did I?" He brings the cup to his lips then cusses because it's so hot.

"No, I guess you didn't."

"Paige, a lot of shit went down before I ended up in prison. My mom was dying. I got mixed up with the wrong people and started doing drugs and shit and then there was Jolene who left me because Gerard swooped in and enticed her with fancy shit while I was busy screwing up."

"So, he didn't really steal her then. Sounds like she wanted the shiny things, Alex." I take a careful sip from my mug then return it to the table before blowing more annoying strands of hair out of my face.

"That's the pot calling the kettle black don't you think?" He raises his eyebrows at me. "Listen, Gerard made it pretty obvious he wanted her. Right from the get-go over expensive lunches and inviting us into his rich fucking circle of friends."

"Well, that explains what I am to you then. Gerard was right last night. You're playing with me to pay him back."

"No. I'm not and I wasn't." Alex huffs "I was never going to bring you into this, but I think you need to know about her."

God, it's like a repeat from last night.

"Did Gerard tell you Jolene had a baby?" He presses himself back into the chair and arches his eyebrows, looking smug. I understand what Alex is trying to do, I just don't know if it's because he cares for me or that he still has a vendetta against Gerard.

"Yes. He told me. He also said it's not his. He said Jolene tried to trap him so, I don't care that it backfired, that's just dumb." Annoyed that my hair keeps going in my face, I pull it out of its ponytail and use my fingers to comb it before tying it back again. Alex watches me, staying silent for a moment with a dirty look on his face.

"But—that's bullshit." He cocks his head. "Grace is his. It's just, Jolene can't prove it. At least—not in the conventional way." Alex rubs a hand over the back of his head grimacing. I shift myself until I'm sitting on the edge of the couch, frowning and waiting for him to go on.

"What do you mean? It either is—or it isn't his, Alex. A paternity test would have proved that."

Alex puckers his lips

"She, Paige, and her name is Grace."

"Sorry, it's just what's this got to do with you accepting money, anyway?"

"Paige, as soon as Gerard found out Jolene was pregnant, he wanted her to terminate. Jolene refused. She told him she wanted the baby and he couldn't make her get rid of it. She begged him to believe that the baby was his. I was locked up by that stage, but she kept calling, breaking down in tears and shit. At first, I didn't give a flying fuck. That was their shit to deal with, not mine. But then she started getting sick with the pregnancy, ended up in hospital a few times with a threatened miscarriage. I started thinking Gerard was doing something to her, so I let her keep in contact. After she had Grace, she got sick again, something to do with retained shit, I dunno. She was sick for weeks in hospital and as soon as she was better, Gerard tells her he wants a paternity test done."

I get to my feet and fold my arms firmly over my chest. Alex watches me pace. "Yeah and?" I prompt.

"The test came back that Grace wasn't his."

"So, what's the dilemma? Those tests don't lie, Alex. Jolene cheated on him." There's a moment's pause before the realization hits me. My hand goes straight to my mouth. "You mean… Are you telling me the baby is yours?" I mutter through my fingers then slump onto the couch, staring at my cooling mug of tea.

"Fuck no. Like I said, that ship had sailed. But. Jolene swears she never screwed around. That Grace is his. She reckons he somehow had the test swapped."

"Why? No, don't bother answering that. I know why if it were true, but come on Alex, this is not some movie. He might have influence, but no way." I'm shaking my head trying to hold back the laughter. Shocked that Alex of all people would fall for Jolene's lies.

"No shit, Sherlock. But it's hard not grasping at straws when you're desperate. The only reason she was trying to get Gerard to accept responsibly is because Grace is sick and her medical bills are piling up, otherwise Jolene would have been long gone. Next thing we know, he meets you and you're married." Having gotten that off his chest, Alex sucks in another deep breath then reaches for his coffee.

Well, that slapped the smug expression off my face. "I'm sorry. I didn't mean to be…"

"I don't know whether to believe her or not, Paige. But that's why I took the fucking money. To get dudes off my back and help Jolene a bit. Even if Grace ain't Gerard's, it's the least I can do for Jolene since I was a cunt of a boyfriend. And it's the least Gerard could do. You'd think he'd have more heart. Those bills would be chicken feed to him."

"Yeah, but if it's not his?" I shrug. "I mean, it's nice of you to want to help out but can you honestly expect Gerard to pay when Grace is not even his? She cheated Alex, and how bad do you think I feel now? God no wonder he's pissed at me. I feel so bad," I mumble under my breath.

"Don't. There's more to him than meets the eye. But for the time being, I'm willing to roll with it 'cause he's gonna pay me well for this gig." Alex finishes his coffee and goes over to the sink.

"What's wrong with her? I mean, Grace." I reach for my cup. Hoping, praying that Jolene is just desperate and Grace isn't Gerard's somehow. Gerard rigging the test? That's a stretch.

Alex runs a hand over his chin. "Tay-Sachs. It's a hereditary disease."

"Hereditary? That can't be right." I frown at Alex, my thoughts flipping all over the place. But then… Maybe that's why Gerard never wanted children with me. That sort of makes sense, but if that's the truth, Grace would be his. I make a mental note to look it up later.

When Alex comes and takes a seat next to me on the couch, I place a hand on his thigh. "I'm sorry, Alex. I wish I could help somehow."

"I shouldn't have gone there with you guys. You know the three-way. It's just brought all this shit to the surface." Alex is so close, his words whisper across my left temple giving me goose bumps. I twist so we're looking at each other, our faces only inches apart. I know I should get up and go home. Spending time with Alex and hearing all this about my husband from him isn't right. But, as I watch his lips move, explaining how he should just walk away from it all, that Jolene's not really his problem, I'm wishing he'd just lean in closer and kiss me. Something about the way he cares makes me crave him even more.

"She was young and gullible, like you." Alex brushes the back of his hand against my cheek and then cups my chin. "He uses people, Paige." He pulls back abruptly and lets himself fall back into the couch. "I'm just pissed off the robbery turned to shit. I had the money right fuckin' there." Alex gestures, cupping his hands. "I'd be sittin' pretty by now. Wouldn't have to work and I could've given Jolene money and pissed off somewhere. Go and stick a headstone on my mom's grave, you know? I owe her at least that much seeing I wasn't there when she needed me the most."

"I think you're being too hard on yourself. You're not responsible for everyone." I say, sobering from Alex's tender moment and resting my head back on the couch. "But you've got my mind spinning. I just can't believe Gerard has kept all this from me and he wouldn't help you or Jolene out. He's got money and you're his brother."

"Stepbrother, and we hardly spent any time together. I was two when my mom hooked up with Eric and they only stuck it out until I was six. He doesn't owe me a thing, really." Alex sighs, and we stay silent for a long time, lost in our own thoughts.

"Argh! Why is life so ugly? You're the only nice thing about it now." I twist my head, hoping to see something in his gaze that will tell me how he feels. That he's not angry at me or still playing the revenge card.

His eyes rove over my face, then he looks back to the ceiling again.

"Don't fall for me, Paige. I ain't right for you either."

Well I guess that answers it then. All I can do is nod and

change the subject. "Do you really believe Gerard would switch the results to shirk his responsibilities toward Grace?"

Alex arches his eyebrows and lifts a shoulder. "Anyway, I'm not gonna convince you. I'm just taking advantage of whatever he throws my way."

Does that include me?

Alex gets up from the couch and pulls me to my feet. "You should take a look at your gallery. If you're not leaving the asshole, you may as well enjoy the lavish life he's got planned for you."

"Alex." I tug on his hand to make him look back at me, then reach up and stroke his face that looks like the weight of the world is carved in it. "You know it's not my fault what happened to Jolene. But if I can help in any way?"

Alex heaves a sign. "I know. Don't worry about it. Everything is cool." Grabbing my hand he leads the way. I follow, feeling somewhat wounded that Alex sounds bitter and thinks it's an easy decision to divorce someone who has always, until I cheated, been kind and decent. He bought this house for me. Encouraged me to follow my passion. Tried to turn my cheating into a good thing. Learning that Jolene, the woman before me, also cheated makes me feel so ashamed that I'm even here with Alex. Guilt should be kicking in but it doesn't. Instead I squeeze Alex's hand tighter.

When we reach the front room that's being turned into my gallery, Alex turns on the lighting and leans against the wall. I move to the middle of the room and stare up at the hundreds of miniature lights in the center of the ceiling. Then at the rows of spotlights placed at strategic intervals a foot away from each wall. For a moment, I imagine my photographs on the wall, some of my favorites and then one's I haven't even taken yet. Then all I'm doing is staring at blank walls with a sinking feeling.

"You don't seem that happy, Princess." Alex crosses his arms and strolls toward me.

"It's beautiful but…" I look at the floor.

"But what?" Alex stops a few feet away from me. I inch closer, desperate to just fall against his chest, have his arms wrap around me.

"Everything about me and Gerard—it's all a lie."

Alex shrugs. "I don't know. Is it?"

I can't help it. I need him to comfort me. Closing the distance, I fall against his chest and breathe him in, absorb the ocean and soap, his warm musky maleness. When my hands meander over his broad back, he stretches and puffs up his chest. I wait for him to put his arms around me and pull me in tight. When he doesn't, I look up. He has his hands clasped on the top of his head just staring down at me.

"Shiiit." He shakes his head. "What are we doing, Paige? Are you sure you want more secrets to live with?"

I scoff. "I think it's destined to be the story of my life." Letting my arms drop, I straighten myself in front of him before my hands gravitate onto his chest. My eyes are searching his, questioning what I'm doing but then I think about the check Gerard gave me sitting on the table at home. Alex is right. I could easily get out of the city. Alex could come.

And then as if reading my mind, he says, "You understand if we do this, it stays between us. And! I don't want anything serious, all right?"

I take a step back. "I can't help the way I…"

"You can't use me as a life raft to get out, if that's what you're hoping to do. It doesn't work like that. You don't get to use me that way, Paige." Alex grabs my shoulders and brings me close again. With our eyes locked, he seems to ask a million questions that I don't have answers for. My chest feels tight, but I can't tear my gaze away either.

"I seriously don't need trouble, Paige. If you want out, you need to leave him on your own accord. Jumping from him to me and thinking something serious can come out of it—nah." He shakes his head. "It never works out. I'm not saying I don't care about you. I do—a lot. But I'm not setting myself up to be the go-between guy."

I nod my head in understanding until he brings a hand up to still my face, brushing my lip with his thumb, letting his hand slide until he is cupping my jaw and tilting my face upward. He squeezes a little too roughly and I wince. "You're bad news, Princess."

"You're the one who brought me here," I mumble. He lets go of my face then grabs my ass, pulling me closer and grinding himself against me. A rush of heat invades me from the way his pupils dilate and the twitching at his groin.

"I don't want you to think of me as easy though, Alex."

"Easy? You're far from being easy." Alex jerks me, crushing me against his hard body and wrapping his arms tightly, pressing all the air from my lungs, which he catches and sucks in when our mouths collide. His tongue tastes every millimeter of my lips, gliding, prodding, forcing my lips apart so he can kiss me deeply and I moan into him. His hot hand slides beneath the stretchy fabric of my pants to feel my flesh and his lips tug at the corners, making me realize he's smiling.

I pull back to scrutinize him, thinking he's teasing me, but he looks happy not smug. When he comes to kiss me again, both hands cup my ass and he scoops me up, guiding my legs around his waist. I cling onto his neck for support and before I know what's happening, we're back on the couch and I'm straddling him, kissing feverishly, his face held tightly in both hands. I can't get enough of him. My need is so bad, I'm aching everywhere. I murmur how good he feels, and how badly I need him against his closed eyelids.

"You and me both, Princess," he says, kneading my ass and pulling me into him. I press harder against him, rocking, and running my hands over his shoulders, chest, and arms. I want to rip off his shirt, kiss his tanned chest, lick and suck on his nipples. There's nothing I wouldn't do for him.

Desperate for his touch, I grab his hand and force it onto my breast, then shove it down so he can crawl under my top and touch my skin. He knows me, can read me. He knows the perfect way to handle me, a way to silence my overthinking mind until I'm floating in euphoria.

There are no secrets with Alex. He searches my eyes and sees me. Caresses my breast to tease me, causing my nipples to peak beneath my sports top. His eyes dart there, his imagination feasting on what he can't see, and he growls in what seems like frustration. Dipping his head, Alex nips at one bud, leaving a moist patch of warmth on the fabric in his wake. His chest rises and falls beneath me, matching my own heavy breathing because I can feel him growing erect and swelling within his shorts.

Our lips become urgent for each other again, both of us losing control. His hands dig into my armpits, trying to lift me off so we can go further, but I keep clinging to him, not wanting to break his passionate onslaught. I move my hips and grind against his bulge, dry humping him just to get closer. The smell of him is so overwhelming, I can't control myself. I murmur into his mouth over and over, my fingers clawing through his hair.

When I open my eyes to search his, we're both breathy and sweaty. Then Alex lets go from under my armpits and wraps his arms firmly around my waist, forcing all the air in my lungs into his mouth, as he pulls me in tightly. He breathes me in, chomping and devouring my sensitive lips. He helps me press down, rubbing me firmly against himself.

His hands going onto my ass again, tilting me back and forward, and I can smell our sexy scent it's so strong,

"Oh, fuck, Paige," Alex exclaims, our lips finally unlocking. His hands become aggressive with my hips, using them vigorously to rub and rock my pelvis.

He is so goddamn powerful—he has me panting again. His arms, his thighs, his strong hands take control as he grips harder. I wince in pain, but I love it. There is no calmness about Alex, just pure, raw, primal lust. I'm so lost in his rapture I can no longer hold on to him and he can't control himself. He becomes frantic, working me back and forward over his cock still contained in his shorts. My pussy clenches and yearns for his penetration, driving me insane. I reach between us desperate to free his cock, to somehow tear a hole into my lycra pants so he can enter me, but he pulls my hand away and grabs my hips in both hands again, rubbing me excitedly.

"I want you in me. Oh fuck," I wail, feeling myself drawing close to climax, my clenching hole dying, screaming for penetration, which only arouses me more.

Alex dives onto my neck with his mouth, kissing and licking and sucking me everywhere, tasting my skin with his tongue.

"Jesus, Paige, I'm gonna come," he moans. I feel him tense then shudder, his pelvis working into micro thrusts and his vocal release sends me into delirium. Throwing my head back and pushing myself onto his still-pulsating cock within its confines, I tremble in frustration and lurch backward so Alex needs to manage my balance or I'll fall off his lap. With a hand supporting and clasping my neck tightly, Alex runs his palm down between the valley of my breasts until the heel of his hand is pressing against my pelvis. He digs his thumb in and presses against the lycra fabric, pushing into my aching center. When he targets pressure on my clit with his fingers, I moan out and spiral over and into relief.

Staying on his lap, I wait for my thumping heart to slow and wait for my arms to gather strength. They feel devoid of blood because I can't seem to move them. Alex pulls me up so I'm sitting, still cradling my neck in his large hand. I can't speak, only stare back a little shocked. His eyes are glazed and fixed on mine. He's no longer searching but seeing me. The depth I see is mesmerizing. Then something happens inside my chest. Like my aorta is ripping apart. I groan out in pain and bury myself into his neck, my arms gripping him tight.

What the hell am I doing?

4

DEMONS

When I first heard Gotye sing, I felt his pain. Drama. I think I like the drama. And as Alex drives me home, it seems I'm hell-bent on getting addicted to a certain kind of sadness too.

No sooner are my desires satisfied, my thoughts are back on my husband and how I can maintain the external status quo of a married life while suffering the turmoil of loving another man. I shake my head and stare out the side window. I'm a full-fledged cheater, inside and out.

For minutes, Alex and I stay silent as I glance out at the ocean, trying to focus my mind on things I need to do. I can only digest the smaller things and the mundane. I still need to appease Donnie who is waiting on my submission. That reminds me, I still need to take photos of the shipping containers for the prints I intend on donating.

"Alex, remember how I mentioned taking photos of the shipping containers?"

Alex nods but keeps his eyes on the road.

"Is your offer still available? You know, to take me to the port?"

He glances briefly. "Are you sure that's a smart idea, given Gerard's feelings about us?"

"He doesn't need to know. I'll tell him I went with Annabel."

"Well, I guess if you enjoy playing with fire, then sure. Thursday next week, around midday, works for me."

"Perfect. Thanks, Alex."

When his attention goes back to the road, I take in his profile. His strong jaw, his recently clipped hair, his neck only minutes ago I was kissing. I reach out and touch his upper thigh which startles him. He looks down at my hand then back up at me with a grin.

"Are you going to keep seeing Jenna?" The question comes from nowhere.

"I'd hardly say I've been seeing her," he scoffs, glancing between me and the road with a twisted half-smile. "We had sex, that's it. But saying that…"

"I know I get it. You don't have to spell it out," I interrupt. "I understand what we are, what that was." I pull a face at him. "Just go with the flow, right?"

"That's not what I was going to say, but sure. Let's go with the flow."

I remove my hand and begin flipping my phone over and over in my palm. Gerard hasn't rung, and I'm wondering if he believes I've left him. Mentally, I think maybe I have because I've been thinking of ways to help, not just Alex, but maybe even Jolene. And as though I've been thinking aloud, I go on to explain myself to Alex even though he never asked.

"I know I should leave him, Alex. I've just got to find the right time, you know?"

"Well, that's your call, I guess. I've said my piece, and I'm not here to dictate your life." Alex uses the indicators and exits the highway toward Point Dume. Within minutes, the midday traffic slows us to a crawl, and his hand reaches out to squeeze my knee before resting it casually on my thigh. With a wink, his fingers tap, on both my leg and the steering wheel, in time to the music that's playing, and my stomach does that peculiar fluttering thing.

"What if I cash the check and give it to you, Alex." I watch for his reaction. He stops tapping and frowns, so I go on, "You could give the money to Jolene for Grace. I'll just tell Gerard I tore it up."

When Alex smiles, I instantly realize my stupidity. As the light go on inside my head, he raises his eyebrows.

"Right. He'll know I cashed it."

Alex nods. "Don't stress about Jolene and Grace. They're not your problem, okay?"

"I know. But I don't know how to handle all this, Alex. I don't know what to think anymore," I say, almost absentmindedly, turning away to stare out my side window.

"You'll figure it out. Just see things for what they are."

I laugh. "That's not helpful, Alex."

"I think it is. Woman always overcomplicate things."

"Maybe—some things are complicated to begin with."

"Like what?"

"You honestly don't want to know." I rest my head on the glass, watching the craggy cliff face blur past when Alex picks up speed again.

I'm not sure if I frustrate Alex or he's respecting my space, but for the rest of the trip home, he remains silent. When the truck pulls up outside my front door, I finally look at him, hoping he'll give me a smile. When he doesn't, I reach for the door handle and go to get out. Suddenly Alex grabs my neck and pulls me toward him. "Just fuckin' leave him. I care too much to see you get hurt, Paige. And he will hurt you," he says, sounding certain.

"Alex, you don't understand."

"Yeah, I do. You don't want to give up this. Is that it?" Alex screws his face up and juts his chin toward the house.

Sighing away the threatening tears, I make a move to get out of the truck again, but Alex grabs onto my wrist, his expression softening. "I'm sorry. It's just... Fuck!"

"I know. Me too." I nod because I understand. This is just not fair. To anyone.

Alex tugs on my arm, coaxing me to come closer and when I do, he grabs my face in both hands and kisses me. Not a hungry, desperate kiss, but soft, beautiful and all-consuming. Just like the night of Jenna's party when he kissed me in the hall. A kiss that makes me forget everything. A kiss that makes me act on autopilot until I've crawled closer and am lying between Alex and the steering wheel, holding tightly to him as he awakens the sensitive nerves of my lips with the gentle brushing of his own, making us hum and vibrate. When he pulls away, it's only for a brief second before he's kissing my neck and jaw and under my chin, making me beg internally that time would cease to exist, just so we can stay like this forever. Why does Alex feel so right when everything about loving him is wrong?

When we part, he's staring down at me and shaking his head. He exhales heavily, the warmth of his breath stirring over my hair. "You're turning me into a lovesick weakling, Paige. You do it to me every time. Even when you don't mean to."

I close my eyes and rub my forehead with my palm. "Why can't this just be easier?" I groan falling into his chest. "I don't know what I want. I mean I want you." I look search his face then pull a weak smile. "But I don't want to hurt Gerard." I lift myself into a sitting position again but stay close. "It's going to take time for me to work this out, Alex."

"I just don't understand the hold he has over you."

His question scares me. It feels like my core is being strangled. Or is it a shrinking, shriveling of my insides? It's like a black hole wants to consume all my energy into its dense center. I remind myself about last night and I'm sure I've paled.

"I wish I could explain, Alex. I really do. But there's just… there's too much. I feel… Oh God. Seriously, just don't. Because this is stupid and wrong. I already feel so ashamed. People will get hurt and I'll be the one to blame and just— just forget about me," I ramble on, then pull away from him. Losing confidence because I realize I don't have the courage to tell Alex the whole truth about myself. Knowing he will be disgusted in me.

"Ashamed? Are you saying you feel ashamed around me?" Alex reaches for me, but I slide out the cab quickly.

"No. Not of you. Of myself. I have a past, Alex. And anyway," I snap. "You said you don't want anything serious with me."

"We all have a fucking past, Paige. You're not exclusive and I've told you shit because I trust you. Why don't you trust me?"

"Because mine is messy. I will repulse you." I slam the truck door shut mouthing, *'I'm sorry'* before quickly turning and walking away.

When Gerard gets home around seven, he finds me sitting on the couch, sifting through a thin pile of wedding photos I found in the bookshelf cupboard when I went looking for evidence of Jolene. I look happy enough in them, but I don't see myself. I look like a paper cutout, a one-dimensional young girl. I've been trying to work out if I changed myself to suit Gerard or whether Alex is right, I don't know who I am. Because it's only today, after being with Alex, that I realize I've been hiding behind layers of self-loathing, and I married a liar.

As soon as Alex had driven away today, I took myself and the ten-thousand-dollar check to the bank. When the bank teller kept tapping away at his keyboard, then looked up with a tight smile, I knew the check had bounced. Gerard had no intention of letting me go, and now I need to lie about trying to cash it and hide the ache in my heart.

Remaining in the doorway with his briefcase in his hand, Gerard stares at me as though he's looking at an apparition, and when I say "Hi," he slumps, then drops his case to the floor and beckons me. I hesitate for a moment, then toss the photos on the table and go over to him.

"I'm glad you're still here," he sighs, wrapping his arms around me. "I'm so sorry, Paige. I promise to be a better husband, a fairer man. You've put up with a lot lately, but you're still here." He loosens his tie then plants a small kiss on my forehead. I smooth my hand over his face, thankful he's finally remorseful, and regardless it's tight, my smile seems to calm him.

"It's all right. I've been doing plenty of thinking too." I move away and take my place back on the sofa. Gerard ventures farther into the living room, pulling off his tie and draping it over the top of the sofa before collapsing into the cushions. He looks as drained as I feel, his day surely having been fraught with doubt.

"What were you doing with these?" he asks, picking up a handful of photos and flicking through them quickly, then tossing them down.

"Just looking."

"Why?" He strokes my head then goes toward the bar.

"Because of what we talked about this morning." I gather the photos into a pile. "I realize I took so much for granted when we got together. I trusted that I knew all there was to know about you, and well, you have a big past, Gerard." Having stacked the photos, I take the last remaining sip of my wine.

"I know. I should have told you everything, and I've been desperate to call you all day, but I couldn't. I couldn't bear the thought of you not answering." Gerard reaches for a glass and places it gently on the wooden top, studys it before settling the sharpest blue eyes on me again. "I had a million things I wanted to say to you, but everything sounded like lame excuses, and I didn't want you to stay because you felt obligated. But you're my life, Paige, you always have been." He keeps his attention on me from behind the bar, his regret and admission seeming genuine.

Fuck. I know I'm frowning. I can feel the tight lines in my forehead, and I've drawn my mouth into a pucker. After thinking on it for hours, I managed to kill the moral police and I had a plan in place. I'm glad he's not in a bad mood, but I hadn't expected him to be full of remorse—it makes my deceit insurmountably worse and has me questioning if he really has done anything so unforgivable. Is it really a crime that he kept his past from me? Who doesn't do that? And what about what I got up to today? I force my face to relax and smile, remind myself that Alex needs help. I'm intent on fixing that, even if it is underhanded.

"Would you like another wine?" Gerard asks, holding up the bottle.

"No, thank you. I'm never drinking too much again," I huff out.

Gerard pauses pouring a Glengoyne. "I'll only have one," he reassures me, then continues pouring the amber liquid over ice. "Oh, and a funny thing. I'm glad you didn't try cashing that check today. It would have been rejected." He lets out a chuckle, but still, I flush with heat. Is he for real? I resist the urge to feel my head looking for an implant he might have had surgically placed while I was drugged out or something.

"I realized later I took it from a redundant checkbook." He pulls a mock embarrassed expression. "That would have been awkward for you. I'm—sorry that I overreacted this…" His sentence trails off. "You didn't try, did you? I mean, how presumptuous of me. I figured you were here because you want to be."

He slides down next to me and places a hand on my thighs then breathes out heavily. "Paige?"

"No, I didn't. I tore it up, it's in the bin."

"Oh, that's a relief. So, what did you get up to today?" He takes a sip from his glass.

"Nothing much. I'm cooking lemon chicken," I tell him, avoiding a direct answer.

"Lovely. Do you mind if I turn on the news?"

I pass him the remote. As he goes through the channels, I pick up the photos and put them away, disappointed but not surprised by how little interest he took in them.

"Did you work with Alex today?"

"No. I told him I wouldn't be working with him anymore." I try focusing on the TV to avoid his eyes, but I can feel him glaring at me, and when I look, he's frowning.

"You shouldn't have done that. I was being a jerk, and what about your gallery? See. Look what I've done."

"No, it's understandable. You shouldn't feel you need to compete." I place a hand on his shoulder as I move past him. "I'm just going to check on the casserole."

"By the way, you look lovely. I appreciate you getting dressed up." Gerard calls after me, referring to the body con dress I'm wearing. Personally, I think it makes my breasts look too heavy, but Gerard has always liked it.

"Well, I gave a lot of thought to what was said last night and this morning, and you're right, we need to work together on this marriage. I failed you. I need to make up for that," I shout over my shoulder as I walk off and into the kitchen.

Grabbing mitts, I give the casserole a stir before switching off the oven. The table has been laid out with a floral centerpiece, and I've brought out crystal and silverware from hiding, something Gerard would appreciate. When I return to the living room with a small platter of nibbles I'd prepared earlier, I catch Gerard looking at my phone. Instantly, I'm racking my brain over what my latest texts have been to Sheree.

"I hope you're hungry. I've got homemade bread to go with the casserole," I say, placing the platter on the coffee table.

Gerard puts down my phone then takes another sip from the glass he seems to have refilled while I was checking on dinner. So much for him not drinking too much.

"Did my phone ring?" I press on the device to light up the screen, hoping to see what he was viewing, but it's on the home page and nothing seems amiss.

"No, I was just looking. Homemade bread, you have been busy, haven't you? Have I got time to finish watching the news and take a shower before dinner?"

My heart is pounding, and I feel hot all over which will turn my pale skin scarlet. "Sure." I distract myself by picking up a book. After pretending to read for a few minutes, I summon some courage.

"Gerard, I need to ask you something, and I'd like you to be honest with me, it's important."

He turns, looking concerned. "It's not about a certain

person is it, because I really don't want to discuss it anymore."

"We need to, Gerard." Putting my book down, I turn to face him.

Heaving a sigh, Gerard places his empty glass on the table then helps himself to the hors d'oeuvres, his eyes never leaving the television. After several mouthfuls and me burning a hole in his temple, he looks at me.

"What do you want to know—what is there to know? She played me. We had a good relationship until she found herself pregnant. End of story."

"And you're sure it's—I mean, are you sure Grace is not yours?"

Gerard's smile is wide when he chuckles. "Honey, you don't need to worry about *Grace* or Jolene."

"You're certain?"

Gerard turns on me looking as though I'm daft. "Yes, Paige I'm certain. Now please, can we drop this? I'm sorry, but it's none of your business, anyway." Standing, he tells me he'll have his shower. I pick up my novel again and flick through the pages trying to swallow my appendix back down my throat. Who the hell is telling the truth? I involuntarily groan a little too loudly before Gerard is out of the room, making him turn back.

"What now?"

He's got to be lying. I know he's lying. I need him to be lying. Or else it's Alex, who's not telling me the truth.

"Nothing, it's just. Like I said, I've been doing a lot of thinking today, about what you said, and I'm sorry about last night, it was totally my fault you got angry," I mumble into the pages of my book. "I want to be a better wife to you, but to do that I need to accept your past and who you are. Or I should leave."

"No."

"Then we need to talk about what's important to you." I twist my head so he can see my face. "But why don't you have a shower first?" I smile. "I'll dish up dinner then tell you what I've decided."

Over dinner we talk about Gerard's work and the upcoming fundraiser. I inform him that Sheree has returned from vacation, and while away, her boyfriend proposed.

"I'm thrilled for her, Gerard, she's had a lot of bad relationships before Darby came along." I glance at him as I scrape the plates and put them in the dishwasher. I understand he's probably disappointed that I've stayed in contact with Sheree, so I'm not surprised he doesn't seem interested in the news. Gerard grumbles under his breath about the information but still, he helps me clean up before darting into his office for several minutes. When he returns, he is carrying a large white envelope. For a moment, I panic that he will hand it to me, that it contains divorce papers or something. Thank God he doesn't notice my worried look, which I hide by drying the bench for the second time.

"I'm leaving this on the counter, Paige. It's not urgent, but I'd appreciate you passing it on to Annabel when you see her next. It's for Stuart. Something I looked into." He lays it on the kitchen bench before reaching out a hand for me to take. Tossing the tea towel aside, I let him lead me upstairs. "Well, tonight has been a far better night than last night, hasn't it?" he asks, switching off the lights as we go. "Earlier, you said you had something to discuss. Do you still want to talk?"

"I'm going to blame the alcohol for last night." I smile up at him, though my insides are churning. "And yes, I do want to talk. It's about your—particular sexual taste." I try swallowing the damn ball in my throat that doesn't want to go away, praying to God what I'm proposing doesn't backfire.

"Oh." Gerard frowns. "All right, but let's wait until we get into bed then."

While we brush our teeth, I stare at our reflections. We're not the same people, Gerard and I. We used to laugh and joke with one another. Now, I don't know how to behave. Once upon a time, my heart would swell at the sight of my husband. His perfect features, his radiant smile, and his electric blue eyes. His predictability. I want to think I'm wrong about him, but how can a man who hides the truth from his partner of five years be genuine? A man who, rather than help someone out from the kindness of his heart, turns a blind eye. I need to remind myself that Jolene cheated, just like me, and he has every right to be angry and not care, but why is my bullshit radar beeping. There's something about Alex's and Jolene's theory that rings true. Gerard never wanted children. I know this. And he's a clever, resourceful man. He offered Alex money in exchange for sex. Last night he tried to… And the other week he allowed Jamison to… *Eww.* I spit the toothpaste froth out of my mouth and eye Gerard again, feeling angrier by the second until the anger turns to a profound sadness, and I'm asking myself all the what ifs.

What if Alex never arrived? What if I'd never cheated? What if I hadn't agreed to the damn ménage à trois in the first place? And what if Gerard is hiding something else?

When we're done brushing our teeth, I turn him to face me and surprise myself by how calm I'm able to act. Reaching up, I push his hair away from his forehead and smile. "I've always loved you, Gerard, and you've given me almost everything I've ever wanted."

"Why do I get the feeling you're about to say something I don't want to hear?" he asks, lifting my chin. "Are you planning on breaking my heart or mending it? We could make love," he says, smiling and raising his eyebrows.

"No, not tonight," I say, smoothing his graying chest hair with the palm of my hand. "I'm a little sore from last night, to be honest."

Gerard flinches. "Oh well, another night then." He pulls away and climbs into bed without me.

Staring from the bathroom door, my heartbeat cranks up several notches. I quickly weigh up the pros and cons before I take the final plunge, the pros winning out in the end. But still, I'm nervous.

"Gerard—I want to make you happy. I know I've been standoffish about your..." I search for a kind appraisal for his fetish and lowering myself on the end of the bed. "Likes," I say pointedly.

"All right." He leans up on his elbow looking dubious, then pulls himself higher until he is sitting.

Crawling over the covers, I slip in beside him, then take my time fixing the blankets around me.

"Well, go on, what is it?" he pesters, growing impatient with my stalling. But my heart is racing beyond belief. What if he was lying this morning? What if watching isn't really a kink but a way to catch me out wanting to cheat? Is this something I really want, or should I just leave? Move on and find someone else. Maybe once I'm free, Alex will want me. But searching Gerard's eyes, I know I'm delusional. Gerard would never let me be with Alex. He'd stalk us and make life hell. No, this is the only way it can happen.

Gerard lays down again and rolls over. "Well, when you're ready, let me know, because right now, I'm beat. Goodnight," he says, over his shoulder murmuring that he loves me.

I know he's still waiting, dying to know, even though he's pretending to act uninterested.

"I've been thinking about this all day," I start, making

Gerard roll onto his back to look at me again. "And I've decided that you're right. Who wants normal, and what woman wouldn't want her cake and eat it too?"

"What are you getting at, Paige? Just come out and say it. I'm tired."

"I guess what I'm trying to say, is if you want to be a voyeur or cuckold or whatever they call it, then I should be more supportive. I cheated on you, and you forgave me. It scared me to do it again because I thought it would ruin what we have. But I think I understand now that if we don't adapt to each other's sexual needs, then that is what will wreck our marriage."

Gerard rolls to face me. With a deep breath, along with his nodding, he seems to take it all in. Then he purses his lips. "I imagine you have limits on this proposal?"

"Yes," I say, slipping farther under the blankets. "It can only happen when I'm in the mood. It's not to be forced, and I can't have sex with someone I'm not attracted to. Now, I know last night might still be raw, but if you want honesty, which I'm sure you do, I'm going to confess that my first preference would be Alex again. I know him and what to expect."

Gerard inhales loudly and flops onto his back again. When it seems like he's doubtful, I add. "I know he's a player, Gerard, I get that now. I guess I just got momentarily caught up in his attention. I never said I didn't love you. I just admitted I had feelings for him, which is how it works with women. I can't just screw anyone—I need to like them. But you and me—we have a life together and I don't want to lose you because I'm not open-minded enough. I'm suggesting we do it because it's something I think you," I shrug, "or maybe both of us, need."

"Right." Gerard looks to the ceiling again. I study his face, relieved that I've gotten it all out. This could work. We all get what we want. That is, of course, if Alex demands payment, and that's if I can convince Alex it's a clever idea. "And what if Alex says no, like last time?"

"Pay him. I don't care. I'm over the shock. I mean, what's the difference between buying a vibrator or getting a gigolo?" I shrug again, though inside I'm cringing at my analogy. Alex the vibrator. I'm sure he wouldn't like being referred to as that, and now I wish that I could take it back. Gerard might use the reference against me somehow.

"And what if he still refuses?" He narrows his eyes. "How does that work out fair for me?"

A solid lump forms in my throat that takes some effort to swallow down. Quick, think. "Well—I suppose we'll find someone else then. So long as I find them attractive and they are clean, then meh, let's just have some fun. But I think keeping it simple would be better for everyone, don't you think? Ask Alex first. If he doesn't seem interested, offer him money. If he still says no, then we'll go from there."

Seemingly happy with my decision, Gerard nods. I need to force a smile because inside I'm backpedaling, wishing I hadn't given him the option of someone else. What if Alex does refuse? The sensation of ants crawling under my skin has me slipping under the covers for relief, but Gerard's silence isn't helping me either.

He raises himself up on one elbow, his piercing eyes I was once so madly in love with, scrutinize and look disturbed which causes my mouth to go dry.

"Well, that's not what I expected." Gerard smirks "And you know what? I think I might just need to think about that for a bit, Paige."

Shit. Shit, shit, shit!

"Sure." I peck Gerard a kiss goodnight and switch off the lamp. "Whatever you want Gerard, I'm not fussed either way."

I slide down into bed thinking what a goddamn idiot I am, not to mention what an A1 liar I've turned out to be.

Minutes later when I'm just drifting off to sleep, I get an electrical jolt to the heart. The worst thing possible suddenly occurs to me. This morning when Gerard told me about Jolene, not once, did he mention the baby's name. But stupidly, I had.

5

BETTER

"It's a life-changing event," Annabel announces, pinning a piece of paper faceup against her chest as though she's a sandwich board.

You can say that again. I cross my legs under the table studying Annabel's concerned expression.

"It's too strong, ain't it?" She slides the flyer she has designed toward me. Taking it, I gloss over the lengthy description but I take very little in. I can't stop thinking about Alex and the longer she's here, the closer I'm getting to cracking open at the seams.

I hand the flyer back with a reassuring smile. "No. I think you need to hit hard. "

On the outside, I have become the perfect actress—all smiles and pleasantries. Behaving like a good friend and doting wife, but underneath I'm an untrustworthy cheater because I've been crazy preoccupied thinking about Alex and my plan, all week. I haven't been in touch with Alex. I'd made it clear when he dropped me off last week that I was no good for him and if my plan is to work, I've got to play it cool and not let my feelings ruin it. I had hoped to at least get a glimpse of him when he came to do the gardening though, and then when he did turn up, trust me to be out shopping. I only knew he'd been because the lawn had been mowed and he'd dropped off some supplies to build the arbor over the fish pond.

"Oh God, Paige, I've been busier than moths in mittens, and I've still got more to do. Can you believe it's only two weeks away? And I'm so nervous this year!" Annabel shakes her hands in front of herself, then squeezes them into fists. When she moves around the table, unloading her tote and spreading everything out for me to see, her red flats keep skidding on the floor. Any second, I'm expecting her to slip over and fall on her ass.

"Annabel, please. Sit down for a minute." I feel guilty watching her because I haven't been as supportive as I normally would. Her hair is pulled into a loose bun, so she must have been flustered getting ready this morning. She dabs a hand over her sweaty brow and pulls at the neck of her black short-sleeved turtleneck sweater before her brown eyes are darting around looking for, I assume, the air conditioner, which is on full bore.

She's not her usual self.

"Oh, I can't, there's still so much to do." She lets out a groan.

"Well, where's my list? Delegate. No one is expecting you to do all this on your own." I glance down at all the piles she has made. "I mean, what is all this? You've taken on more than last year."

Taking a seat, she looks triumphantly at the piles of Manila folders. "Well, it's giving me a sense of worth. I know my job's not very demanding, and I should spend more time with Katie, but you know...?" She leaves the rest unsaid. "Caterers and the menu." She slaps a hand on one pile, and I nod. She taps the next pile. "A list of requirements. You know? How many chairs, tables, marquees, et cetera. All the furniture, fixtures, and props? And this," she reaches forward then hands me a cream folder, "contains the list of items for auction and who donated them. Each one of those needs an official 'thank-you card' please. I've already arranged for the paper to run another editorial promo, but…" She presses her palms together in prayer. "*We* are needed at the hospital on Friday at ten for photos with the children before the paper can run the story." She looks at me expectantly.

"As in tomorrow, Friday?" I ask.

"Oh hell. Slap my head, you're right. That is tomorrow. Golly gosh, the days are flying faster than green grass through a goose."

"You'd like me to go to the hospital with you?" I'm surprised when she nods. "But you're the one who's been doing all the work, Annabel, not me. I've just been your sidekick, really."

"No, you've been helping just by letting me bounce things around and getting your input." She taps my hand. "Besides, you're my girlfriend. I enjoy doing things with you."

"Well, I'd love to go, and tomorrow works well for me." Although thinking about my commitments to Donnie, I'll need to stay up late if I'm to get my work done. The list of 'thank-you' notes are no doubt larger than life. But if I can generate a generic message, get them printed and posted by Tuesday, it should be fine. Focus, Paige, focus. Your friend needs you.

"Great, that's settled then, shall I pick you up?" she asks. But instantly, I'm thinking 'no,' because it presents an opportunity to slip by the beach house under the pretense that I need to use the bathroom or something immature like that?

"No, I'll meet you there. I have a few things to do first." Christ, so much for playing it cool, 'cheater extraordinaire.'

"Right, then." She taps the table. "How about a coffee first, and then we'll get started?"

"Sorry, of course, coffee coming up." I push my chair back.

"No, sweetie, let me get the coffee. You have yourself a peek at that folder in your hand. I'm sorry, but you've got your work cut out. We were positively inundated with donations. I say, it's quite impressive. I'm amazed by everyone's generosity. It's so nice." Annabel heads toward the coffee machine.

I open the folder and sift through excel spreadsheets that comprise three letter-sized pages. There must be at least two hundred names and businesses on there. "Christ," I mumble under my breath. I don't want Annabel to feel bad but holly heck, I will be busy. She obviously saved the best for last.

"Paige, is this for me?" I turn to see her holding the large white envelope with her name on it.

"Yes, Gerard wanted me to give to you. I think he wants you to pass it on to Stuart or something. I'm not sure if you need to sign anything, but I'm positive he would have left instructions on sticky notes in there. Gerard *loves* his sticky notes." I let out a chuckle.

"You should entice him one night then. Plaster them over your naked body like a road map, 'Touch here first, now—here, and here, and now—here.'" Annabel points to various parts of her body, lastly poking a finger at the crotch of her jeans, then laughs. It feels good to laugh with her. I'm reminded of our carefree days, pre-Alex. When there were less stressful things to consider. I glance at the shed and shake my head. One wrong turn taken, and everything goes to shit.

"No, I'm sure your delish-dish husband doesn't need Post-It pointers though," she mumbles, throwing the envelope back on the bench. I let my smile wan. "I wonder why he didn't give those papers to Stuart himself. Golly, they've been seeing each other every other day. I can't wait for that to be over with. I just hope the partnership works." Turning she gets cups downs.

"Partnership? You mean you're investing in a new business?"

"Stuart wants to buy shares in an existing construction company owned by Ronald. He's fixing to sign papers—Friday next week, I think," she explains, filling two mugs with coffee. "Milk in yours, Paige?"

"Thanks. Well, congratulations then." I take a mug from her when she brings them over. "But I thought that went awash when you never spoke about him again. You've obviously changed your mind about him? I thought you said he was a little on the sleazy side," I remind her.

She places her coffee down then pulls her chair closer to mine before sitting.

"Well, between you me and the cat's scratchin' post, I actually find Ronald a whole lot sexier now. With his pinstripe suit and dishy ties." For some reason, the way she describes him gives me chills "I love the way he talks to me," she continues in a whisper as though we're not alone. "It's like no one else is in the room. Even though it's all business, he's all eyes on me. And he's got this cute little scar on his lip, makes me want to kiss it all better." She touches my hand then giggles before changing the subject.

"So, how was Jenna and Nadal's party? Can you believe I was better that day, but then we couldn't get a sitter for Katie? I suggested we just take her along, but no, Stuart was fixed on staying home. Come to think of it, I should have left the two of them and gone on my own," she says, more to herself than me.

"Well, Katie would have been bored, Jamie and Erica were imprisoned in their rooms with a sitter. But I agree, you should have ditched her and Stuart and come. I missed you, but it was a good night, considering." My face instantly heats up realizing I slipped up. "What time did you say we needed to be at the hospital tomorrow?" I pick up a random folder, paging through and trying to recover.

"Considering what?" Annabel takes the folder from me, then shuffles others around, putting them, I assume, in some order before we go through them.

"Oh nothing. Just some guy was a bit…" I search for the right word.

"Come on out with it," Annabel presses. "A bit what?"

"Touchy feely." I screw up my face.

"Oh, one of those? Well, I reckon as long as they touch and feel in the right places, honey, I don't care." Her eyes go wide, and she throws her head back laughing. "I'm just jokin', sweetie." She taps my hand. "I hope you put him in his place then. Right, now, why don't we get started?"

For the next two hours, we brainstorm and tackle the tasks left to do. With the fundraiser only a couple of weeks away, we need to get as much sorted today as possible. When Annabel finally puts the last of her folders in her tote and we are saying our goodbyes at the front door, we hear before we see the roar of a motorcycle that's coming up the driveway.

"Who's that?" Annabel twists and stands beside me, watching as the manned bike crawls toward the house.

"I don't know." For a brief, stupid moment I think Gerard might have sent some random guy around to get to know me, and my stomach flip-flops.

Annabel and I stand there on the front porch, looking goofy as the bike pulls up meters away. The rider, dressed in black leather pants and jacket, kicks out the stand with his boot, switches off the engine and only then, does he remove his blue and black helmet. I'm not sure about Annabel's mouth, because my eyes are transfixed, but I know mine falls slightly agape in surprise. Yep, Annabel's mouth might not have dropped open like mine, but when she grabs hold of my arm, I gather she's just, if not more, excited than me.

"Hey." Alex rests the helmet between his thighs then combs his hair back with his fingers. "Am I too early?"

Annabel looks from Alex to me then back again. I'm standing there smiling, my face no doubt lit up like a darn Christmas tree.

"Too early for what?" Annabel looks back and forth between us, looking as confused as I feel. It takes a moment and the raising of Alex's eyebrow before I catch on.

"Ooh—Yes—that's today. Sorry, I forgot all about it."

"What's going on, y'all? What am I missing?"

"Alex is taking me to the Port. I've been meaning to tell you every time I see you. I'm going to donate a series of photos for the auction. I quickly fill Annabel in on my idea. "Gerard didn't want me going alone, and well… Alex agreed to take me." If my expression doesn't convey how I feel, my smug tone does.

"Got room for one more?" Annabel looks toward Alex, widening her feline eyes and licking her lips. I can't believe how she flirts with him. Alex laughs, and I think he might be on the verge of blushing.

"Sorry." He shrugs a shoulder then taps the two helmets.

Dying to be alone with Alex, I grab Annabel into a hug to move her along. "I'll see you tomorrow at the hospital."

"Oh, all righty then." Her words come out so slowly, it thickens her southern accent, and I catch Alex's smirk before he palms it away and looks around the yard. "I get it. You need me to go. Well—I'll see you tomorrow then. At ten," she reminds me, shifting the weight of her tote from one shoulder to the other.

Nodding, I wave my hands to usher her along when she keeps looking from me to Alex.

"Okay, I'm goin', I'm goin'. Bye, Alex." Stepping off the front landing, she keeps glancing over her shoulder as she heads toward her green Camry. "Stay safe if you're going out on that thing," she calls out, pointing at the bike. "And don't do anything I wouldn't do." We both laugh at her. Then she's walking backward to deliver her last warning. "And if you can't be good, at least be careful."

"Annabel!" I gasp.

Alex purses his lips and looks down at the helmet he's nursing, then glances up at me.

"She's joking, she doesn't know anything, I swear," I reassure him in a whisper beneath my smile.

I wave Annabel off as she drives away.

"Well," I say, pulling my dress out at the sides. "I suppose I better get changed if we're going on that."

"So, you'd like a ride?" Alex smirks at his own insinuation.

"Maybe. But definitely on the bike."

Alex chuckles. "What a wicked tease you are, Princess."

"Where have you been hiding this thing?" I ask, stepping off the porch and taking hold of the handlebar. I read the bikes badge then trace my finger over the embossed surface, showing I'm impressed.

"Nowhere." He dips his head to watch my hand that lands on his knee.

"Nice leathers," I say, sliding my hand farther up his leg. His thick thighs, clad in black leather, straddle the seat, and I won't apologize that I'm drawn straight to the bulge between them. He is a sight for my sore eyes and my equally aching pussy. If it weren't so improper for all to see, I would climb right up there on his bike and lift my dress so he could take me. When I look up, Alex's eyes are twinkling, and he smiles, but he's shaking his head.

"You're trouble, that's what you are."

"In trouble or am trouble?" I tease, then slap his leg. "Waiting here, or inside?"

"I think I better wait here." He nods slowly. "Wear something practical."

"What, like a short skirt and no underwear?" I shamelessly flirt, taking each step up the stairs backward because I don't want to take my heated eyes off him.

"Christ almighty," Alex breathes, shifting on the seat.

Once inside, I sprint up the stairs, and minutes later, I'm in a pair of black leather jeans that I haven't worn in ages. I grab a scarf and quickly use ChapStick on my lips, then braid my hair. Butterflies are doing wicked things to my insides that I almost forget my camera. Throwing it in a small backpack, along with my phone and the lip balm, I'm done. I've never ridden on a motorcycle before, and I'm practically tripping over my feet as I tumble down the stairs, taking two at a time.

After locking the house, we helmet up.

"When we get onto the highway, make sure you lean with me around corners," Alex yells through his helmet. "And hang on tight." He scoops a hand around my rear and pulls me closer to his ass, then tugs on my arms, making me wrap them tighter around him. In response to his advice, I nod against his back, reveling that I'm so close to him. His Yamaha Road Star vrooms and vibrates beneath me as Alex twists on the throttle, making my heart race and my body tingle all over. Annabel would be seething with jealousy right about now, I think to myself, and I'm half tempted to ask Alex if he'd mind stopping by Jenna's because there's just something I've got to tell her that just can't wait.

"You ready, Princess?" Alex asks.

I'll always be ready for you, Alex. "Yep." I holler back, my hand dropping to squeeze his crotch, and then I'm squealing as Alex lets go of the clutch, and the bike leaps into action.

I can't wipe the smile from my face. Alex is a confident rider. From the moment we take off, I feel safe in his hands. Weaving and dodging the city traffic, I can understand and am grateful he thought to take me on his bike because the traffic is heavy this time of day. Whenever we stop at lights or traffic jams, I relax my grip and look around at the city sights. It's different from being in a car. Strangely, it's more realistic. It's as though traveling by car puts you in a cocoon and separates you from the outside world. But on a bike, you become one with it.

We take around an hour to reach the Port, and when we get there, Alex needs to drive around in search of the containers I saw on the news. Having made calls late last week after asking Alex, I was assured there were no caveats on either taking the photos or getting permission to be around. We were free to wander so long as it was within the normal pedestrian thoroughfare.

After extracting my head out of the tight-fitting helmet, I take a big stretch and hand my helmet to Alex, who balances both on the bike seat.

"That was so much fun. I've never been on a bike before." I'm sure I look a little giddy, and when I reach out and stroke the front of his jacket, Alex covers my hand.

"I thought you'd like that. Nothing like a bit of torque between your legs," he says, giving me a wink.

Laughing, I refrain from giving the comeback that's on the tip of my lips. Instead, I roll my eyes at him, then pull my backpack and jacket off. Now that we're stationary and dressed in leathers, it becomes sweltering in the sun. We look around the Port with interest, momentarily watching a large crane unload a huge blue shipping container as it swings in a non-existent breeze. There are forklifts buzzing around, making unrealistic turns and looking more like a wind-up toy than machinery that can lift a ton.

"I didn't know you owned a bike, Alex," I say, getting my camera set up and changing lenses.

"It's not mine. I borrowed it from a buddy. I used to own a bike. Before prison. Had to sell her, of course." He kicks at the asphalt and rests his hands in his front pockets then glances around again.

"That's a shame. What sort of bike was it?" I ask, even though I know nothing about bikes.

"A 2010 Thunderbird Triumph, the perfect shade of red. Fuck, I loved that bike." Moving closer to me, our eyes cross paths before Alex folds his arms and peers at what I'm doing.

"Well, thanks, I got a real buzz out of that, and I'm looking forward to the ride home."

Crouching, I rummage through the camera case in my backpack in search of a cloth while Alex stands above me, his feet shuffling as he looks about. "I've never been here before," he tells me. "That's a shitload of containers right there. You'd reckon they'd lose track of what's fucking what."

"Yeah," I agree, standing and wiping the lens to my Fujifilm X-T3. "You should go over there so I can focus my lens." I point at one of the heart-adorned containers, wondering if he's gullible enough to believe that I need a human subject to focus my camera. The truth—I just want a good photo of him.

Alex peels off his jacket and lays it across the handlebars of the bike. His deep red tee is tucked into his pants and the graphic on the front claims Budweiser to be 'The King of Beers.' I wait as he saunters over to the container, a grin plastering my face until he turns and I look serious again.

"Yeah, that's it. Right there is good." I bring the camera to my face and start clicking endlessly while struggling to keep a straight face. He moves around with his thumbs hooked in his pockets, obviously self-conscious, and at one point, he runs his hand through his hair. When I've taken about *a hundred,* I put him out of his misery.

"Thanks, that worked." My laugh is contagious and Alex becomes animated.

"You were playing me then, weren't you, you bitch?"

I mock gasp at him. "Alex, language, please. But you're right, auto-focusing." I wiggle the camera at him. "I wanted a keepsake." I'm sure I'm looking smug.

"Yeah, well, don't let that husband of yours see them. Does he even know you're here, with me?" He walks back and stands behind me and out of the way as I put the camera to my face again.

"Don't worry. What he doesn't know won't hurt him."

"Is that right, Princess?" He runs his hand over my leather-clad ass. "You look good in leather, I bet you'd look even better in a latex body suit with a zip opening right about here," he teases pressing his fingers into my butt and making me lurch forward with a gasp.

"Behave," I say, wiggling my ass away from him and returning the camera to my face. "Has Gerard called you lately?" I ask, sending my heart into a flutter.

"No. What for?"

It takes all my strength not to pull the camera away and explain everything. "Nothing. I was just making sure he's been speaking with you, that's all. You—are still talking to each other, aren't you? I mean I haven't wrecked your relationship, have I?"

"No, we're cool, although I should tell him what a dumb-ass he is for trying to fuckin' rape you."

I hold in a lungful of air for a moment before answering, wishing I hadn't told him about the fight. "I'd hardly call it rape, Alex, he bound my hands and was rough, that's all," I explain, though the memory makes my stomach twist. "Besides, he can't know I told you about that."

"Whatever. But I bet you were scared in all the wrong ways." He sounds a little offbeat.

I take the camera away from my face and nod at him. "I was," I confess searching his eyes. "But it wasn't your fault," I add, sensing he still blames himself.

Alex grunts. "Yeah, well, if it ever happens again, kick the fucker in the balls, that'll sort him out until I get there to kick his ass. Don't let anyone do that kind of shit to you without a fight." He pushes his hands in his front pockets and rocks on his heels. "Are you nearly done? I've got things I need to do."

"Just a few more." I say, resuming my task.

"Sweet," Alex says seconds later, making me look around. "I'm getting a drink. Will you be all right here for a minute?" he asks. He's spotted a store over the road that's tucked in amongst some derelict buildings. It looks as though it's been recently improved going by the bright blue paint and new flags advertising Civil Coffee.

"Sure. I'll have a water, please." I reach for my backpack.

"I've got it," he says, brushing me off before walking away. It's just as well he offered to pay because my purse is nowhere to be seen when I go looking for it. In my excitement to see Alex, I must have left it behind. I keep my eyes on him until he's on the road edge, enthralled by the way he moves. The way his beefy shoulders rotate with his swaying arms. And, argh, the way his ass fills those leather pants. With no audience, I let out a distinctive sigh. He may not be as tall or as handsome as Gerard, but by God, he's insanely sexy.

I take as many shots as I need, then look around the dock through my lens, taking random shots of cranes and people in the distance, hoping I'm not breaching any laws. Zooming in, I spot a cat laying on a pile of flat cardboard boxes on a pallet, its belly pointing to the sky.

"Paige!"

I spin around and Alex is waving me over from the front of the store. Packing up my gear, I throw my backpack over a shoulder and make my way across the road. By the time I get there, Alex has re-entered the store and is paying for his purchases. When the bell chimes behind me, I almost miss the greeting that escapes a petite ash blonde standing in front of Alex.

"Oh my God! It is you, Paige." She peeks around Alex's frame after dropping change in his hand.

In partial shock, I mutter Kelsey's name. My old roommate comes from around the counter, smiling. She has her hair in a messy bun that's tucked beneath a hairnet, and she's almost devoid of makeup. She looks paler than when we lived together, and her small frame is overwhelmed by a large apron that reaches past her knees. Kelsey had been aspiring to become a dancer, and I'm disappointed to find her in the industrial side of town and not on a stage. Looking tired, her mahogany eyes are shadowed by hollowed sockets. She moves in quickly and wraps me up, albeit in small arms, into a big bear hug. She smells of fried food and sickly sweet sugar.

"I was watching from here and I saw you guys pull up at the yards. Obviously, I noticed your hair, and thought—shit no, it couldn't be Paige Guthrie, but this guy said it was you." She glances at Alex then back at me. "Cool. So how ya been? You look amazing." She takes a step back to take me in, her hands clasping hold of mine, her thumb rubbing over the large diamond on my wedding finger when she notices it. She looks up and raises her brow, then smirks in Alex's direction. "What have you been doing, where do you live? Did you end up going to Bali?"

Kelsey fires off question after question in an excitable rant, reminding me of the plethora of dreams I once shared with her. Travel and taking photos. Writing and starting a blog. Riding an elephant then adopting it so I could set it free. Smiling, I tell her to slow down then introduce Alex, glancing at him over my shoulder. "I'm just here taking photos for a collection piece I'm working on. For a fundraiser. I finished my studies and I do a bit of freelance stuff, nothing too exciting," I tell her.

On the fringe of my view I catch the frown Alex throws my way before he excuses himself, saying he'll wait outside.

Kelsey moves away and acts busy, straightening a few packaged sandwiches in an open cabinet fridge until Alex has closed the door.

"How long have you been working here, are you still with Fin?" I ask, drawing her attention back to me then unhitch my backpack from my shoulders and lower it to the floor. "You look good, Kels," I add, looking around the small interior of the fast-food outlet.

Kelsey becomes self-conscious and smooths her hands over her apron before crossing her arms. "Thanks. Believe it or not, Fin and I are still together. We live about six blocks that-a-way." She gestures to the left with her head. "He's hot." Her eyes dart to Alex, who is standing on the curb, waiting to cross. "Better than that older guy you had the hots for back when we lived together. Sometimes, I miss that apartment and you."

"It was good wasn't it? And yeah Alex is nice. He's…"

"I'm sorry I bailed out on you like that, Paige." She shakes her head and looks at the floor for a split second. "You know, it's been eating at me ever since." The color in Kelsey's cheeks deepens and she looks as though she's on the brink of tears. I take a step closer and reach out to stroke her upper arm in reassurance.

"It's fine, everything ended well. I'm glad you're still with Fin, and you seem happy. It's no big deal." I smile, but she doesn't return my gesture.

"No, it wasn't the right thing to do, Paige." Screwing up her face, she looks thoroughly annoyed. "I was chickenshit, but that guy creeped me out, and I didn't want trouble. I hope he didn't turn out to be evil or anything?"

"What do you mean, what guy?"

"That dude you liked from the café."

For a moment, I struggle, remembering my old work friends and old boss, Aymil, wondering if I ever found him creepy. Then I realize she's talking about Gerard. Instantly, the hairs on my arms stand, and for a moment, I feel disorientated, reliving the sick feeling when Kelsey said she was moving out. How abrupt she was, and how I'd thought it had something to do with me. That she was tired of me leaving dirty tissues on the coffee table and using the last of her favorite nail polish, annoying habits that often grate on thrown-together strangers.

"Do you mean the lawyer, Gerard?" I'm looking straight at her.

Kelsey's eyes go wide. "Yes," she exhales in a high pitch. "Him. Good-looking but creepily intense. I'm glad you didn't fall for him."

If my face has paled, Kelsey doesn't comment. She glances around the shop then settles her eyes on me again but shuffles. Her arms and hands are so restless, she unfolds and refolds them, finally stuffing them in the front pocket of her apron, which seems to give her the confidence to continue. "He came around one night when you were at class." She leans in. "Said he knew about me and my dirty habit," Kelsey whispers, referring to the occasional pot smoking habit she had. "He said he didn't appreciate me influencing you, and he suggested I find somewhere else to live."

"Are you for real? How the hell did he even know about that?" I fan the top of my tee that's getting soaked at my armpits.

"I thought you must have told him. I was so pissed off at you I didn't bother explaining."

I jerk backward, shocked Kelsey would think that of me. "Kelsey, I would never. I didn't even talk about you. Only that I lived with you."

"Well, he threatened that if I didn't move out, that I better watch my back. That he knew the local cops that cruised our area and whenever they raid a place but find nothing, they just go ahead and plant drugs, so they don't look like fools. Then he said, 'And they might not just find marijuana either. Do you know the offense for pushing cocaine, Kelsey Jane Ramirez?' That's what he said, swear to God. He knew my entire name." Her arms come up to clutch herself, and she quivers deliberately.

I'm rendered speechless and feel a real shiver crawl up my spine. I look from Kelsey to outside where Alex is resting on the seat of his bike. I gloss over Kelsey's face and survey the store, lost in thought as my insides shrivel into my bowels. That's exactly how he phrased Alex's name the night of our big fight. Alexander John Perna.

"Are you all right?"

"Yeah, I'm fine. Sorry that happened to you, Kels. What a jerk, hey?" I retrieve my gear and swing it onto one shoulder. "So how long you been working here, you didn't tell me?" I ask, eager to change the subject.

"A little over two years. The pay is shit, but the tips are a-plenty." She glances behind her into the kitchen where I assume her supervisor must be. "Do you know how many dock workers there are? Hundreds, this place is so busy for lunch, and they don't mind tipping even though it's small. It's in the numbers, Paige, not the amount." She nods looking pleased with her smarts, and her logic makes me smile.

"That's good, Kels. What about Fin, what's he doing?"

"Loving me." She laughs. "He keeps applying for jobs, but, meh, you know the stats."

I agree with a nod and give her a tight smile. "I guess I better go, can't keep lover boy waiting," I joke, pulling a face to hide my awkwardness. "It was nice seeing you, Kelsey."

"Yeah, you bet. Drop in again, let's have lunch one day," she calls out as I make my way to the door. "Hey! You never told me where you live now."

"Oh, still in LA, nowhere special. Say hello to Fin for me. I'm happy for you, and I hope you're still dancing?"

She nods and a huge smile splits her face. "I am. I've gotten a few good gigs too. Ever heard of Ava Max?"

"Really?" I'm genuinely surprised. "Good for you, I knew you'd get there. See you around, I guess." I wave, letting go of the door and my composure, my face falling at last. I can't move. I'm frozen at the curb, watching the passing traffic as a blur in front of me.

Maybe Kelsey corrupting me was a genuine concern to Gerard? I survey the asphalt at my feet. But we weren't even seeing each other. Why would he threaten her, why wouldn't he just say something to me, tell me it was something to consider? Why make her move out? Why wouldn't he encourage me to move in with someone else? No wait, he did. Him! I know the truth, it's there, right there under the surface, bubbling like toxic waste, ready to infect me. But I don't want to accept it. Was that his plan? To get me alone so I became vulnerable and needy, so I'd turn to him for help? Damn, I should have asked Kelsey when exactly he threatened her. Was it before or after he asked me to move in with him? I turn back and stare at the shop, ready to ask, but then I realize it doesn't matter when. He threatened her. Forced her to move out.

"Paige. What are you doing? We need to go," Alex hollers, curling his arm for me to hurry.

My intake of air enters in shudders. Is absolutely everything built on lies?

It seems like I float across the road to repeat incoherently to Alex the story Kelsey just told me.

"Here." Alex offers me the bottled water when I collapse against the shipping container and slide down so I'm out of the sun. "Have this, and then we better go. Have you had lunch? I think you need to eat."

Taking small sips of icy water, I stare at my knees then at a pacing Alex.

"Shit, are you sure that's what she said, and she wouldn't lie?"

I nod. But my entire body is stiffening because all I can think about is the man who held me at knife point. Digging into my memory, I try to recall his height, his build, the sound of his voice. No, no, I'm certain it wasn't Gerard. But he could have paid someone to do it. In an instant, I'm on my feet and doubling over. "Oh Christ." I choke out a sob. "It was him. I know it was him. He got rid of Kelsey so I would struggle and then he sent someone around to scare me. He played me, and I fell for it. Oh my God, I've been so stupid." When I look up, I feel deathly pale. "What am I going to do, Alex?"

"What do you mean, sent someone to scare you?"

"There was a break-in and a guy with a knife." I fill Alex in on what happened then try disputing the idea that Gerard orchestrated it. Alex remains quiet until I'm finished ranting then pulls me into his chest.

"Come on. We can't stay here." Alex leads me over to the bike. I jerk him to a halt. "Alex, please. What am I going to do?"

The gravity of my situation seems to weigh Alex down to the point where I notice his shoulders droop. "Look. I don't think you can just trust that girl."

"But why would she lie?"

"I don't know. Maybe it isn't as dramatic as she's making out. He might have said he cares about what happens to you and that police often raid on a whim and he didn't want you caught up in it. Maybe that girl…"

"Kelsey."

"Whatever. Maybe she was stoned at the time and got paranoid, the truth got distorted. Who knows, Paige?"

I'm nodding the whole time he's talking, desperate to believe what he's saying. "And the burglar?" My eyes send out a plea for him to convince me of another explanation. "Do you think that was just random?"

"Yes. Now come on, let's get out of here." Turning abruptly, he strides over to the bike leaving me to amble along behind him in doubt.

Alex tosses my jacket at me and when I join him at the bike, he shoves a helmet in my hands and even before I've buckled it up, he's thrown a leg over the bike and brought it to life.

"Are you okay? You seem angry," I ask.

"I'm fine, but we need to get going."

Alex waits until I get into position behind him and take hold of the sides of his jacket. He throttles the bike a few times, letting it roar beneath us as if venting. Something is wrong with him. When I lean in, I feel every muscle beneath his jacket tense. Behind my helmet, I try to numb my emotions, but tears threaten. The more I know about Gerard, the more helpless I feel and the greater the gratitude I have for Alex. I squeeze him tighter, silently thanking him for being there for me. He relaxes a little, and with a reassuring pat on my arm he yells through the helmet, "Just hang on to me, Princess."

Oh, I will, Alex. You can be sure of that.

6

EVEN IF IT HURTS

We speed along the highway, and before I realize what's happening, Alex has pulled up outside the beach house. He waits for me to dismount before he's pulling off his helmet and explaining himself.

"My buddy needs his bike back by three. So, I'll take you home in my truck after we have some lunch. Is that all right?"

I shrug. "Sure. It's not like I'm looking forward to going home."

I follow him as he hastily makes his way toward the side of the house and up the stairs.

"I'm just going to get changed first. I suppose you'll get hot in those clothes," he surmises, unzipping his jacket and peeling it off.

"I should be okay," I say, as he unlocks the door then makes a beeline toward his room. I stay behind in the living area and take off my jacket, looking around to see what changes have taken place since I was last here. A new kitchen has been fitted with all new appliances, and he has some magnetic scrabble tiles adorning the stainless steel fridge door. Someone has spelled out, 'ALEX IS A LOSER', which makes me chuckle. Helping myself to a glass of water, I'm staring absently out the window when Alex shouts out making me jump.

"Now don't get weird on me, but do you want this to wear?" Alex enters from down the hall, holding up a dress. He has changed into the same clothes he had on the morning at the hotel.

I get close enough to inspect the garment. "Lost property box," he explains sheepishly.

"Fine." I glare at him before taking it out of his hands. "But only because I'm roasting alive in these pants." I go into the bathroom to change. I need to wear my boots, but surprisingly, they go well with the floral sundress. I look a little country, so I let my hair loose and give it a tousle to shake out the waves.

When I emerge, Alex is already at the door as though in a hurry.

"Let's walk along the beach. Do you have time?"

"I'll make time." Mentally I ignore the pile of 'thank-you' notes but grimace when I think of Donnie's voice booming over the phone at me again. I really don't have time but this opportunity with Alex, I just can't pass up. Besides I really need to get him on board if we are going to help Jolene and Grace.

Taking off our shoes and shirking our responsibilities, we make our way closer to the water's edge where it's cold, firm and easier to stroll along. It's nearing midday and the beach is quiet. There is just the slightest breeze that does nothing to cool the day down, and the waves are barely rolling in. They look more like the waves on a lake. The kind that are caused when people ski. Ripples that normally soothe the senses but for some reason cause me a kind of agony I'd rather not interpret. The shushing sound seems to demand that I be present, but not here. It's somewhere else that screams of a memory I need to keep suppressed.

I feel so real, so authentic being with Alex, and yet at the same time, fragmented, like pieces of me are falling away. It's uncomfortably confronting. Gerard was everything I ever wanted, a man I adored. But the woman who loves him isn't the real me. It's a version of me who is still reluctant to push the veils aside. I don't want to see the truth about him because it means I have to acknowledge the truth about myself. Images of Gerard confronting Kelsey are disturbing but also flattering. That he'd go to such lengths to be with me is like saying I'm the only woman on the planet he wants to be with. Gerard wanted to see other men have sex with me, to the point of paying, is both derogatory yet empowering. Him showering me with love, gifts, and forgiveness makes me feel worthy. So long as I say I'm his.

And then, there's Alex. And suddenly I'm free-falling. I don't know him. Sometimes he's scary. It's like he has a metal detector, but he's searching for lies. And lies is what he'll find if I let him look too deep. There's so much rot down there. Decay I don't want brought to the surface. Gerard pulls me away from my past, whereas Alex pulls me back into it.

"You're quiet." Alex nudges me with his shoulder. He doesn't reach for my hand, though I wish he would. But when I shrug, he seems to slow our pace to invite conversation. "Come on, what's on your mind? I can see the cogs turning."

I smile at the sand and then kick some up with my feet. "Where did you grow up, Alex?"

He turns and looks at me, perhaps surprised by my random question. "Portland, Oregon."

"Where did you learn to surf then?"

"Cannon Beach mostly. My mom was raised there, so we had family in town. It's nice. We spent just about every vacation there, seeing as my old man was tied up in the military."

"No wonder you're so tanned. Aw, you were a beach baby. Tell me more."

Alex stuffs his hands in his pockets, taking his time to answer as though thinking of what might interest me. I make deep toe prints in the sand, waiting for his reply.

"My mom surfed."

"Really?"

He nods, looking proud.

"She's been dead ten years now."

"It must have been hard watching your mom go through cancer," I sympathize, understanding the subject is close to his heart.

"Nah, I was too much of a prick back then to notice what she was going through, thankfully she had some good friends."

"What's the age difference between you and Gerard?"

"Eleven years."

I do the math, making him thirty-one.

"You know, Gerard never mentioned you until a couple of weeks before you arrived. Why do you think he did that?"

"I dunno. Maybe because after our folks split we didn't see each for like, I guess—seventeen years. I was six when my mom and me took off, and the next thing I know, Gerard's living in LA working at some law firm. He was always super smart though. He tracked me down somehow. He encouraged me to get into a trade. I was just bumming around before that."

"What trade did you do?"

Alex huffs. "Not even one lousy year in mechanics. Then my mom got sick and Jolene happened and well you know the rest." It's obvious he's not comfortable talking about the lowest parts of his past.

"What's your mom's name?"

"Talia." Instantly I picture a petite blonde with a super tanned, fit body and big blue eyes.

"Was she pretty?" It's a strange question to ask, but he answers in a heartbeat.

"She was. She had hair like yours, long and wavy, except hers was dark." His description sends me off kilter.

"Really?"

"Mmm, and green eyes. She was beautiful. Even after chemo. Secondary cancer took her within a year. I miss her. We were close before I went through my dickhead stage," he confesses with a pfft.

"What about you? Where did you grow up?"

I groan and flick him a look. "Colorado, the cold state." I pause for a second. "In a town called, Ponderosa Park. I'm certain the place is only notorious because of my mother."

"Why do you mean?"

"Can I just say, she liked penises an awful lot and leave it at that?"

"Sounds like my kind of lady, a cock worshiper hey?" he tries joking.

"Trust me, she's not any kind of lady." We step our way over a section of rock that cuts through the sand, careful not to land on any slippery sections. "My guess is that, like most of us, she had a bad childhood," I continue when we hit the sand again. "She never talked to me about it though. She was always drunk, and I mean hammered. My dad left when I was eleven. He'd had enough of her, but I can't believe he left me in her care, if you could call it that. I guess in that way, Gerard and I are alike I suppose. I think I was just lucky to have my close friend Sheree. Without her and her—," I stammer, and a rush of new heat hits my cheeks. "Without Sheree, I think I would have ended up dumped somewhere. Maybe even dead. Her family cared enough to know if I went missing, and my mom counted on that. Gerard…" I catch myself babbling and stop.

"Gerard what?"

Kicking at the sand, I watch it land ahead of me, then look at the ocean. "Nothing. He just hates my mom and even me talking about that time in my life."

Alex slips my hand into his. It's only then I realize just how much I blurted without intending to. Embarrassed, I can't look at him, even when he squeezes my hand. The action seems to work on my eyes instead and I need to clamp them tightly to avoid tears.

"There's a café just up these steps." He indicates toward the sand embankment. Feeling relieved by the distraction, I pick up my pace and chatter about the convenience of shops to our beach house. Anything to not talk about my past anymore.

Alex leads the way to a small establishment surrounded by large palm trees. It's not a flash place, more like a hippy's shack. The long wooden tables are surrounded by a multitude of different styled chairs that look like they were picked up from a secondhand shop, although the ones that are upholstered, that don't have bums on them, look newly restored.

The shop is almost packed to capacity, but everyone is talking in hushed tones. There's music playing in the background, and I can hear the busy kitchen from out front. Making our way to the counter I notice the specials menu, a small chalkboard with script writing that suggests, Organic Banana Bread, Poached Free-Range Eggs on Sourdough, or the 'Chef's Special,' Vegetarian Eggs Benedict. Having skipped breakfast this morning in my haste to get the basic house chores done before Annabel's arrival, my stomach grumbles.

"Alex," squeals a girl behind the coffee machine when she

notices us walk in. She's tall and slender with straightened brown hair, that's pulled into a low ponytail. She either has naturally thick eyelashes, or she's fallen victim to volumizing. Either way, her moss-green eyes simply pop. Or it could be because Alex gives her an award-winning smile, showing off all his teeth. My female instincts suspect they've been intimate. I shuffle uncomfortably and cross my arms.

"How was Byron Bay?" he asks, then turns to me. "Brontë went to Australia."

I nod at Brontë who grins then ignores me.

"It was beautiful. You would love it. I learned to kitesurf." She jiggles on the spot excitedly while frothing milk in a stainless steel jug. "We met some other backpackers the first day there and hooked up with them. They were Irish and sooo much fun. Every day, we did something different."

"Brontë, how's those coffees coming?" A burly looking guy sings out from the kitchen. "Your order's up."

"Fine. I'll be there in two," she shouts out breezily. "What can I get you guys?"

I look at Alex sheepishly. "I didn't bring my wallet."

"It's cool." He grabs some menus then addresses Brontë. "Come take our order?"

"Sure. Not a problem." She gives him a wink. I feel she may have picked up the term when in Australia. It sounds a little cheesy to me, but Alex rewards her with another flashy smile, making me want to pinch him.

When we're seated at a tiny table for two, Alex hands me a menu, and because I'm starving, everything sounds delicious.

"Do you suggest anything in particular?" I quiz.

"The oatmeal cakes are good, but so are the real eggs benny."

"Real eggs benny?"

"I like my bacon."

I laugh "Okay. Good to know. I thought you said you didn't eat breakfast. Obviously you come here often, and for breakfast, as in the morning after the *night* before, I suppose."

Alex tries to hide his smirk behind his menu, but his eyes give him away. "Aren't you married?" He frowns playfully.

"Anyway, we're here for lunch, so what's good? I'm starving. I missed breakfast, can I order big and fix you up later?"

Nodding, he studies the menu without making any more suggestions. I chew on my bottom lip then say, "Brontë seems nice." I stare at the menu as though I'm still deciding on what to eat then peek over it. Alex fixes his gaze and smiles. Then turns serious.

"She's all right."

I put my menu down slowly and stare at him.

"You and her. Have you been an item?" I know it's not my place to ask, but I can't pretend I don't care. Alex pulls his chair in and props his elbows on the table and hunches in closer.

"That—is something, you, don't need to know—Mrs. Whitmyer." His mouth turns up at the corners, broadening into a sensual smile. Then his ankles are at my feet, sliding them apart. I can't tear my eyes off him, and when I try to draw my knees together, he bumps against one. "I'm very hungry too, Paige." His admission is lustful and clearly not about food.

"Alex," I gush, looking around the café.

"Paige," he torments, sliding a hand under the table and rubbing my thigh. Oh God, Alex don't do this but please keep going, my muddled mind whines.

My breathing intensifies, and everything around blurs into obscurity. Alex is all I see, and when Brontë come up to the table she startles me.

"What can I get you guys, have you had time to look at the menu?"

"I'll get the usual and coffee thanks, Bront. Paige, what will you have?"

I notice he shortens her name affectionately, adding to my suspicion that they are familiar. "The pumpkin and pine nut salad sounds nice. Oh, and coffee for me too, please."

"Sorted," Brontë declares, popping her notepad in her apron pocket and collecting the menus from us. "I'll bring water. Tap or distilled?" she asks casually, then rolls a shoulder and winces. Before we have time to answer, she adds, "I think I'm nearly due for another massage, Alex." He looks from me to her, then tries to hide his amusement.

"No problem. Next week is good, and tap water is fine, I think. Paige?" he asks for my approval.

I nod absently and knock his knee with mine.

"Back soon." Brontë turns on her flats. Alex watches her walk away but starts tapping my knee with his own, making me realize he's watching me through peripheral vision. I shift out of his reach, making him turn and witness my sullen expression. It seems to give Alex pleasure because he laughs.

"Lighten up, Paige, she's a client. Not that you should care." He raises one dark eyebrow.

"But I do."

When he reaches under the table and strokes my knee again, I pull myself in closer, desperate for his reassuring touch. "Client?" I question, thinking how Gerard paid him to have sex with me. Is Alex saying he's an escort? I feel my face flush, and I must look shocked because Alex gets serious.

"Massage, nice hands, I love to caress." He waves his hands at me. I giggle then playfully groan.

"Don't tell me you're a masseuse as well?"

He nods.

"Oh please, really?"

He nods, and a stupid grin splashes across his face. He's totally enjoying tormenting me. "Mostly weekend work."

"Argh, Alex you're killing me here. So, what made you take on that? A chance to feel up as many women as humanly possible, I imagine."

"No. I do men."

Now it's my turn to raise an eyebrow. "Oh really." Instead of being embarrassed by my insinuation, he gloats back.

"Yes, really."

We both peel into laughter. Then he's taking hold of my hand and starts playing with my fingers.

"No, seriously. I took courses in prison, went with being a personal trainer. Figured I might as well get something useful out of my time."

"Wow, you really are a man of many talents, aren't you? You realize I will have to book a massage."

"Mmm, that could be tough." He tilts his head.

"Water," Brontë interrupts and Alex lets go of my hand. She lingers while filling up our glasses, and I get a sense that she now feels me as a threat. She confirms it when she pulls a tight smile at me before walking off.

"Oh my God, did you see that?" I whisper across the table at Alex when she's gone. "Is she someone you're seeing, Alex?"

He chuckles and looks smug.

"No, really. I'd love to know whether my bitch radar is working or I'm the one being the bitch."

"Yes." Alex straightens in his chair. "Yes, your radar is working. I've never slammed one into her, but I get the feeling she wouldn't mind if I did."

"Oh." I glance at Brontë behind the coffee machine and she glares back. I should feel sorry for her. Both she and Alex are single. Am I in the way? I sigh then look at Alex feeling confused again. What am I doing?

"So," he begins. "Just so we're clear here. After lunch, am I taking you home, to the beach house, or are you going to a friend's, or maybe you should buy a gun?"

"A gun?"

"To shoot your husband and get him out of the way?" If Alex didn't wink and pull his cheeky grin, I'd think he was being serious.

"No, none of those things, because I have a plan, Alex," I say, pushing my hair back then gathering it into a loose bun in preparation for when I eat.

"I'd rather you plait that." Alex leans in smiling. "Or buns so I can use them as handles while you deep throat me again. Fuck you give good head. Mmm." His pupils seem to dilate and turn his eyes a darker shade. "No, I think I need to take you to the beach house," he murmurs then shakes his head to dismiss the daydream.

"Alex!" I look around the restaurant to see if anyone has overheard him. "Don't talk so loud." I shift in my seat because the desire still lingering in his eyes has set me on fire.

"I just like getting you all hot and bothered, Princess, makes your eyes sparkle." He twitches his eyebrows. "Endorphins. They're God's gift to humanity, and the more we use them, the more we make, and then… the younger we feel," Alex declares with comical confidence while sitting taller.

"So young and so wise." I lift my glass of water and toast him then press my lips together and put the glass back down. I need him to take me seriously.

"My plan," I say, reminding him what we are meant to be discussing.

"Yes, so what's this plan you have?"

"Please promise you won't get angry at me."

Alex leans back into his chair to make room for his arms

to cross his chest. The longer he stares at me, the more his head shakes like he's reading my mind.

"You were serious the other day." Alex nods. "You're thinking of extorting money out of your husband just so you can sleep with me guilt-free. Aren't you?"

The heat that sprints to my neck prickles. When it reaches my jaw, my cheeks become sponges, drawing all the hot blood in. There's no point denying it, my face says it all.

Sitting straighter, my eyes dart for a moment then settle back on Alex. "You said you took the money so you could sort your debt and help Jolene, right?" I can't stand him glaring at me. I reach for my water and gulp it down then refill the glass. Alex drops his arms and pulls his chair in tight. Leaning in on his elbows, he comes right up to my face.

"I don't—want to fuck you—in front of your husband. I didn't the first time, and I don't care how much money he pays me—I won't do it."

"But why not?" I whimper, throwing my head back in frustration before snatching hold of his hands. "Alex, please, can't we do it this way, just for a bit?"

"Why? So you can test the waters maybe?" He sits back and huffs. "What am I missing here, Paige?"

My gaze falls on the table, locks onto the cardboard coaster that reads, 'Don't cry over spilled milk, it could have been wine.' I wish I had a damn wine. I also wish I could be honest. Why does shame have to make you dishonest?

I groan and catch my face in my hands. "Please, Alex. If I said it was something I really wanted to do? And the money could go to Jolene. And you could get out of debt," I say, trying to convince him.

"Jesus, Paige. Where are you going with this?" Alex's eyebrows knit so tightly, they become a mono brow.

"You could tell him you'll only sleep with me if he pays you." Alex goes to object, but my fingers to his mouth shush him. "Make it clear to him you don't want me any other way. That way he won't think of you as a threat. I mean, why can't we all get what we want? And let's face it, there could be worse things my husband spends money on."

"No, Paige."

"Please, Alex, you have to. I told him if you wouldn't agree, he should offer you money."

"Fucking Jesus, Paige."

"Well, sorry." I fold my arms and glare at him. "But wasn't it you in the hotel who was trying to encourage me into his kinky shit in the first place?"

"Don't turn this on me, Paige. You're an adult who makes her own decisions. And that's not what I was trying to do in the hotel. I was trying to point out Gerard's a manipulating asshole. Seems like he's rubbing off on you, sweetheart."

He just doesn't get it. "It's not that simple," I whine. "I don't have anything Alex. Nothing! Every—single—thing is in Gerard's name. My car, the house, the credit cards. They were all his before we married and stupid me signed a prenup stating if the marriage ends within two years, I forgo the right to half our accumulated earnings and alimony. We've been together five years, but married only nineteen months." I snatch up my phone. "Even my damn phone is in his name. I'm stuck. I can't even get a decent amount of work out of Donnie, it's chicken feed. I can't just turn my back on everything and walk away with nothing."

"He gave you a check. Cash it."

"It bounced."

Alex jerks his head back.

"Look. What I have with Gerard is—complicated."

"Do ya think?"

I trying pleading with my eyes. "Please, Alex, if Gerard calls, tell him you'll sleep with me for the money, give it to Jolene for Grace. Because if you don't, I said..." I bury my face again then mumble through my hands. "I told him to ask someone else, so he wouldn't be suspicious." I peek through my fingers.

"Oh, Paige."

"Well I thought you'd say yes," I groan, reaching for his hand with both of mine.

There's a mixture of confusion, disbelief, frustration, and a whole lot of disappointment distorting Alex's face. But in the center, his penetrating green eyes look calm and give me hope. Shaking his head, he pulls his hand free and grabs my jaw gently.

"If he asks, fine, I'll go along with it. But in the meantime, you dig yourself out of this shit in case he doesn't offer the money. Tell him you changed your mind. That's all you gotta do. Undo it, Paige, because I'm sorry to say it, but that was a super fucked up idea."

Letting go of my face, we sit back and stare at each other with forlorn expressions. Then we need to make room for Brontë as she places our plates in front of us. A little too abruptly, well at least mine anyway, and with a triumphant smile I might add.

Then we eat in silence.

NEVER BE THE SAME

When Alex drops me home straight after lunch, I run upstairs to shower and change into something I know Gerard will appreciate. I decide to order takeout, so I can concentrate strictly on my work. Pre-ordering from Kora's Kitchen, an amazing restaurant here in Point Dume, I decide on filet mignon for Gerard and duck à l'orange for myself, to be delivered at seven.

I work on my assignments for Donnie first, then make a start on the generic 'thank you' message that will go on each card. I search online for someone who can have the cards printed in time and try my hardest to not think about Alex and our discussion or how stupid I feel. Alex was right. It was a ludicrous idea. My saving grace is that Gerard hasn't mentioned it since, so I'm hopeful he's forgotten about it.

With the laundry done and folded, I'm feeling relieved that I've caught up with most of my work. Making a mental note that tomorrow, before I go to the hospital, I will organize the printers, and everything will be on track for the fundraiser by Wednesday next week.

I busy myself with a few other menial tasks, then wind

down with a wine to wait for Gerard. When I enter the kitchen to reclaim wine glasses from the dishwasher to restock the bar, I see that Annabel has left her letter from Gerard behind.

I curse aloud and glance at the clock. It's past four and I know that by now there's not a chance Annabel will still be en route picking Katie up from school. I also know if I don't get the papers to her, Gerard will be annoyed. Concluding I have time, I decide to bring them to her and show her the photos I took today, hoping for her input.

Keys, backpack, and phone in hand, I lock up and leave. Our neighboring area where Annabel lives gives the impression of being middle class, but that's not true. Well-established trees give it an air of old-world charm which is reflected in the price tags. It's the older part of Point Dume where the houses are big and have character, but the yards are small because they've all been subdivided.

When I arrive, I'm grateful to see she is home. Katie and her friend, whose name I don't know, are sitting out front with their iPads. It's depressing that they're in each other's company, but they'd rather stick their faces in front of a screen instead of talking to one another.

"Hey, girls," I call out as I approach the two six-year-olds. Katie stands and greets me with a hug. Still in her school uniform, Katie's blonde hair is tied back in a ponytail but looks like a mouse has been scratching through it. "Heard of skipping ropes?" I ask.

"Aunt Paige, skipping ropes are for babies," Katie says, rolling her big blue eyes. My heart swells every time she calls me aunt and she is instantly forgiven for being rude.

"Mmm. Well, I know I was still skipping rope at your age or doing crafts. Like making pom-poms," I chirp.

"That's for babies too," Katie's friend informs me.

"Well, okay then," I say, leaving them to their exciting one-dimensional iPads.

"Mom's inside, I think she's getting drunk."

"Mmm, I better check on her then." I open the front door and let myself in. "Annie," I sing out, envelope and backpack in hand.

"In the kitchen."

Katie is right, Annabel is cooking and drinking, and from the look on her happy face when she sees me, I can tell she's had a few.

"What's the occasion?" I point to the wine cooler in her hand.

"No occasion. De-stress medicine. Doctor's orders."

"Has something happened?" I ask, concerned. I pull out a barstool, getting ready to sit.

"Don't sit. Come with me," she demands, putting down her drink and heading down the hall to her office.

"Look." She points to her computer screen. "When it rains, it damn well pours."

I look at her screen and recognize her online marketing website dashboard. "See that?" She taps the screen. "One hundred and fifty inquiries Paige, one hundred and fifty! For months—nothing. Now five days away from the big day, I get inundated, so typical. I'm turning it off and not looking at it until after the fundraiser but still, it's here," she taps her head, "in the back of my mind. I was hoping to go on a vacation after the event, but do you think Stuart will let me once I tell him about all these potential clients?" She looks at me expectantly.

"Three words, Annie."

She looks confused.

"Don't tell him."

"Very funny. It's not likely he won't know. It's all because of Ronald Klaneski. He asked me for some business cards months back and now look." She shakes her head at the computer screen before settling back on me. "Anyways, what brings you here all gussied up?" she asks, leading me back to the kitchen where she picks up her drink again.

"This." I pick up and wave the envelope at her. "You forgot Stuart's paperwork, and I thought you might like to look at the photos I took today."

"Ah yes, your little photo shoot with Alex," she drawls before taking a slug from her wine cooler. "Want one, sweetie?" Annabel offers reaching for the fridge. "Then you can tell me what's goin' on with you two."

"Um, I really think you ought to slow down on these." I laugh and reach out to take the wine from her. "You'll be drunk by the time Stu gets home otherwise."

Annabel moves out of my reach. "Don't try that trick on me, honey. I'm fine. What I want to know is what's going on, are you doing that hunk of a man on the side or what?"

"Stop it. Now, have you got time to look at these or not?" I try acting serious to ward her off.

"Sure, let me put this pie in the oven, and we'll take a look," she says, pouring an egg mixture into a dish.

"I see what you mean now." Annabel is standing behind me nodding as I play around on her computer, explaining my idea as I go through the shots I've taken. Most of them are repeats, so I breeze past them quickly so I don't bore her. Then the images of Alex appear. Annabel makes me slow down, commenting how hot he looks, and she doesn't mean from the sun that's casting just the right amount of shadow across the corrugated Corten steel to create an unusual effect. "What's going on with you two?"

"Nothing, we just went to take photos. You just saw them." I close off the file.

"Oh, don't you dare pee on my Gucci's and tell me it's raining, Paige. I ain't stupid. I can see you're into him, and all I'm saying is watch out for that man. I can feel in my bones he's the love 'em and leave 'em type. Don't ruin what you have with Gerard, sweetie. He's your real catch." From behind the office chair, she squeezes my shoulders. "Unless of course it turns out Alex has a foot-long schlong who can go all night long." Annabel laughs so hard she draws tears from the both of us, though mine are laced with sadness. The fact she admires Gerard so much, I feel she might turn against me if she knew the truth. Moments later, we have the attention of Stuart who has arrived home and is wondering what we are doing.

"I'm going to go, Annie." I rise from the chair and give her a squeeze then greet Stuart and tell him about the paperwork from Gerard that I left on the kitchen bench. As I brush past him, I catch a smell of wood and steel and his hair has flecks of debris through it. I resist the urge to fluff his black curls to set the fragments free.

I say goodbye to Katie on the way out, who is now watching television, and soon I'm buckled in the car and gripping the steering wheel. I shake it fiercely, then thump my head against my knuckles because I can't stop thinking of Alex. I keep seeing his image on the screen, like it's burned itself into my mind's eyes. Then his voice is in my head. His erotic innuendos and suggestive compliments, and parts of me where his hands have imprinted themselves, come alive and start tingling and luring me to go to him. Suddenly, overshadowing it all, is his disappointment in me today. I want him to know how sorry I am for putting him in such a ridiculous position. I don't care what Annabel or anyone else thinks, they're wrong. Alex cares for me. I know he does.

I turn on the engine and look at the clock. I don't know what spurs me on because I'm not sure what a quick visit will achieve, but without being conscious of it, I'm soon breezing down the highway and heading for Las Flores Canyon. I don't think at all, just run strictly on adrenalin and lust.

When I arrive at the beach house, I bang my fist on the peeling door. My heart is pounding and my breathing heavy even though I haven't even exerted myself. And I'm sure my panties are already wet just thinking about touching Alex. *"Endorphins keep you young."* I knock again. Harder.

As soon as Alex opens the door, I pant, "I'm sorry I was so stupid."

"Paige, what…" I don't let him finish, just lunge at him like some desperate nymphomaniac and kiss him, my arms wrapping around his neck. His masculine and salty scent drives my finger through his dry and gritty hair. As soon as I've had my fill of his lips, I take his hand and pull him inside the house, leaving him to slam the door hastily with a stumbling foot. I tug him farther down the hall, like a mother dragging her child to the bedroom for time out, except I'm dragging him there because I'm desperate for his touch.

As soon as we enter the living area and I see he has company, my heart comes to a screeching halt. My eyes dart back to Alex. He smiles at me, then his friend. The look of embarrassment must be written all over my face. "Oh God, I'm so sorry." I pull my hand out of Alex's and face him, hugging myself not knowing what to do. Alex looks down at me with a smile and pushes his hair out of his face. Then he glances at his friend.

"Give me a minute, Tony, I think it's an emergency," he says, taking hold of a sweaty hand and pulling me through the rest of the living area and down into his room. Closing the door behind us, Alex folds his arms over his chest.

"What's going on?" His eyes narrow, looking me up and

down, taking in the floral fitted dress and heels I'm wearing. Now that we are alone, my nervousness rushes my breathing again.

"I needed to see you." I step closer and grip onto his belt, holding his gaze. He searches my eyes. "I wanted to tell you how sorry I am for putting you in an awkward position. It was dumb of me." I keep jerking on his belt but don't go for his buckle just yet.

"Are you going to do something you'll regret, Paige?" he asks, shifting my loose hair over my shoulder and studying my features, before running a thumb across lips I've licked.

"No," I say, pulling on his belt and undoing his zip.

"You're becoming a reckless woman, Paige, be careful who you play with," he warns, his hands finding my ass when I push down on the waistband of his jeans until I have freed his already erect cock.

When our flesh connects, his rod twitches on my open palm, enticing me to look down and bite my lower lip in wanting. I kiss him quick before sliding down onto my knees and pumping him with my fist. He lets out the first of his appreciative murmurs and his body slackens.

"Oh, Paige baby, you're a naughty girl for coming here and doing this to a man." He strokes my head with both hands, petting me gently, his fingertips digging in just a little as an urgency in him ignites. "Fuck," he cusses when I blow on the tip of his cock, cooling his pre-cum before my tongue extends to lick him clean. He can't help himself. He takes hold of my head more firmly, desperate now for me to take him in my mouth. It excites me that I have this effect on him. The thrill that I can unhinge him so easily acts like an addictive aphrodisiac so powerful, my body reacts instantly. I moan and spit on his warm knob then roll my palm over him and look up before slowly taking him into my mouth, sucking over the head, keeping my palm wrapped around and stroking his cock gently.

Alex lets go of my head and falls back against the door with a thud, his shoulders supporting him, his pelvis forward in complete and utter surrender. I go wild on him and tug on his pants, set his ass and sack free. My hot mouth stays locked on his cock sucking and bobbing hungrily while drinking in his smell. His raw musky male scent makes me ache all over and I'm certain if I wasn't wearing panties, my lust would be running down my thighs.

Twisting and turning my head erratically, I am salacious and give him everything I've got. I want to inflict as much pleasure as my mouth might deliver. He gets harder and grabs my head again, moaning and groaning in abandonment, not caring if his friend in the living area overhears.

"Oh yes, please take me all the way down, Princess. Fuck," he cusses as a beg for more when I allow him free reign with my head. Using me as a warm vacuum to extract the very pleasure from him. With both hands now firmly gripping my head, he bobs me as quickly as I can take. My eyes are watering as I snatch tiny morsels of air in his wake, but I'm in euphoria with him. I want nothing more than to give him anything and everything he wants.

He stills. And when I moan around his cock with pleasure from his impending release, he shudders out, "Oh fucking, shiiiitin' holy hell." And his whole body vibrates while I clasp firmly to his thighs.

I pull back just slightly so I'm able to swallow his seed, then let him rest in my mouth until he becomes grounded again.

When he is calm, he slowly takes himself out of my mouth. Cradling my face he stares down into my eyes. He has an almost haunted look, and his eyes glass over making me frown. Is he about to cry? But he smiles at me warmly then lets me go. I sit back on my haunches giving him the space he needs to pull up his jeans and fasten his belt. Neither of us saying a word.

Offering his hand, he gives me a megawatt smile that's infused with endearment and I can't help but feel adept.

"You're fucking beautiful, Paige." Alex pulls me into a hug and kisses the top of my head, smoothing my hair before tilting my face to kiss me. Long and gentle.

"I have to go," I say, breaking free from his embrace and stepping away.

Snatching me back, Alex presses my head onto his chest, holding me there so I can hear the thumping of his still galloping heart. I squeeze him tightly around the waist before tearing myself away and reaching for the door handle. "I really need to go. I'm sorry about interrupting you and your friend."

Alex huffs and rattles his head. "No, you're not, you little liar." He grabs me from behind and away from the door to give me a bear hug. "I enjoyed that surprise." He kisses my temple, my ear, and then my cheek before spinning me in his arms and lifting my chin so he can kiss my lips again.

"I'll see you next week, Princess?"

I suck in my surprise, relieved Gerard didn't hire someone else. "Are you coming to garden?"

There's a quick frown before he smiles. "No, I mean I'm coming to your fancy money-spinning event," he replies, opening the door for me.

"You're going? I didn't think you wanted to." I look over my shoulder at him as we walk down the short hall back toward the living area.

"I'm invited, aren't I?" He reaches forward and pinches my waist, making me giggle and quicken my pace until I hit the open space. My eyes dart around for a moment before landing on Tony, who is still sitting on the couch but now with a phone in his hand. He looks up.

"Hi and bye," I say, power-walking toward the front door, not allowing time for an introduction even though it feels a little rude.

When we're at the front entrance, Alex pulls back the door just enough to let me slip through. He leans over its edge, looking down at me. It seems he can't seem to wipe the silly smile off his face and I feel myself blush from his intense gaze.

"Kiss me again," he whispers when our heads pass, only inches apart. My body flutters all over when I look at his beautifully shaped lip and when I kiss him, it feels like I'm seeping right in to become part of his skin. My body, no, my soul cries out to be naked with him. To press together every inch of flesh so we have a memory of each other. It's such an intense sensation, I feel it twist my insides. Nothing has ever felt more divine, and when I pull back and look at him, he is staring right into me with his dark, sensual eyes. It's in that instant I know for certain I am in love with Alex. This very real and gorgeous man.

"See," he says, shaking his head. "You do it to me every time, Paige."

Throughout the drive home, I don't know whether to laugh, scream or cry. I think at some point I may have done all three and remarkably I arrive home just as the delivery van is dropping off our meals. Scooting inside and turning on lights, I rush around to set the mood for Gerard's return. I've barely changed out of my wet-from-desire underwear, and into a fresh pair, when Gerard is calling out from the hall, announcing he is home.

"Hi," I say, coming down the stairs, calming myself with each deliberate step then follow him as he heads for the bar.

"How are you, honey?" Gerard asks over his shoulder.

"Good, great." I sidle up to the bar to join him. Watch as he pours his scotch and then a wine for me. "I've been busy."

"Oh, doing what? Did you give those papers to Annabel like I asked?"

"I did," I reply, taking the half-full glass of red from him. "How was your day?"

"Well, I've had better." He combs his thick hair with his fingers then gives his neck a good rub. Picking up his glass, he comes from behind the bar and starts pacing in front of the bookcase. He's agitated and within seconds, before my legs give out, I'm sliding my butt onto the barstool.

Guilt, I was once told, is a useless emotion. I'd like to add guilt is also an illusionist that can distort the truth. The mind plays games, because before I know it, I'm responding to stimuli that aren't even there.

As always, I feel the prickling heat rise in my neck. "What happened?" I ask, one hand soothing my nettled skin. I bring my drink to my lips, my breath unsteady in the glass and I hold it longer than necessary to my mouth, still watching Gerard as he paces.

"I was disappointed by some news I got today. But at least it wasn't as bad as a case one of our associates landed. He scored a client today. A man in his late fifties." Gerard shoots me a look. "He married a much younger woman. A very good-looking young woman who had nothing before he fell in love with her." He downs the rest of his liquor and comes back over to the bar, quickly dumping in ice and pours a full glass again.

I get up and slink over to the couch and curl my legs beneath me. Wishing I hadn't asked for an explanation of his shitty day because it's sounding more like an analogy for a betraying wife because the Big G illusionist is messing with my head. But Gerard couldn't know about my day. Could he? Then I'm thinking of how he found out Kelsey smoked pot. Then I'm wondering if I should ask him about it. Then I'm thinking full circle because I'm picturing my mouth around Alex's cock and the look in his eyes when I left.

Gerard perches on the edge of the stool I vacated and rubs his knees with both hands. "The young woman he married caught him cheating with numerous women and even some men. She has proof of this so it would normally stand up in court regarding their agreement. A divorce would ensue and substantial alimony in her favor would override their prenuptial agreement. You know what they are, don't you?"

Gerard gets up and grabs his drink, then sits down with me on the couch, still eager for my attention. "But you see, there are a couple of factors that could help our client. One. The young woman he married was not biologically born female and we could argue she never disclosed this to her husband, because let's face facts, it's his word against hers. And two. He also knows *she* has *cheated* on him." Gerard takes a mouthful from his glass and murmurs into it. "Oh! And it was with the mechanic they use to service her nice car. That he paid for." Gerard laughs and reaches for the remote. "I wonder if that sucker knew who he was fucking."

I have no idea what to say. So, I don't say anything until he asks for my opinion.

"It's all a bit of a mess don't you think?"

"Yes, I guess it is," I say, uncurling my legs and crossing them.

Gerard holds the remote at arm's length, pushing buttons and sipping his drink, then puts down the remote to loosen his tie.

"Lucky for me, I've never cheated on you. But if I did, I

hope you'd never take me to the cleaners. Christ, who wants to air dirty laundry like that?" He pats my leg and a smile dances on his lips before he fixates on the television. "So, what kept you busy all day?" He puts down the remote having found the station he was intent on finding.

"I—handed in some extra work to Donnie, so I'll be free to enjoy the fundraiser on Wednesday night and…"

"Oh, yes. I'm glad you have reminded me about the fundraiser night. I've organized another…Mmm, how did we term it? Play night, I think." He wiggles his eyebrows.

I can't help that a smile curls the corners of my mouth and any residual shame I have from giving Alex a blow job slips away. We all get what we want, I reaffirm to keep my moral demons away.

"Yes, play night."

He's so casual about the whole thing his eyes barely leave the television set. Why has this never bothered me before?

"So, are you sure you'd be okay with that? You haven't thought things over and changed your mind, have you? And just so we're clear, I asked Alex like you wanted." He twists his head to look at me briefly and forces a smile.

For a moment, I think about the lecture Alex gave me in the café. Here was my chance to bail out. But with the afternoon still fresh in my mind and my body desperate for more of Alex, it's really a no-brainer. Alex said he was invited. Gerard must have called and he agreed.

"No. I haven't changed my mind. I'm willing to try it and see what eventuates."

"Great," he says, patting my leg, still giving most of his attention to an innate object instead of an overly aroused me. How could life get any better? I shift in my seat. That is— until I make some changes.

"I'll go shower. Do I have time before you serve dinner?" Gerard gets to his feet and helps himself to another drink.

"Yes, I ordered in tonight, so it's just keeping warm in the oven."

"Oh." He sounds surprised. Or is it disappointment? "Why?"

"Well, I had so much to do today, and I just thought to take the pressure off..." I trail off, annoyed that I feel the need to justify my actions when it's not a big deal.

"Right. Well, just don't make a habit of it, you know I love your cooking." He makes it sound like a compliment when in truth, he's asserting his dominance. Something I'm only just realizing he's been doing all along. "I'll be fifteen minutes. Then we'll eat." He gulps down his drink then bends to place the empty glass in my hands, confirming I'm a hundred percent right.

I sink back into the couch the second he leaves the room, sipping slowly from my glass in an attempt to blot out the uneasy feeling Gerard left behind. Instead, I begin fantasizing about Alex, him kissing every inch of my starving body. Five days and counting. I let out a sigh. Then I need to down the last of my drink to obliterate the fact—my husband will also be there.

8

MAD WORLD

When Sheree was fourteen, her dad bought a boat. He said he wanted to teach Sheree and his wife how to waterski, suggested it was something they could all do together. He said he would rent a lake house so they could stay whenever they liked. He told Sheree he'd tow her behind on a tube to start, then show her how to ski properly. He then suggested Teresa, his wife, drink piña coladas and get a suntan. When he was done with his announcement, he wrapped an arm around Sheree's shoulder, which she shrugged off. I felt so sorry for him that day. He was so excited, and both Sheree and his wife Teresa couldn't have cared less. "Do you even know how to ski?" Sheree had asked, screwing up her face before his wife shook her head and wandered back inside the house.

They changed their tune soon after, and weekends out at the lake became normal over summer. And in the spring, Sheree's dad fished. I was lucky enough to almost always get asked to go along.

Around that time, my mom broke up with Carlos, and he moved out. That didn't mean he was gone though. Most mornings, he arrived reeking of stale cigarettes and beer, searching for food. As he grumbled about nothing to eat, she complained about the sudden lack of clients, and that's when I realized Carlos was her pimp more than he was ever her boyfriend.

I still had a crush on Peter Moriarty at that stage; it was before the incident in the park, and Sheree had started dating a guy named Dan. He was tall and had blond hair like Sheree. He played football, and his parents owned a wheat farm ten miles out of town. Dan also had horses, a pool table, a heated swimming pool, and a bunch of cool friends who brought along weed, cigarettes, and beer. So, it wasn't long before Sheree started spending weekends at Dan's learning how to ride, drink, play pool, and smoke. All in that order.

That left me mostly at home in my room while my mom watched re-runs in between servicing men because Sheree never seemed to ask me along, not that I cared. Well not entirely, because I knew I wouldn't fit in anyway. Dan's friends wore designer clothes, drove pimped-up cars, and got promised vacations in exchange for good grades.

It was on one of those days when Sheree was at Dan's that her dad came to our house for the very first time. When I opened the door, my lunch literally rose to my throat, thinking he was there to see my mom as a client.

"Is your mom home, Paige?" he asked, reaching up to support himself against the door frame. He always smelled and looked clean, and on this day, there was something more, something different about him that made my heart race. I stole a quick look behind me, and when I turned back, his intense gaze seemed to roam all over my face and the small smile that graced his face, seemed suggestive. Millions of thoughts ran through my head. Like, could I ask that he wait there so I could tidy the house? And should I warn him that Mom's had the clap? To whether I should tell Sheree that he'd been around to see my mom. Then I thought of his wife, that it would destroy her if she found out, and I would be banned from their home, and my friendship with Sheree would be over.

"Um, yeah. But why?" I grimaced because I was knew I was being rude to ask.

Over my shoulder, he scanned the kitchen, making me turn and look. There were flies hovering over dirty dishes and a bin full of decaying scraps, and there was no escaping the pungent smell of beer and ash from the overflowing ashtrays. I could have died of shame, I was so embarrassed.

"I suppose I should ask you first anyway," he said dropping his arm away from the door frame and grazing the top of my arm, causing me to spin and re-establish eye contact. "I'm going out on the lake later, and I noticed last time we all went, you seemed keen on fishing." His observation was true. After hours of quiet patience and remaining focused, hooking a fish was exhilarating.

"As you might know, Sheree is at Dan's, and Teresa is visiting her sister. But I thought you might like to come along. I should check with your mother first. See if it's okay with her." He smiled, and as always, it felt like someone was sitting on my chest because I was longing for my own father. But he har long since gone. "That is, if you want to. I won't be offended if you think I'm not cool enough to hang out with, but your company would be nice, that's all."

I stood there wishing more than anything that he was my dad, that it wouldn't be weird to hang out with Sheree's father without her. I wanted to go so badly. Just then, my mom came to the door.

"Well, hello there Sheree's daddy," my mother drawled, eyeing him from head to toe in her dressing gown with her hands on her full hips.

"Hello, Mavis, how are you?"

"Better now, I can feast my eyes on you. You're a very handsome man, Richard, even better up close, come on through." She stepped out of the doorway, and if there had have been a rock close by, I would have crawled my way straight under it.

"Oh my God, Mom," I groaned, letting my long hair spill over my face. "He's here to see me, not you."

"Well, is that right?" she said straightening herself, no longer looking so pleased.

"I was asking Paige if she's like to come fishing," he explained.

She squinted what was the most striking feature about her, her emerald, almond-shaped eyes, which she ruined with heavy fake lashes.

"I just thought I'd check with you first," he clarified, leaving out the part that we'd be alone.

"Well, it ain't like she's never been before," she replied, moving away to find her cigarettes.

"I can't. I've got tons of homework," I lied, glancing at my mom then back at him. If I disappointed him, he didn't let on, but I still felt bad rejecting him. The truth was, I knew if I went with him, I'd want to tell Sheree about it. And if she were anything like me, she'd be annoyed that I was vying for her dad's attention. She'd already snapped at me a few times for things I didn't think were my fault. Just the same, her friendship meant more to me than fishing.

"Suit yourself," my mom said before waddling away, her heavy hips swinging, looking back to see if Sheree's dad was watching, which he wasn't. He was still staring and questioning me when I turned back to face him.

"I'm sorry, I would but, like...you know?" I leaned back against the door frame looking at the worn linoleum floor, "I think Ree would get dirty on me. She's like that."

"She wouldn't have to know. I've never told her about you

sleeping in the shed," he reminded me, making my stomach drop. "But I suppose that's different isn't it?" I glared at him for too long, giving him the impression I would change my mind because he raised his eyebrows and smiled encouragingly. I felt sick knowing he held that over me, because I was sure Sheree would think I was weird for still going there.

I shook my head and took hold of the door. "Sorry, but I can't."

"Well, maybe next time then. When Sheree can come too." With a nonchalant shrug he left, pushing his hands deep in his pockets, seeming not to care. I was left feeling both confused and disappointed.

It was later that same day that Carlos came around. My mother was with a client and I was in my room listening to music and daydreaming about Peter Moriarty. Suddenly, my door flew open, and Carlos tumbled in, asking me what I was doing. He stood in the center of my room swaying, with a beer in one hand and a joint in the other.

I sat up on my bed, concerned how badly he was wobbling. I yelled at him to get out and called him a hopeless drunk, annoyed that he was stinking up my room. Wishing then that I'd gone fishing with Sheree's dad so I didn't have to put up with the dregs that made up my life.

Ignoring him, hoping he'd go away, I fell back down. I resumed my lotus pose, which was flat on my back with one leg cocked over a knee and staring at the ceiling. In a flash, he was at me. "You, rude little fucker," he swore through gritted teeth, hitting me so hard across the head, my foot fell off my knee and my ears started ringing.

As soon as I was upright, his beer went sailing across the room, and he was on top off me trying to pin me down with his weight, grabbing my jaw in one hand and tilting my head so far back it was painful trying to scream. His weight crushed my chest as he secured my arms beneath his knees, leaving only my legs to flail in space. Beer breath slipped between his contorted lips where he held onto the spliff. When he had me pinned and gasping for breath, he sat up on me and chuckled. I tried screaming out to my mom, but the sound came out more like a wheezing tire, leaving me even more breathless.

"You got a big mouth for a weak little girl, haven't ya?" he said, pinching the smoke between his fingers and taking a large drag before blowing it straight in my face, snagging my jostling head to keep it steady for maximum effect. I tried not to inhale, but with his weight still on me, I was already on the verge of passing out.

"You should get high, girl. Then you might let me fuck you. You still a virgin are ya?" His arm reached behind himself as if feeling between my legs would somehow give him the answer. My reactive jerk startled him, and with his weight better distributed I heaved with all my might and sent him off balance. I let my lungs roar for all I was worth and pulled myself out from beneath him.

Next thing I knew, my mom was there and some strange guy she'd been shagging. I didn't even stay long enough to hear anything anyone said. I just ran straight out the door, and I kept on running until my legs were burning and I was all out of tears. I found a reclusive spot behind some fallen trees on the fringe of the pine forest just outside of town. It was the first time I seriously considered ending my life. I felt disgusting, unloved, and pointless. I had no one to turn to except Sheree, and she was with Dan and it seemed she was all but forgetting about me. I stayed away until I was so tired and cold, even my fears had numbed.

When I got home around midnight, my mom and Carlos were sitting at the kitchen table still awake. By the collection of empty bottles in front of him, Carlos was still drinking, and my mother had her elbows resting on the table, nibbling on her thumb with a cigarette posed millimeters away. I froze at the door when they both looked at me.

"Sit down, Paige," my mom demanded.

"Not while he's still here." I folded my arms and leaned against the door, acting tougher than I felt.

"See what I mean?" Carlos said. "She's turning into a smart mouth who doesn't understand her place."

"My place? You don't even live here anymore, so why are you even here?" I marched ahead with as much bravado as I could muster. I'd almost reached the entrance to the hall before Carlos was dragging me back by my sweater and pulling me onto his lap.

"Your ma asked you to sit down."

"Mom," I yelped, struggling with Carlos when he snagged my legs with his, keeping me on his lap with an arm tightly around my waist so his free hand could go exploring.

My mother just shook her head, took long deep drags on her cigarette, leaving me busy slapping at Carlos's wandering hand.

"Tell him to let me go!" I screamed, squirming to pry his arms apart but my mother stayed mute, looking thoughtful behind a cloud of swirling smoke for the longest time.

"Mom," I screamed so loud the neighbors should have heard.

"You're gonna need to start paying your way around here soon, Paige," she finally spoke, tapping away ash but not looking at me. The implication in her tone made my blood run cold. Stunned into submission, I stopped fighting Carlos for a moment, until he took advantage of my passive state and drove his hand down onto my crotch making me scream.

"Do you know how much a virgin cunt makes, Paige?" he said in my ear, pinching me there—between my legs.

When I managed to leap out of his slackened grip, every vulgar word I possessed came spewing out my mouth. When I looked back at my mother, she refused to look at me. She just got up and walked straight out of the room.

My fear was amusing to Carlos, and I could still hear him halfway down the street when I ran off to Sheree's, where I knew I could sleep safely.

My mother was a negligent person. She was also extremely indigent, and desperate people do insane things at times—which was something I later found out.

9

OVER

I'm finding it hard to stop staring at my reflection. I look beautiful. I'm even prepared to be vain and say I look stunning. My hair is pinned into a beautifully styled loose chignon. I've spent time in the salon and I now have an even all-over tan. My makeup has been perfectly applied, complete with thickened lashes, and a shimmering blush. My gold earrings are exquisite, delicate chains with tiny diamonds embedded within the links. They make a gentle shushing sound whenever I shake my head and I feel overly indulgent when my matching jeweled nails catch the light as I stroke and play with the chains.

With a descending hem line, my deep-red knee-length crepe ballgown reaches the floor but still shows off my legs. Cinched in at the waist, the bodice rises into my collarbone with shoe-string straps, creating an almost halter-neck style. After slipping into a pair of nude understated heels, I take hold of my matching clutch and complete the look.

"Perfume?" I say aloud as if the bottle has ears, and search over the shelves for where I last put it.

"Are you talking to me?" Gerard asks, coming out of the bathroom in his tuxedo and into the walk-in closet.

"No, just myself." I find my favorite Chanel bottle and mist my wrists and elbow crook with the delicate scent.

"Look out Jenna Martin," Gerard says, coming up behind me and encircling my waist, his chin dropping onto my shoulder with a smile. We stare at each other in the full length mirror. He's happy and jaw dropping to look at and for a moment I pull the veil over all the truths he has become. When he presses a freshly shaven cheek against mine, murmuring that I look gorgeous, my throat turns dry and I have to close my eyes to conjure a smile. Inside I feel like crying. If only I'd never cheated, I would have remained blissfully unaware of his faults and happy with this man.

"Perfect in fact," he adds, then inquires if I'm almost done.

When I nod, he reaches around my waist and squeezes. "I always knew you'd be the woman of my dreams, Paige. I saw the potential in you the moment I laid eyes on you, and you can't imagine how much I appreciate that you've accepted me for who I am, and what I like." He places a gentle kiss at my temple. Standing straight, he steps to the side and flicks at his jacket. "Now, if you're ready, I think we should go. You wanted to be there early," he says, fixing his bow tie. "I'll go downstairs and check if the car has arrived."

I look at myself one last time. Suddenly I don't feel so beautiful anymore.

An hour later, when we arrive at the event, the limousine driver comes to open my door. I wait for Gerard to take my hand. There are people mingling everywhere on the lush lawn overlooking the ocean and waiters are weaving around with trays of hors d'oeuvres and champagne. Snatching up a glass the moment one is offered, I follow Gerard as he leads the way toward the marquees. Several tents are joined to create one, and once inside, we're treated to the sight of floating heart-shaped balloons that create a red ocean above our heads.

Dominating the floor area are at least one hundred round tables covered in white linen surrounded by fabric-covered chairs with a bow fastened at their backs. In the center of every table there are long atriums, and tall glass vases with fairy lights spilling over to create a waterfall effect. There are just as many people gathered in small groups between tables, if not more, than there were outside.

"Wow, it gets better every year." I'm in awe of the setting, transfixed by the glamour and excited for the evening to get underway. I smile to myself when I notice the band setting up near the dance floor, wondering if Alex will ask me to dance.

"It does, and you played a hand in it. Be it half-hearted this year." Gerard pulls me in at the waist. I'm sure he must feel me stiffen because he kisses my cheek attempting to soften his cutting remark. "I didn't mean it the way it sounded. Do you see anyone we know?" Gerard swings his head in all directions before guiding me through the crowd. I catch pieces of excited conversations as we pass gathered groups both large and small until we are standing nearer to the bar.

Looking to spot Annabel, I'm also curious where Alex might be and I open my mouth to ask why we didn't just pick him up, considering the beach house was on our way. But when Gerard spots someone and waves, I snap my mouth shut. It's probably better I don't appear overly concerned anyway.

"Well, I'm not sure about you, but I'd like a drink at the

bar. Would you like to come, or do you need to see Annabel?" he asks.

"Would you mind? I'd like to check how she's holding up under the pressure."

"Go ahead, I'm sure I'll find you again," he says. He stops briefly to greet people he recognizes before I go on my search, secretly hoping I run into Alex.

Smiling and nodding to people in my travels, I walk through the large marquee with purpose, touching tables and pushing in chairs, trying to feel at least a little helpful given Gerard's comment earlier and the fact that he's right. Previous years I was much more hands-on.

The stage has a lectern, and there is a big banner against a pleated curtain. To one end of the banner, there is a photo of smiling children, obviously patients, because they have oxygen leads under their noses, and on the other end—why the foundation was founded in the first place—is a heart-warming photo of Claudia McMillan and her baby son Noah before they both died. Noah through lack of essential equipment and then later Claudia from suicide due to despair. Then smack in the middle is the LA Children's Hospital logo, bright and in flight, and splashed across the very top are the words 'Brave Heart Foundation' in bold red letters.

As I move on, waitstaff breeze past me with empty trays, and I notice a flustered organizer talking to them before they re-enter what I assume is the caterer's marquee. She is a small woman in a black dress suit and red scarf. I decide she looks important enough to know where I might find Annabel.

Pointed in the right direction, I find Annabel in a separate marquee, nursing a champagne glass and talking with a gentleman in a dark gray, pinstripe suit. When he looks my way she also glances in my direction, but it takes a moment before she registers it's me.

"Well, it's about time," Annabel sings out, abandoning her companion in favor of me. Gliding over and looking beautiful in a knee-length pale blue dress with folds of fabric falling off her shoulders, she reaches for the pearls around her neck. "But well, look at you." She takes me by the tops of my arms. "You're just a diamond in a rhinestone world, Paige honey." She inhales deeply. "If I didn't love you so much, I'd hate you for turning me green."

"No, you're the one who looks gorgeous. What a beautiful dress," I whisper in her ear when she swooshes me into a hug. I nudge her off when her companion begins making his way toward us.

Annabel spins on her heels when he arrives. With a big grin plastered across her face and looking proud-as-punch, she feeds her arm through his and turns to me.

"Paige, meet Ronald Klaneski."

Ronald holds my gaze and offers his hand. "I like your work," he says scrapping his top teeth against his bottom lip, drawing my attention to the scar Annabel mentioned. He's a lot taller than Annabel but only slightly taller than me with my heels.

"My work?" I ask, confused.

"Your photos, silly," Annabel replies, shaking my arm and setting my hand free from Ronald's.

"Oh. Thank you. I thought they'd be appropriate." I glance over at the mountain of donations that comprise expensive looking cow-hide chairs to crystal vases and light fixtures. "Who's the auctioneer?" I ask, moving around to take everything in.

"A Mr. Sebastián Van der Kleine." Annabel pulls a face. "Mouthful of a name, but he's supposed to be good."

"Can I get you ladies a drink?" Ronald interrupts, obviously not interested in our quiet chit-chat.

"Ain't he just a gentleman? Thank you, Ronald, that would be nice. We'll just wait right here for you." Annabel bats her heavily made-up eyes and wiggles up her nose.

I look from one to the other. My mouth holding an awkward smile because Ronald continues ogling Annabel for an interesting extra few seconds longer before leaving us. When he's gone, Annabel touches my arm.

"Told you he was good-looking. I'm telling you now, Paige, if he were to grab me in a dark alley on a moonlit night, I can't guarantee I wouldn't graciously lift my skirt and let him take me from behind."

"Annabel!"

"Oh, Paige sweetie, you have no idea. He just does something to me every time."

I think I might, but I don't tell her that. Instead, I point out numerous donations that look unique to divert her attention.

"Have you been mingling or just hiding out here all night?" I ask, running my hand over a large plush cushion then pick up a box to peek at what's inside.

"No, I've been out. Got as nervous as a whore in church though, so I'm pretending to guard the goods 'till I'm skunk-drunk. Where's Gerard? Oh, and did you see Jenna? Did you notice what she's wearing?" she asks, rolling her eyes as she drinks down the last of her champagne.

"Gerard is where else but the bar." I shake my head then put down the box that contained a watch and pick up a silver picture frame with a generic image of a mother and baby and smile at it. Annabel studies the photo, then contorts her face at me.

"What? It's a sweet photo," I tell her.

"You know they pay them lots of money to look that

happy. It sure ain't like that in real life. Come on, put it down, you're depressing me. You don't want babies anyways."

Extracting the frame from my hands and putting it aside, Annabel turns me around toward the larger pieces on offer, including my three large canvas photos.

"So, what's Jenna wearing?" I ask, knowing she'd love nothing more than to run her down.

"Oh, you'll see." She inhales deeply and weaves her arm through mine. "If you can't find her, just look for a cluster of men. I guarantee she is in the center holding them all hostage, including my husband."

"Cut it out, Annabel, she's not that bad." I shove her gently with my shoulder. "And you have nothing to worry about with Stuart."

"Did someone say my name?"

Annabel squeezes my arm and leans into me. "No, but maybe he might," she whispers, arching her brows and glancing at Stuart before unhooking our arms and smiling wide for him, leaving me wondering what she means.

We head toward Stuart who's carrying two champagne flutes. Suited up, he looks smart in gray. The color catches his eyes and his curls have been cut since I last saw him.

"I believe you ladies requested these." He offers us the flutes when he is closer. I raise mine in the air thanking him and we exchange pleasantries before he is trying to lure Annabel away.

"I'm struggling to find anyone I know except Gerard, and he seems to have stumbled onto some old friends or clients by the looks," he says, making me curious.

"Oh, all right then, I'll come out," Annabel whines. She downs her champagne in one go.

"Babe, take it slow, you've got speeches to make remember?" Stuart advises, leading her away with me following close behind.

I find Gerard by the raised parquet dance floor, talking to a youngish couple. The lady is wearing a sexy backless mermaid dress that sparkles when she moves, which is a lot because she keeps looking around at the thickening crowd. Her blonde hair has been straightened, and she is fidgeting with her matching midnight blue clutch. Her partner is also attractive. He is as tall as Gerard and manages to carry the tuxedo he's wearing with ease. His hair is cropped short all over. I'd almost call it a buzz cut but not quite, and it's white blond. He is lean from his waist down, but his chest resembles that of a rooster. All puffed up and proud. I approach slowly, hoping to catch sight of Alex before I reach them, but I don't.

Instead, I notice Jenna, and she is jaw-dropping gorgeous in a gold, sequin full-length gown that hugs her svelte form. Her hair is styled into a volumized bob, and she looks to be wearing every rock she owns on her fingers while her hands talk in animation to the crowd. I don't see Nadal anywhere, but knowing his form, he's hunting down young prey.

Having noticed me, Gerard calls out and waves me over. When I'm among them, he introduces me to his companions.

"Hello," I say, tucking my clutch under my armpit and shaking their hands in turn.

"This is Oliver and Falon's first time here," Gerard says on their behalf.

"What do you think, it's impressive isn't it? So, what made you come tonight?" I fire off questions before they have time to answer even one.

Oliver looks at Gerard who is now looking over the crowd.

"We—were invited," he stammers.

"You're not from here?" I say, tilting my head, trying to pick his slight accent.

"Born in Sweden but I've lived in the States over fifteen years now."

"Oh, and how are you liking it?" I address Falon, but she just smiles and lets Oliver do all the talking.

"It's exciting, yes. There are many opportunities here in the States. Gerard tells me you enjoy photography."

I nod.

"And you work for a well-known publishing house?"

"Uh-huh, that's right, just part time."

"Will you excuse us, Paige, Oliver," Gerard interrupts. "I'm just going to introduce Falon around. Falon is looking for work."

She nods, and her round big blue eyes light up when she smiles shyly.

"What do you do, Falon?" I ask, taking a sip from my glass.

"I am a re—cep—tion—ist," she says in a succession of syllables, attempting to perfect her English.

"Well, you're in the right place to establish some reputable contacts." I nod and take a step back. "I'll let you go too, Oliver. You might like to meet some other people yourself," I suggest, already throwing my eyes around in search of Alex.

"No, no, that's fine, Paige, you chat with Oliver. He has an interest in photography as well. I think you'll have plenty in common, and I'm sure the formalities will begin soon." Gerard glances at his watch. "We'll be right back." Falon smiles up at him when he takes her by the elbow and leads her away, which leaves me with an uncomfortable feeling and an overtly attentive Oliver.

Shaking my insecurities off, I turn my attention back to him. "So, you're a photographer then?"

Oliver smiles. "Yes, you could say that." He presses a hand to the small of my back. "Can we walk? I'd like to take in a cigarette before we're asked to sit. Do you smoke?"

"No," I reply, but let him escort me toward the exit, his hand feeling warm on my back. His cologne is something cheap because it assaults my nostrils when the breeze from outside rushes toward us.

"Would you mind keeping me company? We can chat outside."

"Sure, why not?" It's only then that I notice Alex, and he is looking my way. I smile at him and shrug, then pull an 'I don't know' face at him, feeling relieved that he's finally here. I throw my head back as Oliver and I leave the marquee, hoping to get a better look at who Alex is with. But the crowd so thick, I can barely see his face anymore. I'm hoping Oliver is a quick smoker.

"So, what's your expertize in photography?" I ask as Oliver lights up. We are not alone outside even though the air is rather chilly, now the sun is setting. There are several more smokers and odd bods milling about.

"Nudes," Oliver says, catching me off guard.

"Oh!"

"Yes. Erotica, actually." He returns his packet of smokes to his inner jacket pocket. "Does that shock you?"

"Um, no," I reply cautiously, although I'm struggling to understand why Gerard would assume Oliver's interests were the same as mine.

"They're tasteful," he tells me as though reading my mind, then draws deeply on his cigarette and looks down at me.

"I'll take your word for it." I look around hoping to spot a waitress carrying champagne.

"You're shocked, aren't you? I can see you thinking, and you're blushing," Oliver says, making my face hotter.

"No." I pause for a moment then decide to be honest. "Well, yes, maybe a bit. I'm a landscape and clothed people kind of gal myself, so I guess I don't share the appreciation of the human form quite like you do."

"I would love to photograph you some day. Your hair is astonishing. I imagine it's quite long when down, and it would cascade nicely over your equally beautiful breasts. Do you also have ginger pubic hair?"

"Excuse me!" I laugh because he is so forward it's funny. "Do you?" I fire back.

"Only when I dye them." He laughs along with me.

"Well, if you must know, I don't exactly have that much left down there, but what I have is much darker. Now stop flirting and tell me about your wife. Falon is a very unusual name." I twist the stem of my empty glass between my fingers.

"She's not my wife."

"Oh, you're not married?" I ask, just as a waitress zips by. "Whoa, hold up please," I sing out calling her back. She stands patiently so I can deposit my empty glass and grab two more, offering one to Oliver.

"Thank you. Cheers," he says, clinking my glass with his. "No, beautiful, she's my younger sister. I needed a plus one, and she needs to find a job." He gulps down his champagne in one giant mouthful. "She's only here for six months in the U.S., but I suggested she gets work. See what the Americans are all about."

"Can't argue with that."

Oliver walks a little distance away and puts his cigarette out in the bin provided. When he returns, he stands in front of me, looking down and smiling. He is handsome in a clean-cut kind of way. Fresh faced with a broad grin and large white teeth. Typically, Scandinavian I would think.

"This friend of yours, Annabel, Gerard said she is largely responsible for organizing this show."

"Event," I correct him.

"Is she as beautiful as you?"

"Far prettier, I think. Why, are you looking to pick

someone up for the night?" I eye him over the rim of my glass while quenching my dry throat. "Because she's married and committed." I waggle my finger at him. "Now, Jenna on the other hand…" I trail off and laugh at my own joke. After looking around to check who is in earshot, I add, "Jenna will be the one in the center of the room in there." I jerk my head. "Surrounded by a moat from all the men drooling." I giggle again and take more of my champagne, which incidentally is going straight to my head. Oliver smiles and chuckles in encouragement. Using my hand as a shield in a mock gesture to show I don't want to be overheard, I whisper, "She's married as well, but, you might just be right up her alley, I think."

Oliver nods and puts his hand on the small of my back, pulling me closer to his mouth.

"Alley?" he questions, obviously not understanding the term.

I pull back and look at him in the face. "You know laneway, road, path." I drain my glass, acutely aware he is now making small circles on my back and still flirting with me.

"Oh." He nods. "Actually, I rather hoped I'd be right up *your alley*, later tonight, beautiful Paige," he murmurs through puckered lips.

Okay. Now it's gone too far.

I take a noticeable step away from him. "You do know I'm married to Gerard?"

"Oh yes, he explained that." Oliver straightens, still smiling and not looking the least bit ashamed. I'm starting to wonder whether I have an invisible stamp on my forehead that illuminates whenever I'm around philanderers.

"I think we better go inside," I say, feeling overwhelmed by his audacity. I don't even wait for him to answer. Turning on my heel, I walk away as fast as I can, but Oliver seems to keep pace regardless, and again he slips a hand on the small of my back. I sidestep in an instant and out of his reach.

"Please don't," I snap, using my purse to fan my face. I search everywhere for someone, anyone I know.

Oliver grabs my arm. "Have I offended you somehow? If I have, I'm sorry."

I look from his hand to the confused look on his face. "I just need to find Gerard." I glance past Oliver and into the crowd, twisting my purse in my hand and fiddling with an earring, praying Oliver will just leave.

But then he's helping me look, making me feel stupid that maybe I was overreacting to his flirtatious remark. Maybe it's the alcohol that's making me overly sensitive.

Spotting Gerard, Oliver points him out then thanks me for keeping him company. I nod but don't smile, and I'm relieved when he doesn't try to keep me any longer. When he heads off in another direction, I let out my breath and silently forgive him. God, what's gotten into me?

Gerard who has deposited Falon somewhere, is amongst a group of people I don't know. He keeps his eyes fixed on me as I approach.

"Here you are," Gerard says, sliding an arm around my waist. I smile around at the group in greeting but stay distracted, looking through the crowd. "What did you think of Oliver?" he asks.

"Do you know where Alex is, I thought I saw him before?" I ask, ignoring his question. Then, seconds later, when a waitress passes me, I lunge forward and snatch two flutes of bubbles off the tray, nearly causing the whole lot to go toppling. In an instant, I've downed one glass.

"No—I haven't. And I think you should slow down on these." Gerard tries taking the second glass out of my hand, but I move it out of his reach. I attract some attention from the group close by, and a tall woman with no chin, but big beautiful eyes grimaces. When she rolls her eyes and lets go of a big smile, I giggle and salute her with my glass. I then gulp the contents of the second glass down.

Offloading the champagne glasses on the closest table, I hook my arm through Gerard's. "I think we should go and find our table. These shoes are killing me, and I need to sit down."

"Did you talk to Oliver about his work? I thought maybe once the gallery is up and running, you could display his work."

I pivot and glare up at him. "You know he shoots nudes."

"I'm sure they're tasteful," he says, pulling me away from the group.

I laugh so hard it sounds fake. "Who is he anyway, you know that's his sister he's with?"

"Yes, of course I know that."

"Well, do you also know he tried coming on to me?" My voice is an octave louder than Gerard cares to hear, judging by the evil eye he awards me. He looks over my head and straightens his bow tie, then nods in greeting as two males voice his name and pass by, before a third sounds to be getting closer.

"Gerard. Good to see you again." The voice is deep and eloquent, and even before their hands are joined and I have turned around, I recognize it's the perversive man from Jenna and Nadal's dinner party. "Ah, so it is you, Paige," Jamison says. He lets go of Gerard's hand and steps back to appraise me. "Stunning, I must say, and I'm impressed with what you've done here." He gestures around the room in spectacular fashion.

I can't even muster a polite smile. "Well I'd hardly say it was me alone, or at all really," I say, regretting that I told him about the event in the first place. Everything seems to be spoiling my night so far, and still I can't find Alex. Then I'm looking for Jenna.

"Oh, I thought you said you were part of the organization?" Jamison says.

I shrug. "Yeah well, whatever. Gerard should we find our seats?" I say, looking up at him.

If his frown doesn't tell me he's annoyed, the tight grip he takes on my arm fixes that. "Why don't you go check your makeup while I speak with Jamison," he suggests. "Then find our seats and slow down on the champagne, you're getting loud."

Pulling my arm out of Gerard's grip, I glare at Jamison whose smirk reaches both his big ears, before I head off toward the restrooms located outside somewhere, battling the soft ground with my heels as I go.

Once outside, I lose all momentum and stand bewildered between marquees roaring with activity. Voices and music, pots clanging and staff calling out instructions. The sun has now set, and almost everyone has made their way into the main area. The flow of bright traffic lights on the adjacent highway keeps me transfixed in a daze as I try to collect my thoughts. Oliver's comment keeps repeating itself making me feel uneasy. I need to find Alex.

Spinning around, I bump straight into Annabel who is with him. The relief that fills me spills over as I expel Alex's name in a deep sigh. In all my life, I've never been so happy to see someone.

"Why, Paige. Alex and I have been looking everywhere for you."

"Hey." Alex stuffs his hands in his suit pants and rolls his shoulders as if relieving a pinch between his blades.

"I'm sorry I was just getting some air." I take a step closer to Alex and reach out to stroke his arm but catch myself just in time. "Where have you been?" I ask.

"Around. Pretty big crowd. Not my thing but..." He shrugs and glances back at the marquee and the crowd. He is wearing a new suit by the looks, and the soft gray shirt he's wearing emphasizes the rich green of his eyes. When he catches me staring, he winks. My face comes alive with the giddiness that whooshes through me, reminding me how lovesick I am.

"Come on, let's get back inside, they'll be starting the speeches soon, and I need one more drink before I go on," Annabel says, leading the way and unfortunately straight toward Gerard who is now alone but looking straight at us.

"You look nice." Alex lowers his head close to mine, and behind the fullness of my dress I graze my fingers over Alex's and grin up at him.

"Thanks, and you look very handsome in a suit, Alex."

"Don't he just?" Annabel remarks, flicking her head around, surprising me that she even heard. "I almost didn't recognize him standing there with Jenna," she goes on to tell, and my smile slides away.

Alex nudges me and when I look up, he squints his eyes and shakes his head. "Just being sociable and looking for you," he explains, putting my smile back where it belongs.

My heart is thumping inside my chest and it takes all my effort not to just grab his hand and slip away again, but all too soon, we are alongside Gerard. Annabel keeps going ahead of us, informing she needs that stiff drink.

"How have you been?" Gerard asks Alex after they greet each other.

"Busy. Going out a bit. No time for much else, but I'm making progress."

"Yes, I noticed when I stopped by. I hope the builder didn't get in your way. He needs one more day there and then he's done. How much longer do you think before you're finished? We're getting anxious to use the place, aren't we,

Paige?" Gerard slips an arm around me. The skin on my neck comes alive like needle pricks are assaulting me because Alex throws me a dubious look before nodding at Gerard and answering him. I end up staring at the floor. How is tonight going to work if Alex is already crabby that Gerard is being affectionate?

"Yeah, well, I should go and grab myself another beer. How long do these sort of things usually go for?" He crosses his arms and rocks on his heels like he does, looking positively pissed off.

"We can expect to be out of here by midnight, going by our experience previous years," Gerard surmises.

"Right. Well, I will see you at the table then. I've checked, and we're at least sitting together. Later," he says, walking off and leaving me anxious.

SOBER II

S oon after, the night becomes a blur of activities. First, we are ushered into seats and the emcee offers a welcome. There are some long-winded speeches from both LA General's board of directors and Brave Hearts' founders before finally, we are asked to take shifts at the large buffet-style banquet. When Gerard gets caught talking to two doctors sitting to his right, I use the opportunity to take my turn at the buffet after seeing Alex slip away.

Although it's true we are sitting at the same table, unfortunately, Alex has been allocated a seat over on the other side of our table that seats an even twenty. Stuck next to an elderly man wearing a hearing aid, I can't imagine Alex is enjoying himself one bit. I'm feeling painfully guilty knowing he's most likely only here because of me.

Jumping the line and slipping in behind Alex, I get a playful growl from the couple I've encroached on. "Sorry, special needs," I whisper to them, then grab hold of the back of Alex's jacket to get his attention. "Hi."

Alex looks around, for I assume Gerard, before his eyes settle back on me. The way he knits his eyebrows implies I should let go of his jacket. Heat rushes to my face and gets my heart racing. Is he angry because I'm acting too familiar with him or is it because he saw me talking with Oliver?

"Enjoying yourself?" he asks a little flatly, taking a step closer to the food, a plate twisting in his hand.

"I would be if I could shift places," I reply, moving along in the queue, feeling silly now because I don't even have a plate.

"Are you all right, you seem upset?" I ask.

"Ah it's just a bit boring for my taste. No offense, but most of the people here are a bunch of arrogant assholes with money."

"Sorry, I guess Gerard shouldn't have asked you to come."

Alex takes another step forward. "He didn't."

"What do you mean he didn't?" I look back toward our table at Gerard and see he's now watching me. Electrical pulses sap through my entire being, and then my eyes scan the crowd where I spot Oliver with his sister at a table that's still seated and waiting their turn. He is nursing his chin and ogling me. When I look back to Gerard he is no longer seated. I look frantically around taking little steps and moving along behind an aloof Alex.

"Alex." I tug on his jacket again. "What's going on?"

Alex turns to me, looking bewildered. "What do you mean? Nothing. I just hate waiting in fucking queues for food. Reminds me of prison." His gruff reply attracts the attention of the people both in front, and behind us. Alex widens his eyes at the young man behind me. "Murder," he pranks, nodding his head.

"Stop it." I slap his arm then turn to the couple. "He's joking," I assure them, then stare at Alex's back wondering how I can broach the subject of the three-way without causing gossip.

"You might want one of these."

I turn sharply and there is Gerard, holding a plate out to me. I know my face must turn bright red because the heat is stinging the crap out of me. I take it from him without a word and stand dumbfounded not knowing what to do as he walks away.

"Alex."

He turns to me.

"Did Gerard talk to you about tonight?"

"What do you mean?"

"I mean—why are you here?"

"Do you want me to leave?" He looks both hurt and baffled.

"No, but I'm wondering why you came."

"Because I thought you'd appreciate it if I did," he says pointedly. "I'm also interested to see how much your photos make."

"You are? You did?" But I'm still confused. "Didn't Gerard call you and ask if you—we—could," I stammer looking behind me, frustrated that there are people so close that I can't say anything too outlandish. "Did he invite you to party with us later?" I eventually find the right words.

Eyebrows pinched, Alex turns and stares down at me.

"He asked me, and I said no." He's looks around I presume for Gerard.

"Then what?"

"Then nothing."

"He didn't offer you something?"

"Jesus. No, and I thought you were going to give up on that stupid idea, Paige."

"He was just here looking pissed," I say, holding up my plate to my chest. "I thought he was arranging something with you. I told him..." I can't finish my sentence. I slam my eyes shut hoping to block out my own stupidity.

"What's going on, Paige?" Alex says through the roar of chatter that seems to overwhelm me now. But I can't answer, I need air. I feel sick. I'm burning up like I have a fever. I leave the queue and make a beeline for outside, dropping my plate off at the nearest table as I go.

Outside, my hands go to my face. I need coldness. My face is a hot plate, and I imagine my makeup is slowly sliding down my face. I want to go home. I feel sick and the champagne is going to my head even quicker now.

"Paige?"

I spin around and there's Gerard again. My heart is pulsating so hard now it creates a ringing in my ears and I can't hear what he's saying until he repeats himself, taking hold of my forearm and grounding me.

"Are you all right?" he asks. I look over his shoulder and see Alex heading our way. Rushing in, I hug Gerard and glare a warning at Alex with the slight shake of my head. He makes a gesture with his hands that suggests he has no idea what's going of before returning to the line.

"I'm hot," I say, stepping away from Gerard and putting my hands on my face again, pressing my fingers onto my lids, forcing the tears to recede. Gerard says silent. When I realize he's not even going to touch or comfort me, I come out from beneath my hiding place to see his jaw is locked. My eyes are drawn to his clenching fists.

"Are you sick, or are you just planning on ruining the night for us?"

"I don't know." My voice comes out sounding like a whining child until I clear my throat. "Why are you still friendly with Jamison, and who is Oliver? How do you know him and why is he here? Did you plan something with him tonight?" I say in a flurry.

Stepping closer, Gerard takes my shaking hands and

interlocks his fingers with mine. I can feel the strength in his grip, and his eyes have turned a steel gray in the shadows.

"I could ask you the same thing about Alex, now couldn't I?"

I think my heart just seized up, and for a moment I can't breathe. "What do you mean? I thought we agreed to another play night."

"Yes, and I have a night planned with a man I believe you find attractive. He even has something in common with you."

"But we agreed you'd ask Alex first."

"I did. He said no."

"But why didn't you offer him money?"

Gerard's whole face scrunches like he's tasted something foul. "I wasn't going to offer him money again. I figured if he couldn't see what a privilege it is to have sex with you, he's an idiot. So, I asked Oliver instead."

"No. You should have offered Alex the money." I'm shaking so furiously I'm getting dizzy.

Gerard steps back. "Why should I have? Sounds to me like you were planning something with him before even talking about it with me. How else would you know I didn't offer him money, Paige? Are you trying to make a fool out of me?"

"What? No. But there's no way I'm letting anyone else touch me."

He studies me without saying a word, but his lips pucker as if he has a thousand things he'd like to express but has no idea where to start.

"Gerard, you're hurting me." My feet peddle backward, fear stinging my eyes as I attempt to pull my hands out of his tightening grip.

Gerard's mouth turns into a tight line. "You must find it funny playing with my emotions, Paige, because that's all you seem to do lately. You're my wife and the woman I've been loving unconditionally. I've given everything I have to you. And now you've become a lying, cheating bitch, who just wants everything her own way. You promised me if Alex said no, I could find someone else."

"No, I said *we'd* choose someone else."

"Well, I suggest you choose Oliver because *he* is what's on offer. You know there's only so much I will tolerate from you, and it seems to me, Alex is becoming a pain in my ass because you've become obsessed with him. I think he's going to find himself in a lot of trouble soon. He may even find himself in prison again." He tightens his grip, pressing my palms backward painfully. Instantly, I think of Kelsey, knowing for certain now she is telling the truth. "You might think you love him, but I can assure you, he will break your goddamn heart the first chance he gets and leave you with nothing." Gerard lets go of my hands and points a finger at me. "If you think you can run off with him until you've had your fill, then come crawling back to me, you're sorely mistaken."

My mind is racing, searching for ways to dig myself out of this mess. He has me cornered. I don't want Alex to pay because of my stupidity.

"What's it going to be, Paige? Am I to assume you planned this, and it backfired? That Alex is a threat to our marriage and you're no longer in love with me?"

He's putting an ultimatum to me that's a lose-lose. Shit. Shit, shit, shit. I can't think.

"No. How I feel about Alex has nothing to do with him. He's been nothing but friendly. Please, don't take my stupid little crush out on him."

"Good. Well then, I guess we understand each other perfectly." Gerard dusts his suit off as if we've had a physical confrontation. I even feel as though I'm sitting in the dirt battered and bruised. "Should we go back inside and enjoy the rest of the evening?" He takes me around the waist and guides me inside the marquee again. "Now tell me," he tucks me close to his body, "you did find Oliver attractive, didn't you?"

SAVAGES

The hotel we arrive at looks like somewhere families would stay. Ground-level and painted brick, it's nothing like the hotel we shared with Alex. I'm in some sort of altered state because I've drank far too much wine, and champagne. I can't remember the auction. Cannot remember saying goodbye to anyone—the night is a blur. I'm feeling lucky that I still remember my name.

Gerard doesn't seem too worried when I wobble away from the cab and look around aimlessly for where I'm going. Then Oliver becomes chivalrous, scooping me up into his arms before I topple over.

"I need water," I complain into his neck. I look at Gerard as he follows Oliver and me. He's looking annoyed. I guess it's because I'm so drunk, but that's the point. I didn't want to remember this, don't even want to participate. If I pass out, he can't make me do anything.

"I didn't get to eat. Let's go back. I want food, I'm sooo hungry," I call out, then let my head drop onto Oliver's shoulder and shut my eyes. When I'm lowered to the ground, I'm conscious again and standing in front of a door. "Eww, why would they paint it green," I slur, looking around for Gerard. "Where's my husband, Olie?"

Oliver digs into his pockets then produces keys, making me realize it's his room. Was he sharing it with his sister? Are they from out of town? Where is his sister?

"Hey, where are you from anyway?" I ask, reaching out for the brick wall to steady myself.

"Sweden, remember," he replies, having trouble with the door.

"Nooo, Olie, I mean where do you live now?" My eyes lolly all over the place when I try to focus on what he's doing. "Christ, I'm drunk."

Oliver pushes the door open and pulls me off the wall but doesn't answer me. "In we go," he says, helping me inside the room.

"Gerard should have booked. He picks nice places. Where did he go? I want my husband back." I sway and toss my purse onto the nearest surface. "I mean really back. This is not him you know, I think he's..." I tap my temple. "He's been, embodied. Like, like... what's that movie? Remember the one that those people get aliens inside, but they still look like who they are?" I rant about a movie I don't even think I've ever seen, maybe only watched the preview. I stagger back out the still-open door in search of Gerard. Why would he leave me here anyway?

"He's gone to get some food and water for you, beautiful, come back inside," Oliver says, pulling me back into the room.

When he closes the door, I reach for his head. He thinks I'm going for a kiss, but I push his face away and bring my mouth close to his ear and hang onto his arm to help steady myself.

"I need to tell you something because I feel bad, and I don't want you to think I don't like you because you know, you're a really good-looking man and *funny*," I say, tapping his cheek with a finger. "But..." I make him press closer because I whisper. "I want to be with Alex tonight, not you. Him and me, we've got a thing, but shh, don't tell Gerard, because he'll get pissed off if he finds out I told you." I pull a sad pout at Oliver, then drunken tears spring.

"Hey now, beautiful, don't go getting all sappy on me, come here." Oliver pulls me into a hug and smooths my hair.

"But I really wanted to be with Alex tonight."

"You just pretend I'm Alex, because you know what I've been thinking about all night?" he asks.

I shake my head against his chest, my arms encircling his waist, hanging on as though he's a long-lost relative I can trust.

"What your hair will look like spread all over me while you suck me off. Will you let me take it down?" Without an answer from me, he reaches up and fumbles with my pins. I just stand there, half sleeping against his chest, closing my eyes and taking long, deep breaths, feeling totally wasted.

When there's a loud banging on the door, I jump and notice a coolness on my back. Then I realize my dress is gaping open. Oliver eases me away and goes to answer the door. For some reason I'm expecting Alex to join us, but it's Gerard. Rocking slightly, I stay where I am, feeling confused because I thought Gerard was already in the room. Then I'm feeling giddy because everything in the room starts spinning.

I glance around when I get a whiff of fried food, and my stomach lurches. I spin around again until I focus on the bathroom door and make my way for it, moving faster until I reach the toilet and throw up copious amounts of red wine.

Someone gathers my hair as I jerk repeatedly, each heave ending with me groaning louder.

"Why do I drink?" I mumble into the toilet. Then I'm being lifted until I'm standing and swaying on my feet again.

For some reason I think it's Alex. Feeling relieved, I turn around and smile. But it's Gerard. I let my lip drop. "I wanted you to be Alex." I place my hands on his chest. "Sorry Gerard, I think I'm too drunk," I slur, as if it's not already obvious.

"Come and have something to eat and drink," he offers, taking my hand.

"Toothbrush," I say, as if I'm two years old and only capable of speaking minimal syllables.

When Gerard sits me on the toilet seat, I close my eyes and drift into a semi-conscious snooze. Then he's there again, with a toothbrush and paste. He helps me to my feet and hands me the prepared toothbrush then leaves the bathroom. Brushing my teeth in slow uncoordinated strokes, I stare at the blurry reflection which is a very drunk me. When I'm done, I go out and flop on the bed face down, desperate to pass out.

"Paige, honey, have some food first," Gerard says, pulling me up then helping me into a chair at the small round table. He slides some food in front of me. I see Oliver digging into his overnight bag that's on the end of the king-sized bed now. It's only then I take in the room as much as my drunken state will perceive. It's neat, clean, and very standard. There is a mounted headboard and two cheap-looking bedside lamps. My eyes take in the artwork around the room in a daze as I stuff fries in my mouth, washing them down with water.

"I'll just take a quick shower, beautiful, don't you fall asleep on me," Oliver says, going into the bathroom but leaving the door wide open.

"I don't know why he calls me beautiful, because honestly —I'm just a whore really. Did you have to pay this guy or is he paying you?" I question Gerard, trying to focus on his face.

"You're drunk and being stupid. Now eat."

I'm not too drunk to read the angry look that clouds his face.

"No, seriously, I want to know, did he pay you, because I'd loooove to know what I'm worth." I smirk at him. "How much did this pussy earn you?" I sway backward and slapping at my crotch.

"Stop it Paige, don't be ridiculous," he snaps.

I turn my attention back to Oliver in the bathroom. He has undressed, and I become fascinated because men can be so blasé about their bodies around other men. I stay transfixed, zoning in and out of consciousness as I eat.

"He's tall, isn't he?" I ask in a moment of clarity. "He comes from Sweden, you know, but I don't know where he lives. He won't tell me. Where'd his sister go? Don't you want to fuck her at the same time?" My sarcastic laugh doesn't even rouse Gerard's attention. "Wait. Eww, no that would be so wrong, wouldn't it? Aha! No, you should have invited Jenna. I found out she's a kinky girl just like you." I waggle my finger at him and start laughing hysterically. I nearly fall off the chair until I grip the table and steady myself.

Gerard doesn't say a thing. He's too busy looking at his phone, or is that—my phone? I scoff at him then go back to watching Oliver in the shower, lathering his body with soap. The room soon becomes hazy and then I'm just staring straight through him, or maybe my eyes close, I'm not sure, but then I hear voices from my past.

"Get in the car, Paige. And here, put this on and cover yourself up," Sheree's dad had said, shoving Sheree's Broncos jersey at me. I had put it on over my torn and dirty school blouse, wondering first whether Peter and his friends would tell the kids at school what happened before I worried about Sheree finding out I wore her jersey.

"Ree won't like me wearing this," I told him, my teeth chattering and my nose twitching to shake the vile smell of cigarette and gasoline fumes out of my nostrils. I pulled on the jersey feeling comforted.

"Sheree won't know." Her dad twisted me so I was facing him in the front seat of his car. He smoothed my hair again and brushed something off my face. "Did they touch you, you know, down there?" He looked concerned, his thumb grazed my lip which felt swollen.

Then his expression softened and his actions seemed like that of an anxious father. I felt my lips quiver and a warmth spread through me. He really cared. My father hadn't. He abandoned me, left me with my horrible mother who didn't even love me. I was scared, I was aching, I was lonely. Sheree's dad seemed to always be there for me. I wanted to tell him about Carlos. How he kept saying he wished he could claim my virginity, but it was worth too much and how my mom didn't seem to care. I wanted him to know how scared I was. I burst into tears and fell against his chest, needing to feel safe.

"They spoiled you didn't they, those boys?" he asked, taking hold of my shoulders. "Tell me they didn't get to you," he snapped.

I pulled back and stared at him then wiped at my eyes. I was so worried I'd shamed him somehow, I answered in a heartbeat.

"No, they didn't touch me, honest."

"Good. That's important," he said, looking relieved and letting go. I didn't understand what he meant at the time. "I'll take you home, so you can get cleaned up, and I'll talk to your mother."

"No! Please don't tell my mom. You don't know what she's like. She'll go off her nut and say it was my own fault."

"But you're a mess, your clothes are torn, she will know something has happened."

He started up the engine and put the car into gear. As he

drove, he turned to study me every so often while I thought things through.

When I reflect on it now, it amazes me how I didn't realize. Maybe it was because I was still shaken up from Peter Moriarty and his friends and everything seemed to be in slow-motion anyway, but it seemed to me that as Sheree's dad took me home that day, he was driving extra slowly. Watching and waiting for me to come up with a plan of my own, because the moment I turned to him triumphantly, saying, "You could always take me to the lake house. I've got spare clothes and stuff there." His face lit up like a glowworm and his foot pressed down for more speed.

I don't know how I got undressed. I'm on all fours and staring at Gerard who's sitting naked on a towel and wanking himself in the dining chair that I was just sitting on and eating fries. His eyes are alive and reveling at the sight of Oliver fucking me. Where did I go? I don't remember what I was thinking about.

Oliver slaps my ass hard making me bite down on my lip to hold in the yelp, my flesh tingling in the wake of his hand.

"Oh, you have a beautiful wife, Gerard. Her pussy is nice and tight." Oliver slaps me on the ass again in the same place, making me cry out this time. Gerard pumps himself harder, and I feel the tears coming. I clamp my eyes shut. Why am I doing this?

"Get off." I push on Oliver and he falls away from me. But then he's pulling me by the hips. I twist around to look at him. His cock is long and curved and points toward the ceiling and the condom covering his shaft is glistening with my juices. I bury my face into the mattress and expel a groan. I feel like a whore.

"Sit on the edge of the bed, Paige. Here." Oliver pats the mattress, then drags me into a sitting position. When I look at Gerard and shake my head, his eyes narrow into a death stare. His wordless threat is emphasized when he lifts his eyebrows and grins.

He just wants me to be a dirty little whore now. I decide to repulse him by acting as wanton as I possibly can and position myself on the edge of the bed and face him, but then I'm swaying and my eyelids droop again. And then, I just don't care what they do. Alex is angry at me. I tried to trick Gerard and now he is punishing me. I created this mess and if I don't do what Gerard asks, he will take it out on Alex. I know he will.

"I'm a lucky man tonight. Privileged that your husband likes to watch, because I like to put on a show, beautiful, Paige." Oliver rises and stands in front of me. Gerard smiles and sits back in the chair to watch. He fascinates me for a brief coherent moment. His eyes are dark and full of lust. Like nothing else in the world matters except being fixated on me. Shamefully, the attention arouses me.

Oliver smooths my hair, pulling it around so it falls across my breast, then he sits on the bed next to me. When I look at him, he comes in for a kiss. Have I kissed him before now? I don't know because I can't remember, but his lips feel familiar. Sweet like soda pop. I pull away.

"I'm very drunk," I slur, trying to focus on what's going on. How did they get this far with me anyway, and why am I so willing?

Then Gerard reaches forward and takes both my knees and jerks my legs wide apart. I catch my breath in an instant and look at him.

"Keep your legs open, honey," he says, holding onto my knees when I go to close my legs. "I want to see you all wet and aroused. I want to see your pussy winking and begging for cock. There's nothing sexier than a woman flushed with desire, don't you think Oliver?" Gerard is wanking himself slowly in the chair and Oliver is using his fingers to massage himself. They're both staring, watching and waiting for me. I feel my pussy clench and I hate myself for it.

"Oh yes, to be sure," Oliver agrees. "Massage with your tits, beautiful." Oliver reaches out and plays with my nipple. I watch his hand in a daze for a moment then look up at a grinning Gerard. I hate him right now, but I hate myself even more because I'm so weak when it comes to Gerard getting his way.

"He loves me being whorish," I mumble to Oliver and stare straight at Gerard. His pout comes across as mocking but his words are silky smooth.

"You're not a whore, honey, you're sexy. Look, you've got us both hard as rocks." Gerard jerks himself again.

Then, it's as though I'm someone else, like the alcohol has erased all my boundaries. I get aroused because they're fixated, fascinated with me. Their eyes are absolutely feasting on me and my lady bits. My heart flutters because of their expressions. They're both waiting on edge, eager to know just how wicked I can be.

I can't help it. I feel myself thicken, slicken, and become warm. I reach up and caress my breasts, my gaze darting from one set of eyes to the other in a drunken daze. I'm not me anymore, just some woman who has the power to make men worship her.

Looking between my still-spread legs, I see a pool of moisture has begun seeping into the sheet. The sight alone sends shivers through my whole being.

"That's my girl." Gerard says, breathy and pumping his cock a little faster. "Will you suck Oliver off? Do it now while I stare at your perfect pussy," he rushes, as though he is ready to blow his load any second. Oliver stands in expectation and runs a gentle hand over my head. He is not Alex. I want him to be Alex. *Pretend it is Alex.* This is for Alex, so Gerard will leave him alone. He's got no money, and Gerard threatened to send him back to prison, and it's all my fault. But Gerard was supposed to offer Alex money again, we would all have all gotten what we wanted. I would have gotten what I needed. I need Alex not Oliver.

But my hand still takes hold of Oliver to stroke him gently. I don't want to do this. *It's just sex.* I don't want to be here. *Just get it over with.* I should get out of here now. *Just pretend it's Alex, just slip away. Alex is with someone else anyway.* Why didn't he follow me when I went outside? *He doesn't care, you're just another girl to him.*

"Good girl. I knew there was a bad girl in there waiting to get out," Gerard says, making me groan and whimper simultaneously, like I've suddenly been caught out. "Suck him and use your fingers on yourself, Paige. I want to see you fuck yourself," Gerard demands in urgency, obviously aroused because he is controlling the entertainment in front of him. And me, I have become his fallen angel.

In my drunken stupor, I take both Oliver's cock into my mouth and fingers to my pussy, wishing neither action was making me so aroused, but there's something about their hunger and my need to satisfy them. I know there was a reason why I'm obliging, but I'm so drunk, I can't remember what it is anymore. I faux pas on autopilot. I'm a slut at Gerard's disposal.

Bobbing over Oliver's cock like I love it, Oliver pushes me backward so I'm laying back on the bed. Then his tongue is on my pussy, licking and playing with my clit. I groan but get lost somewhere again. Did I pass out? Because now Oliver is sitting beneath me, fucking me and I'm sucking Gerard's cock. He's moaning and holding firmly to my head. Where did I go?

I'd heard a noise, but the sound was out of place. It sounded like an electric shaver. Was someone shaving? And then I remember a man in a bathroom, he's shaving, who was it?

"Oh God, Paige, you suck like a goddess," Gerard moans aloud.

I freeze, push him away then look at his face. Where have I heard that before? I'm still in a drunken daze. Then I'm locking eyes on Gerard who is nodding. "I told you, you were." He smiles. "My little goddess, remember?"

I nod, but Gerard's face is blurring, and he doesn't look like him. I don't know him anymore—he has the eyes of a stranger now. Where did my kind husband go? Grabbing my face, he drives his cock in my mouth and down my throat again, gagging me without restraint. I start sobbing and my jerking must cause Oliver to think I'm climaxing because he chirps out, "Oh yes, beautiful, clamp yourself around me."

I pull away from Gerard again. His cock bounces in protest and he sings out, "Don't fucking stop now." Then I feel Oliver thickening within me. Gerard grabs my face and kisses me as Oliver, who's still inside me, works his way backward on the bed. Then Gerard is hovering over me.

"What are you doing?" I gasp, before he locks his lips on mine again, kissing me with such hunger I become breathless and my hands don't know where to grab to steady his urgency.

Oliver keeps pulsing within me. His cock is so hard I feel the fullness press against my abdominal wall.

Then I'm like putty as my body decides to betray me in favor of their unchecked rapture. Oliver is pulling me down with him as he lays flat on the bed, me splayed facing up, on top of him. His cock slides out. Then Gerard's eyes, thumb and fingers are between my legs, spreading my slickness so Oliver can insert his cock into my ass.

"No, no, no," I cry out slapping my palms onto the mattress. But it's too late. Oliver has filled me to the balls.

"Oops sorry, wrong hole," Oliver whispers in my ear. But he does nothing to correct himself so I know it's deliberate.

Gerard hovers over me, wedging himself between Oliver's and my legs.

"What are you doing, Gerard? No, not together, I can't take you together." I try pushing on his chest but he's so carnal now, he cannot—not enter me. I moan deeply when he sinks himself right in, the feeling of fullness so overwhelming and surreal, my drunkenness evaporates with the heat of our bodies as we meld into one.

"Oooh, honey, yes you can. And God, does it feel fucking amazing," he moans in rapture. And it does. It fucking does feel incredible, and I hate that it does because I want to tell them to stop, but I can't. I'm caught in the submissive sensation as they thrust slowly, taking up every inch of internal space I have. Gerard looks to be in euphoria, holding my legs apart watching in amazement as I'm being fucked in both holes. I can feel their cocks rubbing within me, the friction almost setting my internals on fire. Every nerve ending is electrified as one of them enters, and the other withdraws, getting faster until they are like wild animals pummelling into me.

I feel myself slipping into a space between semi-consciousness and oblivion unable to assimilate the difference between pleasure and pain. And then I am climbing, a brewing eruption like I'd never felt before, caused by the simultaneous rubbing of cocks and Gerard thumbing against my clit. Coupled with the delirium of my mind, I'm mumbling incoherently along with moans. "Oh God, oh fucking Jesus, no you need to stop, but God it feels so weirdly good. Please, oh yes. I mean no, you need to stop. It's too much but it's so good," I mumble, on and on, causing both men to get more excited by my undecided state of mind.

Oliver begins pinching my nipples fiercely, then Gerard's mouth is on them, soothing the sting away. They keep repeating the process until I'm slapping at them to stop. It's too overwhelming, I can't take it all in. Then Gerard is smothering me with kisses along my neck and face, moaning and groaning as his climax draws closer.

"Oh Christ," I moan, "it's too muuuuch." But my plea goes unregistered as both men get faster with their relentless thrusting, frightened perhaps that I will force them to stop at any moment when it becomes too much, as if it isn't already.

With every arousal point targeted now, I am grabbing onto the bedspread, trying to steady the oncoming tsunami. Howling and moaning, my hands fist into balls, clutching at the tangled bedspread, and then I spill over. Climaxing into what I'm sure looks like a convulsive epileptic fit, driving both men wild and closer toward their own cataclysmic ejaculation. Together they pound into me at the same time, both arching with all their might.

Oliver erupts inside me first. Hissing out, "Yeees," then gasping in delight as his cock swells inside my tiny, tight pucker hole before his release.

Wails of pleasure ricochet around the room as I thrash about between them, trying to escape, and then I am shaking uncontrollably as another orgasm claims me. A few more thrusts send Gerard into a spiral of his own. Pulling out just before he ejectulates, he squirts his jism all over my tits, my face, and through my hair.

Oliver holds me tightly to his chest to ease my shaking, then he thrusts into me a final time. I keep my eyes clamped shut. I don't want to see the reality. The reality that I just let a stranger and my husband use me in such a way. I want to block it out because I'm disgusted and confused, lost and disappointed in myself. I'm dirty. A whore, who'll do anything.

"Good lord! That was the screw of this goddamn century, beautiful." Oliver kisses my temple as I lay motionless in his arms.

"I think, Paige is satisfied now, Oliver," Gerard pants.

"I'd like to hope so." I can feel Olivers smile against my face.

I start crying.

"Paige honey." Gerard takes a seat beside us as Oliver sits me up then slides me off so Gerard can put an arm around me. "What's wrong, honey, did we hurt you?" His voice sounds chillingly condescending.

Oliver stands awkwardly but reaches out to stroke my head. I can't stop sobbing. Why did I let them do that to me? Why did I think getting drunk was a way out of this arrangement? It only made things worse. I meant to pass out, not let all my inhibitions go and fucking enjoy it. I'm an idiot. Why do I think I owe it to Gerard to have his way?

I see in my peripheral vision the creamy globs of Gerard's semen in my hair and smoosh it out of sight. I look down at my chest and see the proud trail he has left behind.

"I'm not a fucking cheap slut, you know." I cry louder.

"Oh, darling, that's for fucking sure." Oliver squats in front of me. "Hey, I'm sorry if I've upset you, I thought you wanted this?" He looks at Gerard as though for confirmation of something. I feel Gerard shake his head at Oliver, who then stands. "That, I mean—you, were amazing, Paige, thank you," Oliver says, before going off to the bathroom, I assume for a towel.

My sobbing eases as my mind numbs.

Gerard has me in a tight squeeze, not wanting to let me go. Knowing full well that he has overstepped a boundary now. I'm suspicious that he planned for the double penetration all along. I'm waiting for him to apologize, to say he didn't realize what Oliver was about to do. But, he doesn't, and he's not sorry.

"Paige, honey. I made you climax," he says, without a single trace of remorse in his voice. In fact, he sounds elated.

I shake my head and remain mute. I have nothing to say. Gerard has become selfish, controlling, and unpredictable. He has no scruples. Oliver is standing at the sink washing his face and hands, a towel hitched around his waist. Then he is stroking his chin with his palm, admiring himself, but to me, it's not his face I see, it's Gerard's face, the man who called me precious and then a goddess. I hate his face; I loved his face. When I look at Gerard, my still groggy state melts his face into Oliver's and then when Gerard looks into my eyes before he kisses me, Carlos's face melts into Gerard's. They are all the same.

Making my way to the shower, I pass Oliver on his way out. I don't uttering a single word and I can't even look at him now. I'm not sure what to make of any of it because I allowed it to happen so I could protect Alex. As I turn on the shower, I hear Gerard and Oliver talking quietly in the bedroom. I question whether they are exchanging money. I wait for the hot water. I adjust the cold. I step inside.

Gerard comes in, fully dressed again.

"Are you all right then?" he asks.

I stare at him as water caresses my deadened body. My mind is numb. I reach down and feel between my legs, my pussy is also numb, or is it quenched. I don't know. I feel violated but not. Satisfied but still yearning. From afar, I can feel Alex being ashamed of me. I know at some point during the night he saw me leave with the two of them, but I don't remember where or how.

"Paige," Gerard snaps.

I look up and give him a slight nod. "Fine, I'm fine. I'll be fine," I reply flatly. Every emotion has passed through me tonight ending with me lost somewhere, confused, shaken and so very, very ashamed.

"Good, because you see, now we know, it's not just Alex who can make you come after all," he says with such pride, it's like he's just discovered the Holy fucking Grail.

Well, aren't you just the hero now? I want to scream.

WHEN THE TRUTH HUNTS
YOU DOWN

I'm staring out the side window of the taxi, chewing my lovely jewel encrusted thumb nail deciding what I need to do. *Block it out,* a voice comes from somewhere deep inside. He knew I was drunk and I'm disgusted by who I became in that room with Gerard and Oliver, letting them take advantage of me like that. I was hammered for fuck's sake. Why would Gerard let that happen like that? *He doesn't care anymore, now block it out.*

"You're quiet, what's the matter?" Gerard asks.

"You planned it."

"With your permission. You agreed before we left."

"No, I mean, together like that."

"You seemed to enjoy it, and I made you come, didn't I?"

"I was drunk and out of my mind."

"Whose fault was that then?"

There's silence while we both stew.

"I don't know who you are anymore, Gerard," I mumble against the side window. "And that felt wrong," I add, brushing at tears. One of my false lashes begins to lift. I pinch it and carefully peel it off then toss it on the rubber mat under my feet.

"Wrong how? It's not like we broke the law," he says smugly.

"Yes, you did."

"Me?"

"You let Oliver trespass." I cross my arms and legs and glare at him.

Gerard thinks that's funny.

"When I agreed again, I thought it would be with Alex." I keep staring at him.

Gerard huffs then mumbles to himself.

"What?"

He stays silent for a moment, perhaps not wanting the cab driver to hear any more of our discussion. I haven't even looked to see if he's been watching us in his rearview mirror because I really don't care anymore. About anything. I'm disgusting. I feel like an idiot and it seems to be taking forever to get home. The cab's clock displays that it is nearing three. I don't even know where the night went, and my head is pounding.

"You're unbelievable. You're a liar and a goddamn cheat, Paige. You can't make up your mind what you damn well want, and now you're twisting everything around to blame me to suit yourself so you can stay locked in your little lovesick drama," Gerard blurts out what it would seem he's been stewing on for the last five minutes. Or maybe it's been the last few months.

My eyes shoot to the cabbie, and I swear I see him hunch over. I can't decide if I feel like hurling vomit or punching Gerard. I stare at him, contemplating doing both. Hurl vomit, then punch the fucker in his damn handsome vomit drenched face. Me! Twist things around?

"Fuck off," is all I can manage to say before turning back

and staring out the window again, chewing on my nail until it snaps off.

When we get home, I go straight to the guest room and fall into the bed. Gerard doesn't come looking for me, and I don't give a shit what he's even thinking. I lay there, looking around the room, remembering when it was mine, which seems a lifetime ago.

I feel like I've entered a nightmare. What started out as exciting has turned into a disgusting sex fest. It's got to stop. Gerard needs to stop. No, I need to stop. It's me, Gerard is right. I'm letting this happen. I could have said no to Oliver. But I was drunk. I don't even remember getting in the cab with them. I don't even remember leaving the venue. Did I see or talk to anyone before I left? I wish I could remember more about the night and what happened. What happened to Alex? Livid at myself, I shut it out and start humming a tune then concentrate on counting. Soon I'm drifting, and then thankfully, sleep overwhelms me.

"Paige," Gerard snaps, jarring me awake. I look up at him. My head is pounding and my mouth feels drier than cracked heels. "Here, it's Sheree, she's been calling non-fucking-stop." He thrusts my cell phone at me.

"Maybe you should have answered it then, you coward," I say, snatching the phone from him. I'm looking down at the screen when suddenly, my head is sent sideways when he slaps my face, shocking me blind. My hand glides up to cover my stinging cheek as I look up at him.

"Don't you ever call me that again. You have no fucking idea how hard it's been for me putting up with your disgusting secrets."

Well if nothing so far has killed the smugness in me, that

certainly did. Shaking now, I watch him until he leaves the room. I sit in stunned silence for minutes, staring at the closed door, jolting when my phone springs to life.

"Hey, Ree what's up?" I ask, my voice sounding like a seasoned smoker.

"Hi, sweet pea, how are you? I've been ringing for hours."

"Sorry, I'm hungover." I can't be bothered explaining, just opting to listen instead.

"Oh yeah, that's right the Brave Hearts thingy. How did it go?"

"Can't remember," I say, squeezing my aching forehead with my hand. The sun blazing through the window isn't helping me either.

"Okay, another day for that then. Paige I've been calling because…" she pauses for a moment and I'm grateful because the silence is kinder to my head. "Paige, your mom's in the hospital," she finally says.

"I'm not paying for her," I reply immediately.

"No, it's not that. Paige, she's dying. I'm so sorry, and I feel so bad, you know? I mean it was just the other day that I said that she should just die already, and well God, she must have already been sick because now she's riddled with cancer. They say she's only got weeks, maybe only days," Sheree explains the prognosis.

I'm speechless. My head is throbbing, and I keep getting flashes from last night that are making me feel sick.

"Thanks, Ree, for telling me. I appreciate it. I'm going to hang up now, because I'm pretty sure if I don't, I'm going to throw up on my bed. But thanks for letting me know. Love you." I wait for her to say goodbye, then hang up. I stare at the screen, shocked. My mom's dying. Shit! But then, I just don't care.

I fall back on the pillow and stare at the ceiling just as Gerard opens the door.

"Is everything all right?" he asks, and I suspect he's been listening on the other side of the door.

"My mom is dying of cancer," I say coldly, and when he takes a seat on the bed, I pull my legs up to get away from him.

"Well I guess that's no surprise really."

I let out a heavy sigh and flick back the blanket because I'm desperate now to use the toilet. "They say she's only got weeks or days."

"Do you plan on visiting her?"

"No."

I look for Gerard's reaction to that. He creases his brows at me before I turn and walk out of the room.

"I need to use the bathroom," I tell him over my shoulder because he leaps up and is hot on my heels.

"I won't let you blame me for last night, Paige. You can't think you can go around screwing people and it ends there."

"I don't," I say, rushing to our room.

He keeps coming.

"Good, because it seemed like you were enjoying it well enough, and I would never make you do anything you're not comfortable with," he lies, or says, trying to convince himself. "I can't believe how good that felt, feeling you climax while I was inside you."

He keeps talking to me through the door, even though I've slammed it in his face. "I can tell you. It's been a very long time since I've felt that." He sounds to be in awe.

I'm sitting on the toilet, peeing and shaking my head. I do not need to hear about his other women's orgasms when I've just found out my mother is dying. Men!

"Shut up, Gerard, it was fucking coercion, and you know it." I'm surprised there's no response from him.

I flush the toilet and wash my hands and see the mess that is me. My hair is mattered, and what's left of my makeup that didn't get washed away earlier, is smeared. I'm red from stubble rash, and the slight welts Gerard's fingers left behind. Even my eyes are bloodshot and I'm sure if I peeked at my pussy, that too would be red, because it hurt like a bitch when I peed. I feel dirty all over again.

Moving away from the vanity, I turn on the shower just as Gerard comes inside, looking menacing and ready with his rebuttal.

"You wouldn't have called it coercion if Alex was your ride."

I roll my eyes at the ceiling. "Leave me alone, and don't think for a second there will ever be another ménage, Gerard. Take some of that money you keep nicely stashed away and buy some gangbang movies and watch to your heart's content for all I care, because I am not spreading my legs for your pleasure ever again."

"What!" Gerard exclaims as I struggle with the zip on my dress. He doesn't offer to help, so I give him a dirty look until he does.

"Oh, so now you don't want any sex at all? You're going to deny me, is that it?" He rips the zip down forcefully.

"Yep. Until you go back to behaving like the man I married."

He's still shaking his head when I get under the water.

"You only want Alex? And I'm supposed to be all right with that arrangement, knowing you damn well think you're in love with him. Is that right?" he yells, coming closer to the shower screen and glaring at me. "You're fucking unbelievable. You must think I've got rocks in my head or something."

"No more three-ways, period! Gerard, not even with Alex. You let a stranger screw me, knowing I was hammered. What sort of husband are you? I was hoping to blackout so we couldn't do anything. I was vomiting. I was delirious. You two took advantage of me," I yell. Looking at him through the glass only inches from each other, yet totally separated in every sense of the word, then I hiss, "You're no better than those guys who put roofies in a girl's drink." Turning away, I put my hair under the shower head. "Don't you need to go to work or something?"

Gerard doesn't know what to say. He's never heard me this angry before. Suddenly, he grabs me from behind the screen, digging painfully into my arm. He takes hold of my other arm and faces me squarely, his face distorting, morphing into a man I've never seen.

"Haven't you heard of the fucking term, an eye for an eye, Paige?"

"What—what do you mean?"

He smiles and lets me go. "You're so smart, honey buns, try figuring it out." And then—he leaves. Slamming the door behind him.

Half an hour later, I'm walking up the road in a daze, still trying to understand what Gerard meant by an eye for an eye.

I thought going out for a jog would clear my head, but I'm doing everything but that. My brain is still shrinking within my skull, no matter how much water I drink. It's also pounding no matter how many painkillers I take. I'm beginning to wonder if Gerard, Oliver, or maybe someone else last night spiked my drink.

When I pass Delilah Newton's house, I see she is on her knees and weeding out her dying petunias. Because I normally run, I rarely stop to chat, but when she spots me, she gets to her feet as she sings out a greeting.

"You're out late today love, how are you?"

Resting my hand on her white picket fence, I glance about her small front yard. Most of the house plots in this neighborhood are large, Delilah's is split into four, and each small lot has an elderly resident. She is wearing pale blue slacks and a blouse. Her sun hat is a Mexican sombrero. I smile at her eclectic style.

"Morning, Delilah, your garden looks beautiful as always."

Coming closer, so we are only a few feet apart, she hangs onto her gardening fork in her gloved hands. Without a husband, I'm wondering whether she gets lonely at times but then conclude she's better off without one.

"Oh, not really. Fall's on its way, so most of them are fading away. A bit like me really. Now, before I forget, did a young gentleman call on you the other week?"

When I shake my head, she elaborates. "Several weeks back, I think it was Monday, no, maybe it was a Sunday. Anyway, he was driving a big flashy silver car. He was looking for your husband. He said Gerard gave him this address. He looked a little rough, and he was young. Young compared to me, not you of course, you're still sweet." I flinch because I'm hardly sweet anymore, but then, was I ever? I shudder when I think of last night again.

"Anyway, call me an old fool, but I don't just give out people's addresses to strangers, so I told him I didn't know anyone on this street. I figured if he had half a penny, he'd call your husband. Did he eventually find your house, dear, or did I do the right thing?"

I think of the silver car that was going up and down this road, the same one that overtook Alex and me. Could it have been the same car?

"Yes, you did the right thing, Delilah, and thank you. I'm sure if it was important, he would have gotten back in contact with Gerard."

"Oh good. Now, the other thing I want to ask. Would you

be interested in a kitten? Marianne in 2B has a beautiful ragdoll that's had kittens. They will be six weeks old in two weeks, there are still two darling little boys left. Do you have time to look? I said I'd ask everyone I know. She can't keep them because the landlord only allows us one pet each."

"I think I'd need to talk that over with Gerard first. Unlike me, I'm afraid he's not fond of pets." At least not the animal kind. "I need to keep going, I'm sorry." I'm suddenly feeling an overwhelming sadness. "But thanks for the chat, and I will come back if we're interested in owning a pet." Which I highly doubted.

"All right then, dear." She turns away, her mind already back on her flowers. "Have a nice run or walk, or whatever it is that you young people do these days." She waves me off with her gardening fork in the air.

I take off in a jog, but the thought of the silver car lurking concerns me. Surely if it was someone Gerard knew, he'd have given them the correct address. By the time I get to the end of our road, and I'm resting under the bamboo, I realize how stupid it is for me to be out running. Not only the threat of someone looking for Gerard for God knows what, but also because I'm still hungover and dehydrated.

I turn around and go back down the hill for home, looking at my phone, constantly hoping it will ring, that Alex wants to say something, anything about last night. Did he see me leave? Did I say goodbye? I just can't remember a thing.

When I get indoors, I head straight for the office to work. I need to catch up. I also need to see what I have in my private bank account. I'm feeling the dread that my marriage is breaking down. That Gerard will become nastier, forcing me to leave, and with a prenup in place, I've been extremely naïve about my position. Gerard has always controlled the finances, only allowing me free rein with a limited credit card that he clears every month. My wages from Bazaar have gone mostly on personal things like lunch dates and beautifying myself.

The longer I sit thinking about it, the more stupid I feel. I've been so blind to how subservient I've been, and when I login to my online banking, the truth hits me square in the face. If I wanted to leave Gerard and start fresh somewhere else, I'd be leaving with barely a penny to my name. I curse him and his bounced check then seriously think about forging his signature. Then I look at his fucking bachelor's degree, all framed up, looking like an FBI badge instead.

I'm on the verge of an anxiety attack. How could I have been so stupid? He controls everything. I open my inbox to see if I have any new assignments from Donnie. When there's only one, I know he is punishing me for my tardiness over the previous weeks, no doubt giving my work to someone who really appreciates it. I get on the phone straightaway.

"Donnie, it's Paige."

"How was the Gala, sweetness," he asks affectionately, which is reassuring.

"It was fab, I guess I should have taken photos, but I was having way too much fun," I lie.

He talks to someone in the background and ignores me for a couple of seconds.

"What can I help you with, Paige?"

"Work. As in, I need some, as much as you can throw my way. Now the Brave Hearts event is out the way, I have spare time," I lie again, rolling my eyes, shaking my head and hating myself more.

"Exciting news for us, but I'm afraid—not for you. We have three, yes, three new interns. So cheap labor for us, bad news for you. Sorry, sweetie." He calls out to someone in the background again. My pounding heart starts making my armpits prickle.

"Donnie is this because I messed up the other week? Look, I apologize, it won't happen again. I was just stressed with everything going on." I hope I sound troubled enough for him to care.

"Look, sweetie, in this industry, there's the quick and the dead. When I've got something for you, I promise I'll send it your way, but seriously these new interns are good—and fast," he adds digging the dagger in.

"Donnie?" I moan.

"Must go, love. I've got six sets of eyes on me, and it's not because I'm so handsome, ciao for now."

I stare at my phone. Shit this is bad, very bad. Before I even realize what I'm doing, I hit the call button below Alex's name.

It rings out. My stomach gets tangled in knots and I put my phone down quickly on the desk as though it's diseased. I get up and pace the office looking out at the yard. Leaves are everywhere and the place looks a mess. Why hasn't Alex been coming around to do the gardening? It's so frustrating not knowing what's going on and not having the confidence to make it my business.

I pick up my phone again. Hit call.

"Well, hello, Miss not-so-sweet pea."

I clamp my eyes and fight the rising bile. "What did I do?"

Annabel laughs. "Something I wish I had the talent to do. Does that song, 'Good for You' by Selena Gomez, ring any bells?"

It all comes back in a rush. A dance floor! The dirty dancing with Alex on the dance floor! Jenna crashing in on my dirty dancing on the dance floor with Alex and me getting catty with her. A stunned Gerard, looking on. An 'eye for an eye' spears straight through my brain. Then I remember sitting on Annabel's lap, talking to Ronald and Stuart. Flirting with them and being suggestive with Annabel who was playing along. I remember laughter. The flutes of champagne, being angry with Gerard. What did I tell him, what was it I said? And then I remember.

"What?" Annabel asks, responding to my gasp. She waits patiently, listening to my groans as I relive the night.

"Oh God, I remember now."

What I don't say is that I remember telling Gerard he was a pussy in bed, that he should learn how to fuck like a real man. How crushing, and what a bitch I am.

"I can't believe how badly I behaved. I—am—sooo sorry if I embarrassed you, Annabel."

"Oh, golly gosh no. You were a riot, sweetie. That is until Gerard dragged you away. Which was for the best, I suppose? I imagine you're nursing a wicked hangover."

"You have no idea."

"Oh, I think I might, I'm not feeling so great either. But all in all, it was a huge success. Do you remember the auction when you were bidding on your own work? You were pushing up the price against Ronald who was bidding against you? Everyone was laughing because you just wouldn't stop, but then neither would he," she reminds me, but I only have a vague memory of that happening. Perhaps because the auction was well after the dancing. "How is Gerard? He looked hurt last night, Paige. You had a bit of a yelling match on your way out."

I've put my phone on my desk on loudspeaker, so I can cradle my head in shame, confidently adding belligerent and narcissist to my list of shiny attributes.

"He doesn't like me much today," I tell her, filling with remorse. Spiraling because now I'm questioning my accusations toward him this morning. Were Gerard's words and actions understandable given what I said to him and how openly ardent I was toward Alex on the dance floor?

"Argh, I'm sorry, Paige, I need to go. I'm sloughing through those inquires. One hundred and twelve left to go."

When we disconnect, I try Alex's number again. It rings through to voicemail and I stare at the screen listening to his message. I end the call simply saying, "Sorry." He's screening me, I just know it. He hates me now. Gerard hates me, my mom is dying, and someone in a silver car is looking for Gerard. He's still talking with his ex I bet. And God, what if Alex is right? That Grace is Gerard's child. Fuck! I jump to my feet. When is this going to end?

I walk around and around the house in an anxious trance, letting the horror movie play itself out in my head. Me on all fours and Oliver pounding into me. I start to cry. Both men were inside me. I wail out and slap myself on the head, then crumble to the floor. Rocking, sobbing, moaning. Alex knows and is disgusted in me. He'll never want me now. I need to shut the thoughts out—I need to sleep. But I can't move. I'm just rocking, and then I see him again, Oliver standing in the bathroom staring in the mirror, only this time, he's shaving with an electric shaver and then he's looking at me and smiling. Then he's telling me he wants his face all smooth, so he doesn't *leave a rash on your soft sweet skin.*' I'm paralyzed in anxiousness. My hands feel tied. My legs feel heavy, like I've been running. I'm crying and rocking on the kitchen floor because my mother dying is bringing back memories I want to forget and I don't want to be like her. "Go away, go away." I fist my eye sockets, my elbows pressing into my bent knee as I rock against the island bench. "You should die, you're a disgusting mean bitch. I hate you, I hate you." I lash out. Then it's as though my mother is standing there with Oliver, but then it's Gerard. She's talking to Gerard, and he's handing her money, and she smiles, nodding in slow-motion at me, saying she's impressed. But she can't be there or here. It's not real. I wail and rock. Then

Gerard is walking toward me, rubbing his hand over his smooth face. *'Are you all right?'* he whispers so quietly I can barely hear him.

"What?" I say, turning my head slowly so I can see him. But all I can see is the kitchen floor and it's all fuzzy.

'Oh, precious,' he says, stroking my head and loving me.

'Do you really love me?' I ask, my eyes closing as his hand soothed my head and his fingertips dried my cheeks.

"Are you all right? Come on, get up."

"What?" I say, looking around and seeing shoes. My head pounds with the rushing of blood as I'm lifted to my feet.

"Come on, honey get up. Why are you asleep on the floor?" Gerard asks.

"What?"

My husband holds a wobbling me at arm's length. "Are you okay? Did you faint?"

I look around the kitchen bewildered. The French doors are wide open, and it's dark outside. Gerard follows my gaze and then heads over to close the doors. The sound reverberates around the room, bringing me further to my senses and I rub my face with both hands.

"You're home from work?" It comes out as a question.

"Yes."

Gerard approaches again, looking concerned. "What happened? You were just lying there on the floor. You scared me."

"I think—I fell asleep."

"On the floor? Maybe you're coming down with something?" he says, pressing the back of his fingers against my forehead. His gentle touch and genuine concern remind me how badly I spoke to him. Hanging my

head, I wrap my arms around his waist and press my face into his chest. He places a light hand between my shoulder blades.

"Gerard, I'm so sorry. After you left this morning, I remembered saying horrible, horrible things to you last night." His fingers travel up and down my spine, but he doesn't hug me in return.

"Never mind. I suppose you were very drunk. Let's forget it. Now are you sure you feel okay? Because I'd appreciate some dinner." He shifts away from me and heads toward the living room. I can't move. He's being dispassionate all of a sudden. I imagine he's also been thinking over the last twenty-four hours, maybe the entire month. Maybe our whole relationship!

When the television blares to life I realize he's not coming back. I look at the stove top and then the fridge, trying to get my brain to engage.

After getting a meal started, I go into the office to get my phone. Jolting back, I'm shocked to discover my computer is gone.

I look around the room as though it has possibly gotten up and moved itself. I even bend over like an idiot and look under the desk.

"Gerard," I call out. When he doesn't answer I go into the living room. "Gerard, did you move my computer?"

He looks briefly at me then back at the television. "No. Why would I move your computer?"

"I don't know but it's not there. It's missing."

His head jerks back and he frowns. Then together we go back into the office.

"We've been robbed. Is that why you were on the floor? Did someone hit you on the back of the head?" He reaches, like I do, for the back of my head as though I wouldn't know someone had hit me.

"No. No one hit me. But someone must have come in while I was asleep."

"Didn't you lock the doors?"

"No. I came back from a run and did some work." I don't need to be put on a lie detector. The heat that crawls up my neck in an instant when I remember I was checking my financial situation so I could get away from him, is a telltale sign I was not working at all. "That reminds me though. Delilah Newton, you know the lady up the road with the nice garden? She told me today someone was looking for you. She said he was driving a silver car, and I saw a silver car going up and down the road the other morning when I was out for a jog. Then when Alex picked me up, it overtook us and sped off along Carnies Road," I add hoping to get the heat off me.

He looks at me blankly for a moment, processing the information. He doesn't worry about the car or that someone was looking for him or that someone has stolen my computer. All he heard was the word Alex.

"What do you mean Alex picked you up?"

It's only then I realize my mistake.

"We should call the police." I reach for my phone that's still on my desk. "Maybe whoever was looking for you stole my computer. Who would be looking for you, Gerard?"

Gerard shakes his head, looking astounded. He snatches my cell out of my hand and starts thumbing through it. At first I think he's going to call the police but when his face creases in annoyance I know that's not what he's doing. He's looking for something. I'm not sure what he's looking for, because I can't think or speak because my heart is racing so fast the room is spinning. What's he looking for?

"Today at ten fifteen and then at twelve forty-three."

I feel myself pale. He's referring to the calls I made to Alex.

"Oh, and look he even texted you, "Please, Paige just leave

me out of it," he reads aloud then smirks. I'm stunned that Gerard is being so crass and immature.

Resisting the urge to snatch my phone back I reach out for the desk to steady myself when the room spins faster. I tell myself not to worry, that I have nothing to hide, but it doesn't help.

"Is this why you were so apologetic when I got home? Did you collapse on the floor from despair because you've finally realized Alex doesn't want you, and now you want me again? Ping pong, ping pong. It's like watching a game of tennis living with you." His tone is filled with such disdain, I burst into tears. "Or did you hit the bottle and pass out instead of being my wife and having my dinner ready?" he adds sarcastically, no longer concerned for me or the fact that we've been robbed, most likely because it seems only my computer is missing. He gives me a smug look. "Maybe you gave your computer to lover boy, and you forgot."

"Gerard, why are you being so ridiculous? We've been robbed, this is not the time to attack me over Alex."

"Well then, here." He hands me my phone. "Call the police."

After I take it from him, he leaves the room. I feel like my mind is turning to mush. I'm staring at my phone as though it's a foreign object, looking at the space my absent computer has left behind. Who would take it and nothing else? When did they come in? Why doesn't Gerard care?

After calling the local police department, I reread the text from Alex, scan over it multiple times. Hoping somehow it will read differently, not words that slice my heart into smaller pieces every time I reread it. Finally, I cork my tears and let the anger claim me. I text Alex, asking if he'd please not hate me, that I'm sorry if I've hurt him, just please don't shut me out. Then, I put a password on my phone and lock it.

I tend to dinner and serve Gerard's meal up like a zombie.

I don't eat, but he makes me sit at the table with him regardless. I address the police in a half daze when they arrive two hours later. They ask me to check the house over while they follow me around making notes. That's when I notice the large glass egg is also missing. The police assess whether there was forced entry, which there hasn't been. When they ask where I was at the time, I tell them I was out. And yes, I must have left a door unlocked. The whole time I'm occupied with the cops, Gerard remains on the couch watching his news and drinking his goddamn Glengoyne on ice. That is, until they finally fire several questions at him. Then, it's only as I'm seeing them to the door, that the devil himself decides to incarnate through my husband and scare the living shit out of me.

"Officers, there's one other thing I just thought of," Gerard calls out, rising from the couch and coming toward the front door. The two male officers, now on the front porch, turn back around. The one holding the booklet taking notes, flips the cover back over and gets his pen ready. Gerard saunters toward us and smiles. But there's the tiniest of smirks pulling at the corners of his mouth that only someone close would notice.

My stomach tightens

"We had had a gardener working here not so long ago. Paige, what was his name again?" Gerard pulls a faux serious expression looking baffled. "Was it, Tony or Anthony or something like that?"

I've never had a near-death experience, but I imagine it would start with a sensation in your toes. Like I'm experiencing. A tingle that turns into pain, as pins and needles spread across the soles of the feet. Followed by the sensation of icicles shooting up the calves. Then, an overall freezing takes over from the knees up, until the lungs stop working. Suddenly, you'd find yourself, like me, floating above everyone and looking down at yourself. At my expressionless face, dilated eyes, and waxy complexion. Looking as though you've been plonked there straight out of Madame Tussuad's museum, and time seems to have paused because nobody is moving or speaking or even breathing.

I float for what seems like minutes, an increasing heaviness filling my chest so profound, it makes me dizzy. Then I begin sinking, like a deflating balloon.

"Or was it—Alex someone or another?" Gerard looks directly at the wax figure of me.

I gasp, and instantly I'm sucked back into my trembling body and my eyes go wide.

"No," he says, screwing his face up. "That wasn't it either. Never mind, we'll let you know when we remember, won't we, Paige?"

13

YOU BROKE ME FIRST

It's been said the silent treatment is a form of emotional abuse. That being ostracized goes against the very nature of our social existence and has been known to drive people insane. For me, it's a no-win situation because I'm not meaning to shun Gerard, I just don't know what I need to say. Or maybe I don't trust what I want to say.

Unfortunately, my inability to formulate a rational thought, let alone hold a conversation, causes Gerard to become a tyrant, which only seems to exacerbate the problem. I've been afraid to speak in case I cause irreparable damage to Alex. That is, if I haven't already.

For days after the burglary, whenever Gerard spoke, all I could do was shake my head or nod in agreement then do as he asked. But after a week of his snappiness and derogatory comments, I can't even get out of bed.

When Gerard comes home to a dark, quiet house, even from our bedroom I can hear the panic in his voice. He repeats my name, calling out and illuminating the house as he switches on lights. I pull the blankets over my head and curl up into a ball when the stairwell light turns on. Moments later, his feet thud up the carpeted staircase.

"Honey." He settles down next to me and pulls back the blanket. Keeping my eyes clamped shut, I bury my face deeper into the sodden pillow. "You know you're doing this to yourself, don't you?" His hand runs gently over my head several times before he cups my chin and forces me look at him. "You'll make yourself sick, and if you won't talk to me, how can we fix it?" Searching my puffy, swollen face, he shakes his head and adds a sigh. "Do you need me to say sorry, is that what this is?" There's no mistaking his patronizing tone.

"I don't care. Not about anything anymore." I twist from his grip and mumble into the pillow where I bury my face again. I just want him to go away and leave me to die.

"Because I am sorry. I shouldn't have threatened Alex like that, because it's not his fault you like playing games, is it?"

The mattress rises as Gerard gets to his feet, compelling me to peek. He's working on his tie and kicking off his shoes.

"I'd like to understand what you are trying to achieve though. I mean, the door is right there." He gestures with his hand. "If you're so in love with Alex, leave. Just go! I don't see any bars. Do you?"

Yes. I want to scream at him. Yes, there are bars and walls and a persecutor with the key. But they're invisible, so I can't prove they're there. But I try anyway, just to see if I'm right.

"Maybe it would be better for both of us. I've hurt you and I can't undo that."

He regards me for a moment then agrees with a nod. "No. No you can't undo the damage you've done, but I highly doubt you'd manage out there on your own." Now he's shaking his head, the invisible warden that he is. "No. I think you have become a little too accustomed to the sweet life, and I can't for one second imagine you sleeping in say, a cardboard box." His face loses all expression, his tone deepening. "I bet you regret signing that two year prenup clause right about now." Then he laughs.

"I'll survive. I've got arms and legs. I'm employable."

"Oh, I see. Riiight. You mean as a dish pig?" His eyes go wide and mocking me.

"Whatever it takes."

"Okay but listen—before you go, I'd like you to explain why you're so upset with me when it was Alex who rejected you? Again!" He rolls his eyes then looks amused. "Can you believe he said no twice? Then told you to leave him alone? Ouch, that must have hurt. No wonder you said such horrible things to me. Uh. No, hold that thought." He motions with a finger, then presses it against his smirks. "That's not right. Why would you get angry at me for that? Because you didn't. You got angry because I didn't go along with your plan to ensure you got another session with Alex because I didn't offer to pay him. That's why you're so angry. So how was it meant to work? Alex says no then I say, 'Please, Alex. Here I'll give you money so my wife can be with the man she loves but still live the life of luxury with this sucker.'" He punches his chest.

I've pulled myself up in bed, watching as he undoes the buttons of his shirt one at a time. His eyes dart around the room like he's plucking ideas or thoughts out of the air.

"But you being—just a woman, a young one at that. I honestly don't think you're seeing things for how they really are. Are you? I mean, women tend to get loopy at times, and you must think I'm a total idiot." He pulls a mock grimace.

Beneath the blanket, I draw my legs up and wrap my arms tightly around them, pulling my knees into my chest.

"But I think, if I paint a nice clear picture for you, you will understand how it really is, that it should be me who's angry, not the other way around. Pay Alex, Ha! What the fuck for when I know you're in love with him?" He pushes back his hair and rubs his stubble before he starts pacing, making me wonder again if that's a habit of his before he questions someone on the stand. "Now, feel free to interject at any time if you think I've got this wrong. Offer an explanation or defend yourself and it will be duly noted and taken into consideration. Do you think that's fair?"

I give him a small shrug, my eyes following him until he leans against the windowsill. With his shirt wide open, he crosses his arms over his hairy chest, and I curse my heart when it squeezes because of how handsome he is. I want my old husband back, and for a microsecond, when our eyes lock, I see him. Then I'm looking away because I realize it's not love I feel for him, but a longing to feel special. To belong and be worthy of someone like him.

"No, I want you looking at me as I explain this," Gerard says calmly, trying to pull me out of my reverie.

But his words have resonated so freakishly close to something I am beginning to understand. He's right, I'm not seeing things for how they truly are. I've been in love with the idea of Gerard. That's not the same as loving someone for who they are. My heart slowly slips into the pit of my stomach with the dawning. I love Alex because it's unconditional. He doesn't want to own or possess me. In fact, he wanted me to be free and enjoying things I love, not because it makes him look good but because it makes me feel good. It's why I'm hopelessly attracted to him, whatever the cost.

Drawing in a deep breath, I let go of my knees and cross them. My heart is pounding so hard it's constricting my throat because right now, Gerard holds all the cards, and he's about to annihilate me. He's going to humiliate me some more, then crush me so he can control me. I go to slide back down into the bed, my eyelids heavy and my head hurting.

Do I have sleeping pills somewhere? I should drink his scotch and the vodka and the…

"Don't you dare cower away. Have the decency to sit up and hear what I have to say." The fury in his voice sends me into tears and my head pounds harder. "We were a happily married couple until Alex came along. Agreed?"

Instead of answering him, I draw my legs back up and rest my elbow to massage my scalp.

"Do we fucking agree?" he shouts.

"Yes."

"You." He jabs a finger in my direction. "You were the unfaithful one." He cocks his head looking for another response.

I nod.

"I've never been unfaithful, honest to God, and it took all my strength to become the bigger person and forgive you. I bought a fucking house. A whole, big, enormous house so you could have a gallery by the beach because I thought maybe you were just bored."

"It was a bribe."

"A bribe?" he scoffs.

"Yes, because you also kept waving Alex in my face. You wanted me to cave in so you could get your own way."

"All right, I'll admit, as I did I recall, that the thought of seeing Alex take you was very arousing. I didn't expect that. And I suppose in the beginning, I did think you owed me something. You know, even the score or as they say, 'an eye for an eye.'"

"See, so it wasn't about me."

"Oh, no there's that too. I thought maybe you needed some more experience so you're not such a boring lover," he leers at me. "Get to know your body and needs better. Because, well, you know, your inability to climax sort of shows your immaturity, doesn't it?"

Gerard pushes himself off the windowsill and paces at the foot of the bed. "Yes, I wanted more adventure in our relationship after our night with Alex, and I told you how I felt. To your face. I was being honest. But that's when you," Gerard jabs a finger in the air at me again, "stopped being honest with me. You said you didn't want more, but you were lying. You just didn't want me around. Am I right, or am I right?" He slumps his shoulders and looks deadpan before adding, "Be honest now, because you made me believe that you wanted to explore *our* relationship and *our* sexual tastes. It's hardly my fault your little plan blew up in your face, is it?" His voice rises and he shakes his head before turning away from me.

"I was furious at first," he goes on. "You understand the nature of men, don't you, Paige? That once they claim a woman, they become territorial. We're very primal when it comes to mating, but it seems we can also develop a paradoxical competitive kinship with other men. I suppose that could be why—gangbanging occurs." He raises his eyebrows and pulls a wayward smile. "Now there's an erotic thought."

I think I'm going to throw up.

"When you agreed to a second time, it wasn't about strengthening our relationship, was it?" he asks.

I want to crawl back under the blanket and block everything out but he holds my gaze. Slipping off his pants, he starts pacing in his boxer shorts and socks, flicking his eyes at me every so often, waiting for me to say something. But I know he'll just use it against me.

"I knew you had an ulterior motive," he says.

"Well if you knew, then it's you who is being sneaky and manipulative." As soon as the words are out, I cover my mouth.

Gerard chuckles, sending shivers up my arms. "Now

you're catching on." He taps the side of his nose. "I agreed because you're a transparent pathetic little thing who needed to be taught a lesson. I made you who you are, Paige. I've given you everything and I'll continue to because I love you. But if I don't have your respect and loyalty, what are you even doing here? It's simple really. If you continue to use me, I will continue to use you."

The heat from my churning stomach rises to my chest and threatens to claim my neck.

"I want to remind you that my forgiveness requires you be fucking grateful and treat me with goddamn respect. Is that too much to ask?"

I burst into tears. It's strange when those who say they love you become condescending and intimidating. Strangely, everything they say becomes truth—you look for why they're right. You search your soul and start picking at scabs. Old wounds formed by shame and self-loathing that you ignore daily in the hope they finally fade away. But then you're reminded, like I was. I need him to be right because his low opinion, his accusations, they match what I feel on the inside. There's no fight left in me, just a surrendering, a state of acceptance that doesn't ask me to think or face the demons of my past.

"I wanted to make you happy," I say through sobs. "But I also wanted to help Jolene."

It's not the answer he expects because he stops short then slowly makes his way to the armchair and massages his temples.

"You wanted to help Jolene. How would sleeping with Alex help Jolene? No, the better question would be, what makes you think Jolene needs help?"

"I feel guilty that I came along."

"What?"

"If we hadn't gotten together, you might have changed

your mind about Jolene and Grace and become a family. I thought, well… you wanted to do your thing and watch and yes, I feel comfortable with Alex and Alex said Jolene needed money for Grace's medical bills. He said that's why he took money in the first place, so he could give it to her. You were supposed to offer him money again and… and…"

"And what?"

"And everyone gets what they want."

Gerard stands and starts laughing. He laughs so hard tears come, and every time he looks at me, he laughs harder and does a circuit of the room.

"What, what's so funny about that?" I sit up straighter in the bed and pull the covers tighter.

"That I didn't offer Alex money. Well, that must have ruined your big plans. It seems your shit came full circle to bite you on that tight little ass, didn't it? No wonder you're wallowing away in bed feeling ashamed and humiliated. Jolene doesn't need money for Grace or anything else. And like I told you, the child isn't mine. I already told you that, so why didn't you believe me?" Gerard doesn't even pause to let me answer. "Argh, I know why." he looks to the ceiling then back at me. "Because you'd prefer to believe Alex and martyr yourself. Give yourself an excuse to get together and get money out of me at the same time. How considerate of you."

"No." I snap. "I believed him because he said Jolene never cheated on you. That maybe you swapped the test or something. And at the expense of copping another slap to the face, that sounds more like you. Because children are a nuisance, aren't they? But I know what it's like to be poor and not have a father. I feel sorry for them because—because, I've already ruined Sheree's relationship with a father." I end my rant in a whisper.

"Well, Paige, Grace can't miss what she's never known, can she? And I'm tired of trying to live up to everyone's expectations." He lifts his legs in turn and rips off his socks. "And stop worrying about Sheree. She's a grown woman. She doesn't need her father."

Even though I'm hot as hell, I pull the blankets higher. I've got nothing left to say. I hang my head defeated.

"But hey, what do I know, Meddling Mary? Now if you don't mind, I'm having a shower. Do you think you can at least manage to drag yourself out of bed and order some takeout? Or are you planning on packing your bags and leaving?"

I shake my head.

"Good, because on the weekend, I suppose I must man up, yet again, to prove what a liar your boyfriend is. Maybe then you'll get some sense back in your head and place your loyalty back where it belongs."

It's her smile that shatters me. Not the fact she arrives punctually in a near new blue Alfa Romeo, or the envy I feel that there is an adorable little girl bouncing around in the back seat the moment the car pulls up on our gravel drive. Arriving at exactly ten o'clock, like invited. It's just her smile. It's sweet, sexy, and unpretentious. Then time seems to slow down, and I become mesmerized by her every gesture. The way she peels off her sunglasses and sets them neatly on her head, bats her lashes against her high rounded cheek bones. Lashes so black and thick they put even café Brontë's to shame. How she licks at her glossed lips that look naturally full and a perfect shade of rose. Even through the windshield, she appears radiant with her olive skin and elegant hands, one clasping the wheel when she turns her attention to the back seat of the car.

"See, what did I tell you? Now, does that look like a

destitute mother and sick child to you?" Gerard asks. But I'm lost for words. I've become trapped in a vortex where time is irrelevant. Even when Gerard squeezes my hand, I'm not sure whether I glance down slowly, acknowledging his smug assurance, or it just feels like I do. I look back up as her long, silver-blonde hair is fanning out around the interior of the car when she turns back to face the windshield and smile at us.

When she puts a heeled boot out of the car door and peels herself out, she even appears to be moving in slow-motion, and I can't help it, I'm still transfixed, studying every inch of her while my facial muscles fail in gobsmacked awe. In an instant, I'm catapulted back in my mind. Back to a brick, two-bedroom shack with flea-infested rodents and parasites nipping at my heels. It takes every ounce of strength within me not to turn away and go back inside the house. I feel weak, plain, and insignificant in her presence because she is tall, graceful, and stunningly beautiful. She is —Jolene.

Her black and white Pandora purse slaps against her ultra slim thighs, clad in black leather, skin-tight pants. Then when she turns and bends to help Grace out of the car, the wind picks up her olive-green silk shirt to expose her flawless, not an ounce of fat, waistline, and every bit of confidence I ever had crumbles away.

Still in slow-motion, I glance up at Gerard. My eyes are like saucers I'm sure, because he frowns. And then I can't help it, the words just fall out like verbal diarrhea.

"Are you insane?" I gasp, shocked to my core.

"Excuse me?" Gerard growls. "I thought you said you were okay with meeting them?"

I'm too busy shaking my head to notice they've drawn closer, and before I can moderate my response, that too comes tumbling out.

"But why would you ever let her go?" I breathe. "She's ab…"

"Paige," Gerard says, jerking on my hand then nods toward our guests.

"Hello, Gerard," Jolene says, with that killer smile again, stepping forward to press her cheek against Gerard's, her lips puckering to air kiss, but quickly twisting, making sure she doesn't miss leaving an imprint.

"Jolene," he greets, stepping back. "And hello, young lady." Gerard offers his hand, which engulfs the little girl's when she cordially takes it and shakes it.

"I'd like to introduce my wife, Paige," Gerard says, putting an arm around my waist and presenting me.

"Hi." I offer my hand to Jolene. Devoid of any rings, Jolene clasps with her fingers showing off her perfectly manicured nails whose tips are encrusted with crystals here and there. At least I think they're crystals. From the elegance and perfection of her, they could very well be diamantes, or even real diamonds. "I've been looking forward to meeting you both," I say, my face heating because I feel like I'm welcoming royalty. It's not from the vibe I get from Jolene or Gerard, but I'm almost compelled to curtsy.

Jolene's eyes hold her smile, making me notice feathered straight eyebrows and a high forehead. Jolene is the perfect example of sophistication and beauty, worthy of gracing any magazine. And yes, she simply oozes wealth, making it blatantly obvious Alex has lied.

Grace has inherited almost every feature from her mother. Her slender, hipless physique, the angular face and her large green eyes. The only thing that sets them apart is her strawberry blonde hair. She looks from me to Gerard, looking bored and nothing at all like Gerard. "Do you have any dogs?" she asks.

"Hey!" Jolene says, tugging gently on Grace's hand.

"Where are your manners? Say hello before you go asking personal questions?" Jolene looks back up. "I'm sorry, Gerard." She smiles, but I catch a flicker of, I don't know, something. Was it embarrassment, or fear?

"Hello," Grace mumbles looking at the ground.

"No, we don't own any pets, but we have morning tea." Gerard gestures toward the gazebo where I have food and refreshments ready.

"Lovely," Jolene says, leading Grace along by the hand and scanning over our yard, making comments about the gardens and large jacaranda trees, noting they have plenty of age on them.

She walks straight and tall and doesn't ever struggle when her heels hit the lawn—she just glides along as if floating on air.

With Grace sitting quietly beside Jolene coloring in a book, I learn they live in Long Beach. That after a career in modeling, Jolene now works as an editor for Miss Teen magazine. Of course, she's successful. She and Grace have two dogs, both female Shih Tzus. Grace is an excellent student who is learning piano and is a strong swimmer. It all mounts to disbelief that Gerard could send them packing and settle for someone like me. A common girl from Ponderosa Park with a diploma in pressing a button.

Jolene doesn't embarrass either Gerard or myself by asking how we met, but I shift uncomfortably when she inquires how I spend my days.

"Oh, I just putter around here really. Have a hot meal ready for Gerard, that type of thing." I reply, feeling completely inadequate.

"You're a photographer though, aren't you?" Jolene picks up a scone to nibble on.

I nod and fill her in on my work. Adding our plans about

the gallery, and I'm sure she picks up on my lack of enthusiasm.

"That's not all you do, Paige," Gerard offers, placing a hand on my thigh, which I glance at, surprised. When I look up, he is eyeing me warmly. "Paige and her friend Annabel are also keen fundraisers. They were responsible for the Brave Hearts fundraiser in LA last month," he gushes proudly. I can't help the small smile but surprised look I give him. He squeezes my leg and nods toward Jolene.

"Oh really? I didn't know." She shoots Gerard a quick frown, like she'd expected him to divulge that information prior to her visit. "I wish I could have attended, but I was away in Milan at the time." She looks from Gerard to me. "But I heard it was a success. I think our magazine might have done a small editorial on it." She looks to Gerard again and smiles. Then he's smiling back, making my stomach twist and for a moment, it seems I'm forgotten while Jolene fills him in on her trip.

"Well, I can't take the credit. It was all Annabel really," I say flatly, finally catching on to what's going on. I look over at Grace, who has her head down, still coloring and paying no attention whatsoever. I feel sorry for her. If I hadn't come along, I'm sure Gerard and Jolene would be together. I can sense their bond. The way their eyes connect and how impressed he is. Even when Jolene tells us she is moving away soon, he's encouraging. But the slight tightening of his hand on my thigh under the table, tells me otherwise.

Rising, I announce that I'm going to reheat the coffee, "Would anyone like more?" I don't even wait for an answer before I walk away. The rest of the morning passes in a blur and I'm more confused than ever.

14

WRONG

I become obsessed with getting in contact with Alex. I text him repeatedly, begging him to answer my calls. I need to talk to him about Jolene. I don't believe for one second that Alex lied, I think Jolene is lying to him. Why? I don't know, but he needs to know the truth.

I take daily drives past the beach house, and though I see improvements taking place, I never see Alex's pickup truck out front, so I conclude he's not home. Adding to my frustration, Sheree keeps calling to inform me of my mom's deteriorating condition and trying to coax me to see her before she dies. I won't, I can't.

I spend a day with Annabel when she becomes upset over the partnership with Ronald Klaneski falling through, which leaves her and Stuart thousands of dollars out of pocket from solicitor fees, putting further stress on their already strained marriage. I wish again I could be more supportive, but I'm so overwhelmed with my own affairs, I have nothing left to give. I'm walking on eggshells around Gerard, hoping to stay on his good side just so he'll be civil to me.

After two weeks, I reach a breaking point and the second Gerard leaves for work I'm on my cell phone to Sheree.

"I need to ask you a favor, Ree."

"Aren't you going to ask how your mom is?"

"No."

"Paige."

"Sheree, there's nothing I can do, and she's a horrible person. She doesn't deserve my consideration or commiseration."

"God, pea." There's a long pause, then she sighs. "All right, so what do you want then?"

"I need you to call a number and book a massage under the name of... Tammy Anderson. Just tell the guy, or his voice mail, that name and get an appointment for today at ten if you can. Please don't ask me why. I just really need you to do this for me."

"Really, at a time like this?"

"Sheree, my mom is in your face, not mine. She hasn't been for years. Why should I start caring now? Please, I need your help. I wouldn't ask if it wasn't really important, okay?"

"All right, it's fine, just settle down," she relents, asking for his number. "I'll call back once I've booked it."

"Do you mind texting? I'm just about to go for a run?" I say, fobbing her off. The truth is, I don't want her talking sense into me before I've had a chance to see Alex.

"Fine. But promise you'll call me later."

"I will. Thanks, Ree. I love you—you know that, don't you?"

"I know, and I'm sorry about being pushy about your mom. I just feel bad for her now. She's dying alone."

"I'll think about seeing her."

"Well, try not to think too long. My mom says she not looking very good."

"Did she ever?" I say, before hanging up.

I'm sure Sheree deliberately torments me by not texting back for over half an hour when I'm halfway through my run. Then, finally, she sends confirmation. Panting, I stretch out my quads and calves and read.

'I spoke with ALEX.' Followed by an angry emoji. 'Why didn't u just tell me it was him? U know u can tell me anything.' Then there's a sad emoji. 'I'm hurt u feel u can't talk to me about whatever it is that's going on, but whatever!'

I text back multiple hearts then finish my run in record time, all the while I'm fighting the voice of reason telling me it's ridiculous to believe visiting Alex would somehow absolve me. But I need him to understand how sorry I am. That whatever he is angry about, I can explain. And he needs to know about Jolene.

When I pull up outside the beach house a little before ten, my exhilaration crashes into disappointment. He's not home. At least his truck isn't. Switching off the engine, I realize how stupid it was of me not to clarify where he does his massages. He most likely sets up in the back of someone's shop or has his own consult room. I get out the car to stretch my legs and think.

By the looks of it, Alex has finished painting the exterior. There is still some scaffolding ruining the overall effect, but it looks good, and then I notice it, right there by the parking area. Alex has swapped his rough hand-painted sign with a professional one announcing, 'Future Holds Gallery' in bold cursive lettering with my name below. I don't know how to feel. It both excites and saddens me at once. I draw in a deep breath to collect myself then make my way toward the lower apartment, envisioning an entrance fit for the public, convincing myself that I am the owner and I have a right to drop by anytime.

Afterall, aren't I meant to be setting up the gallery? Though given Gerard's angst toward me lately, I wouldn't be surprised if he punishes me and puts the beach house up for sale.

Lost in thought, I'm looking intently through the bottom level window one moment and in the next I'm almost leaping out my skin.

"Paige, what are you doing here?"

"Holy crap," I yelp, spinning around, locking eyes on Alex as my heart tries to right itself. But with butterflies leaping to life, and a tingling all over when his eyes search mine the way he does, my heart can't decide what to do. God, I've missed him. If it weren't for his stand-offish vibe and his arms folded tightly over his chest, I'd be hugging him in an instant.

"Alex, you're here. I didn't think you were home." I take a step closer to him. "Where's your truck?" I look around expecting him to point it out amongst camouflage, though there's absolutely nowhere for it to hide.

He's wearing commando cargo pants and a pale gray tee that hugs his body, making the outline of his pecks visible. His face is covered in stubble, and if I'm not mistaken, he looks to have lost weight.

"I had to sell it. It was costing too much."

I frown at the believability of that, given its banged up condition.

"Look, it's nice seeing you and all, but you need to leave. I have a client coming. Besides that, you've got a husband. One who gets *irate* because of me."

"I'm your client. Hi, I'm Tammy." I quickly dig out my credit card. "Do—you—have PayWave?" I squint.

"Are you serious?" Alex walks away shaking his head. "Shit," he cusses, heading for the stairs to the upper level with me in hot pursuit. "I was actually counting on that booking, Paige," he says over his shoulder.

"Well, take my card then, because I'm seriously here for a massage." I trot after him as he marches up the stairs taking two at a time.

"I'm not taking your money, Paige. Go home."

When we reach the top landing, we have a standoff. I reach out to touch his chest, but he flinches away.

"What did I do, Alex? Please tell me what I did wrong. I've been calling and texting, why didn't you answer?" My eyes sting, and in seconds, tears need wiping away.

"Why, we're not anything, are we?" His jaw is set in such a hard line that when he adds a shrug and shake of his head, he breaks my heart.

"You hate me, don't you?"

Alex huffs and rolls his eyes. "I don't hate you. I fuckin' hate what you're about."

I can't tear my eyes off him, even though his glare is splitting me apart. His unyielding face, his stiff stance.

I nod. "I get it, and I'm sorry."

"Are you though? Do you know how hard that was for me the other night? Seeing you sitting with Gerard looking like a shackled—I don't know what. A spider monkey or something. Drinking wine but wishing it was arsenic, but it wasn't doing its job. Christ, I've never seen anyone more miserable in their life."

Every tense muscle in me lets go and I physically slump. I'm like a pane of glass to him.

"The only time you came to life was to make a scene on the dance floor. Do you even remember that?"

I shake my miserable head.

Alex goes inside then hangs onto the door, weighing me up as though he can't decide what to do with me. Like I'm a stray cat and he's not sure if he wants the responsibility.

"Please, Alex, treat me as a client, a paying client, that's fair isn't it?" I hold my card out to him again. I need a chance to be with him when he's calmed down.

"All right, I will then, seeing as I had to turn down a legitimate client." He snatches the card out of my fingers. "I'm using the downstairs for massaging." He points to the floor. "Back door is open. Go down, strip to your underwear. There's a towel. Lie face down," he says, then goes off to find his phone or maybe he has a machine. I don't stay long enough to find out, because in a dejected daze, I do as he says and go downstairs.

Alex is using what is to become my office, which is dim because the blinds are drawn. There is a professional massage table in the center. I plonk my handbag on a chair in the corner next to a long bench with oils, towels, and what smells like scented candles flickering. The fragrance is sweet like frangipani, coconut, and fruit. The soft sounds of flutes and trickling water play through a small speaker, and on a stainless-steel trolley, there is what looks to be a Crock-Pot. I walk over and peer inside and see a pile of smooth black stones covered in what I think is water.

My heart races, wondering what it would be like to have his hands all over me. But it's not the reason I'm here. I just want to talk. Alex knocks, I suspect out of habit before entering. When he sees I'm still dressed, he shakes his head.

"You understand you only have an hour, don't you?"

"I just want to talk, that's all."

"I don't want to talk because you frustrate the shit out of me. Either you want a massage, or you go."

I only pause for a split second before I'm undressing, kicking off my shoes and tying back my hair as fast as I can. Anything to stay in his presence. I'm hoping he'll calm down enough so we can talk. Alex moves around the room getting ready, then it seems he can't help himself.

"Do you know I have to leave once I've finished the renovations upstairs?"

"Says who?"

"Says your husband. Just letting you know the repercussions of your actions. Now hurry up." Alex waits with his hands on his hips.

I peel off my shirt and slip out of my shorts, then face him in my white lace underwear. Alex looks me up and down, then shakes his head. He doesn't smile or look even remotely happy, but I notice his loose cargo pants shift around his crotch area.

"You could have at least spared a man and worn granny fucking panties instead of that getup. Fuck me!" He points to the table, indicating I get on.

"Sorry," I mumble climbing onto the massage table then lie face down to stare at the floor. Alex takes a towel and tucks it into my lace underwear, then unclasps my bra.

"You may as well take this off," he says, tugging on my bra. Lifting, I allow Alex to remove the garment that he adds to my pile of clothes on the chair. My nether regions tingle, anticipating his demand that I take off my underwear as well. But when he comes back, he doesn't speak, just places both palms between my shoulder blades.

"Alex, I came because I thought I…"

"Shh. No talking." He takes in three deep breaths.

I try to relax beneath him, to still my mind, but I have so many questions. The next second, warm oil is being drizzled along the length of my back. Alex catches what trickles over my waist and down the sides of my breasts, then distributes the excess over my shoulders toward my neck.

"You've lost weight," he comments, working the oil with both hands over my back, shoulders, and waist.

"So, have you," I reply, unable to relax fully because his

touch feels clinical and impersonal, nothing like the Alex I know.

He works my shoulders and neck, his fingers finding and working out painful knots.

He stops for a moment and places his palms in the middle of my back. "Take some slow deep breaths," he instructs.

I take a breath and exhale in a rush.

"That's not slow." Alex pinches at my waistline, making me yelp.

I try again, blowing slowly through pursed lips, then a third time, with an "Ahh" trailing behind when he takes to my neck again.

For minutes, Alex works on my neck, shoulders and upper back, shifting himself until he is at my head. Warmth radiates off his stomach and into my crown while his balled-up fists knead into the sides of my neck. Rolling and twirling knuckled hands, pushing and digging out years of stuck energy and tension. Alex finishes with my neck by running hands down both of my arms at the same time. Then in a heartbeat, he is everywhere at once, moving around the table, caressing deeply, then fingertipping lightly all over my landscape.

It feels as though he's searching and exploring each muscle, each tendon, each fossilized ball of what could be pain, shame, and fear that's trapped inside my body. At my head again, he lunges forward, scooping down my back, stretching as far as he can reach and exhaling then drawing upward along my sides, careful to not touch my breasts. I register the change in him instantly, making my eyes sting. His hands have become beautiful, caring, nurturing, and loving, reaching a place inside me where the deepest sense of sadness has been residing. It comes from somewhere so deep, I get lost in Alex's expert maneuvers, sliding his hands in long firm strokes up and down my back, catching and removing contorted muscle and sinew from between my shoulder blades and within my collarbones.

Moments later I'm sniffling. In a microsecond, Alex is placing a Kleenex in my hand.

"Happens a lot," he says, resting a hand on my back.

Rising, I dry my eyes and blow my nose. "I don't know what's wrong with me," I say through a congested nose. "I don't even know why I'm crying. I think it's because it just feels so beautiful, like your caressing my soul or something."

"That's the idea." He twitches his head and taps the table for me to lay back down.

I lie back down but keep my head turned so I can see him. "I miss you, Alex."

He avoids my eyes but glides his hands in large circles over my skin, feeling with light fingertips for anything left behind.

"I know," he finally says, tweaking here and there before moving away. I flip my head to follow his movements as he removes a ladle full of stones from the pot and places them on a towel.

"Why aren't you coming to garden anymore?" I ask, lifting myself onto my elbows but fold my arms to hide my breasts.

"That's a stupid question, you know why. Now lie back down, face back in there." He points to the hole in the table, approaching with a handful of stones in a small towel.

I remain quiet, let him concentrate as he places stones strategically down either side of my spine. Using the towel that's hiding my lower section, he covers my back and shoulders then goes to work on the back of my legs with a stone. I toy with how to bring up Jolene's visit. But while I'm thinking, I must doze for a few minutes because the next thing I know, Alex is standing at my head again asking me to roll onto my back. Eyes opening, I'm delighted to take in his sexy face until his serious expression saddens me too much that I shut my eyes again.

Surprisingly, he's delicate with his thick fingers. Circling my eye sockets, then stroking the bridge and sides of my nose. He rubs my upper lip with thumbs, massages my cheeks and works my jaw until my mouth gapes open, slack. I clamp it shut and my eyes fly open to find him smiling at me.

"You're good, Alex. I really don't know what to make of you anymore."

He smiles and shushes me, his hands grabbing both the back of my neck and throat, dragging them down across the top of my shoulder. Fluid, relieving, and every bit nurturing. Then tears sting my eyes again. He touches my lids to make me close them, and my heart is pounding in my ears. Who is this man, and why didn't he walk into the café instead of Gerard all those years ago? My chest feels compressed. I'm so in love with him, it's crushing. Because I've made so many stupid mistakes trying to please both him and Gerard, that I don't deserve him.

"Stop it."

My eyes snap open. "What?"

"You're thinking, just listen to the music and concentrate on your breathing," he says firmly, his hands moving on and over my neck, across my upper chest, before working one hand between my breasts. He presses a finger into my belly button to make me smile. Then his other hand takes its turn down the valley between my breasts. Using both hands, he glides along my hips and sides, going up under my armpits and pulling my arms out to the sides like I'm flying. I feel my nipples pucker, making me self-conscious. Suddenly, he's closer, murmuring against my forehead.

"You know what, Princess?"

I shake my head inhaling the clean scent of his hair,

urging me to run my hand through it, to catch his head and drag him forward so I can kiss his edible lips. But I don't because I need to know what he has to say.

"In another time and place, you would have been mine, and there's no way I'd share you with another man. I'd rather let you go."

"I would never need another man, Alex," I whisper back, spurring on tears that slide down my temples and into my ears. Moving away, and with his back to me, Alex massages my fingers and hand, pressing his thumbs into my palms, smoothing and stretching the backs of my hands with his fingers. My other hand swipes at my leaking face. When he's done, he ends his work by pressing his palm firmly against my own. Palm to palm, he transfers more than just heat, and I can't take it anymore—the need for his love is gut-wrenching. There's a hollowness inside that becomes so painful, I become desperate.

Bolting upright and onto my knees I wrap my arms around Alex's neck where I bury myself. Instantly his arms are around my waist, holding me tightly as my lips explore, working their warm way along his neck and jaw with small kisses. I taste salt and sweetness, making me want to bite him gently. I look at him through dreamy eyes, my lips hovering just under his chin. *Please want me.* I beg internally.

Alex lets out a groan then turns his face to mine, his slightly glazed eyes searching and our chins all but touching.

"Christ, you're fucking killing me, Paige."

The torment I see reflected in his eyes twist at my heart. But I can't restrain myself, my need is too strong, and any selfless thoughts I might own gets buried.

"I love you, Alex. I love you so much it hurts. And I'm sorry, so, so sorry you've been punished because of that."

Alex trails a finger along my jawline, his eyes roving over my face before locking on my lips. "I could stare at your pouty mouth all day and hear those words if I didn't want to kiss you so badly." With a slight dip of his head he is brushing my lips with his own, back and forth across them as though savoring the featherlight caress that's sending shivers everywhere.

In contrast to his tender lips, his large hands cup my ass roughly, his fingers digging in and pulling me closer, pressing and grinding his crotch against my thigh. A joyous moan slips out of my mouth, which he now covers with his own. A deep kiss, hard, but sensuous. And then his tongue is searching for mine. I'm so lost—I don't even notice he has unzipped his jeans until he grabs my hand to feel him. Oh God. Every cell not already awake simultaneously comes alive with the heat radiating from his cock. Then he's gliding a hand down my spine, sliding lower until his fingers slip past the top of my lace panties, making my pelvis tilt of its own accord, craving that he electrifies my insides.

Alex, millimeters from my face, watches me intently, his eyes captivating mine while his hand curls slowly over my ass and when I gasp, he smiles.

"Christ, Princess." He breathes, minty and warm against my lips. "I love that you get this wet for me." And then he's dipping a finger into my core, making me shiver and tighten around him. Our eyes close in unison while we fondle each other, reveling in the heightened sensation. After the previous depressive weeks, I drift into a euphoric daze where his touch is so soothing, I'm barely aware I'm still pleasuring him until Alex groans and stills my hand.

Under hooded lids, I stare into his sexy, dreamy eyes, then reach around his neck, pulling him closer so I can brush my lips over his, teasing him with the tip of my tongue until he responds. Releasing my hand so he can hold my face, his kissing is urgent. I resume pleasuring him, pumping his hot, hard cock. I want Alex so desperately, my whole body starts quivering.

"Alex, I need you inside me," I beg, when our lips part. He responds in a heartbeat, grabbing my legs and repositioning me to sit on the table edge, then pulls off his tee shirt. I reach out and take hold of his strong shoulders, steadying myself against his unbridled passion as his hands take care of my lace panties, pulling and yanking on them until they become curled and rope-like. He looks from them to me and grins. Changing his mind, it seems, he lifts me off the table by the armpits, before turning me around so he can take me from behind. When I reach for my rolled underwear, attempting to push them down and away, Alex stops me. He brings my arms forward and together we grip the far edge of the table.

His body, heated and hard, dominates over my back, and I can feel him breathing heavy. For a second, he waits. His cock, barely in contact, dances and tickles my flesh, making me desperate to spread for him, but I can't because my knees are shackled by my roped panties. I responds to my titillating predicament with wet arousal.

"Oh, fuck, I just want to do everything to you, Princess," Alex whispers close to my ear. I pull a hand free to stroke his head, delighted that he's calling me 'Princess' again. He takes hold of my hand again, clasping firmly, before he thrusts between my clamped-together thighs.

I simultaneously shudder, gasp, and moan. The sensation of him sliding repetitively between my folds and grazing my clit, drives me insane. Pinned beneath him, I wiggle, squirm, and bob on my toes, trying to get him to penetrate me, but he just keeps thrusting through the tight, slick valley he's created. Kissing my ear and head and sighing in rapture, cursing and mumbling to himself that he shouldn't be doing this, that he'll never get over me if he can't keep his hands off. That I feel too good to stop. His delirium feels like warm honey and is so soothing to my ears. He loves me, I know he does.

"Alex, please," I pant, still bobbing and wiggling beneath him, getting hotter and slicker from my arousal and the oil. "Stick it in. I need you to fuck me."

Suddenly, he lets go of my hands and wraps his arms round my waist then stills himself, his cock nestling and throbbing against my clenching pussy. I moan then groan and let my forehead hit the cushioned table. Why is he stopping?

"I can't."

"Oh God, why not?" I let out a frustrated sob. "Please," I beg. "I'm sorry, I promise to leave you alone after this. Just please, I need you so badly."

"No, it's not that, I don't have a condom on me."

"I don't care, Alex. I'm going to implode, just fucking fuck me," I wail into the firm mattress before reaching between my legs, pressing him against me and almost pushing him inside.

"Christ." He steps back and when I turn around, he's eating me alive with his eyes. He's looking frantic and filled with a desire that begs me to drop to my knees, but as soon as I do, he's lifting me up onto the table and pushing me down so he can pull off my underwear. I kick urgently to help shrug them off. Then he's thumbing over my erect nipples, before sucking and licking on my sensitive puckered peaks. I cradle his head, keeping him there, wanting him to suckle and take as much of me into his mouth as he can. I can't keep still. Can't get enough of him. Squirming on the table, I fumble for his cock then complain because he's too far away.

Pulling his face free, he looks over my desire drenched body as though questioning where to start, before reaching for the oil bottle. My breathing is so heavy it sounds like I've been sprinting, and when he moves to the end of the table, with a predatory look in his eyes, slicking his arms, I feel myself peaking and begin panting. I'm so turned on, a few more touches in the right place, and I'll be shattering into pieces.

I hold my breath when he grabs my feet, wondering what he intends to do. Then he's pushing on my ankles, bending my knees and opening me so wide, my eyes prickle and moisten from the saturation of desire between us.

Narrowing his eyes, Alex admires my sex. His chest is heaving along with mine, that is, when I remember to breathe. Wrapping his arms around my legs Alex jerks me closer to the end of the table, then slides his hands down the inside of my thighs, pressing firmly into my flesh, making me want to spread my legs farther still so he will glide closer to the place of yearning. His movements are slow and deliberate, driving me mad with desire. Tracing thumbs over my sharp hipbones, then coming down onto my pubic bone. Then his thumbs reach for and pull upward on my labia.

"Oh God, Alex, you're going to make me come."

"Not yet," he breathes, massaging my folds delicately while rubbing a firm hand just over my pubic bone and pressing. Then his fingers are inside me, quenching me. I let out a long loud sigh and tremble, clenching my internal muscles around his finger, trying to stave off the orgasm that's brewing because I don't want his attention to ever end. But it has the opposite effect, and I become more sensitive.

Then he is doing something inside me, massaging and working his fingers in one spot, making me quiver and squirm then open my legs wider.

"Feel that?"

"Yeees."

"I'm right on your G-spot, Princess, and fuck you're hot in there."

"What?" I ask, breathy and half delirious, practically melting into the table. Then I'm rocking against his hand as he presses, rubs, and does an amazing thing inside my wet, pulsating pleasure zone. I'm losing myself completely. I don't care about anything. I just want to stay with this euphoric sensation forever. I want him to fill me up but to keep doing what he's doing, I can't decide. And then I don't care. I'm peaking, climbing higher, swelling against his fingers, and I grip tighter to the table, my knees bending, my pelvis stilling to absorb the upward spiraling from the pleasure he's giving.

"Yoo woo! Hello, Alex are you there?"

Alex freezes, and my hands cover my face to hold in the wail that wants to escape.

"Shit," he says in a low tone, his head dropping against my leg to let out a muffled groan. His eyes land on me. "I'm sorry, I think it's my next client."

I whimper when Alex extends to full height and moves away from me. It's been weeks since I've been quenched, and even then, it wasn't the way I desired. I haven't allowed Gerard near me since Oliver. And going on how I feel right now with this pent-up desire, I'm not surprised Gerard's been an ass, ready to tear my head off.

Pulling me into sitting position, Alex and I look at each other and draw a deep breath in unison. A quick kiss, and he's putting on his tee and checking his phone before slipping out of the room. I want to go out there and punch his next client in the face. I hear their soft murmurs as Alex apologizes for the delay. Their footsteps sound across the tiled floor toward the back door that Alex obviously forgot to lock, then he's back again.

"Sorry." Looking regretful, he picks up my clothes, politely trying to hurry me along. "Do you want to wait upstairs? I'd reschedule her appointment, but I really need the money, Paige."

"I'll pay you triple," I offer, making him smile. "Quadruple?" I beg.

Alex draws me in tightly, kissing the top of my head then finds my lips again. Everything about Alex feels right. His smell, his touch, his voice, his tone, his face, his body, and oh those beautiful hands. I slacken in his strong arms and sigh. Yep, it's official. I'm in love. I'm so, so in love.

"I can't, she's a repeat client who has referred her friends," he murmurs against my forehead, leaving traces of moisture from his warm breath.

"I see how it is," I huff. "Like me, I bet you wind them all up and leave them nowhere to go, but back here for round two?"

He flicks his eyebrows at me, leaving me guessing. Then says, "Stay. I'll only be an hour."

"Okay, I'll wait." I slip into my shorts and smile at him.

It's the answer he wants to hear, because despite his reservation when I first arrived, he looks pleased. "Drink plenty of water, it helps flush everything out. It will cool you down too." He winks.

I glower at him playfully.

"Can you just tell Erica I'll be five minutes, then she can come in," he asks, pulling off the sheet and gathering up the towels.

"Sure." I stare at him for a moment, appreciating his rugged look, yet gentle soul.

"What?"

I step forward and grab his face in my hands and kiss him affectionately, murmuring my appreciation of the taste and texture of his juicy lips. Then I whisper against his rough face, his stubble scratching me.

"I wish this was a different time and place Alex, because I don't want to share you with anyone either. I honestly hate everyone who came before me. In bed, and on that table." My eyes gesture toward the table before I peck his lips and let him go.

Alex smiles, and glances at the floor. I think it's the first time I've ever seen him blush.

Closing the door, I see through the window, a dark-haired woman seated outside and staring out at the ocean. When she hears the back door open, she glances my way then gets up. She looks classy, attractive, and in her late forties at a guess. She has the face of a homely woman and her eyes are the most striking feature about her. Facing me, I'm amazed they almost match the color of the ocean behind her.

"Morning. I'm sorry my appointment went over and you had to wait."

She looks toward the door. "Am I free to go in?" she asks, brushing off my apology.

"He just needs a few more minutes to change the linen."

Erica turns away and it only takes me a second to add, "If I can give you some advice, I'd tip him big time. I've got friends that have been trying to get in with Alex for weeks now, and the only reason I got in this time was because the other week, I tipped him almost as much as his fee. I got this appointment in a heartbeat." I shrug one shoulder. "It's just a suggestion. Maybe that's why I received extra time today too." Still smiling, I raise my brow.

"Thank you. That's handy to know." Then she must spot Alex at the door because her eyes dart away.

"Oh, he's ready for me. Thank you," she says, leaving me to wander off upstairs to wait out the hour.

15

CLOSE

It could be Gerard or Annabel calling. The bank manager or even the IRS, but I don't give a flying fuchsia, and if my phone, which is ringing and vibrating noisily in my handbag on the couch were in reach, I think I'd throw the damn thing out the window.

Walking around the upstairs of the beach house, amongst the smell of paint and freshly cut wood, I find evidence of a dream built for me, and a life destroyed because of me. Amid freshly painted walls and newly hung light fixtures, tools and unopened packets of modern door handles, is a small collection of boxes with 'MINE' scribbled in black marker scattered here and there, making Alex's pending departure painfully real. In this moment, I both love and hate Gerard at once and I'm questioning my accusation—that he was using the house as a bribe.

Feeling extremely conceited, I dismiss the now silent phone and grab a glass of water and stand at the glass sliding doors. The beach below is surprisingly quiet, given it's a beautiful day. And as I watch the few seagulls scavenge for crabs on the wet sand, I become envious of their simplistic life. Then I notice the outdoor table I now realize Alex must have built. Its rough surface has been neither sanded nor oiled. Just seven long slats of raw wood screwed down to a basic frame. With four cheap plastic chairs surrounding it, it does its best to suffice.

Another thing I notice is how healthy the potted plants now look. Alex is a natural nurturer, and yet, Alex barely owns a thing. No house, no real furniture. No truck anymore and now, because of me, he doesn't even get to complete the renovations downstairs. Why does he even still care about me when all I've ever done is ruin his life? And when he gets upstairs, I'm going to break his heart by telling him Jolene has been lying to him.

Placing the empty glass down, I lay down on the old dusty couch and drape my arm over my eyes to block out the glare of the midday sun so I can concentrate on hating myself some more.

Minutes later, startling me from my doze, my phone starts ringing again. Now in arm's reach, I fish around inside my handbag and pull out my cell that reveals a number I don't recognize. Then I notice I've in fact missed several calls earlier in the day from the same number. Hesitantly, I answer.

Relaying the news of my mother's passing to Alex the second he comes upstairs, I become heated all over. I get up and pace the floor digging my fingers into my hips. My head is swimming in all directions, and I become agonizingly distressed.

"I think I'm going to throw up," I announce.

"If you're serious, you know the bathroom's down the hall," Alex says watching me walk in wayward directions. I don't even understand why I'm so upset, but it just seems that suddenly I need to vent but feel confused as to how much to say.

Needing to be alone, I head to the bathroom hoping to calm myself down. But as soon I close the door, I turn abruptly and throw up in the toilet. Going over to the sink, I hover for a moment gripping the vanity then splash water on my face. I focus on my breathing while staring at my darting eyes. My mind is a hive of irrational thoughts with octopus-like tentacles reaching into my past. Frantically, I find toothpaste then brush my teeth with a finger to help ground myself.

"Paige, are you, all right?" Alex asks, moments later through the door .

"No."

When he opens the door, he finds me sitting on the toilet seat with my head in my hands. He squats beside me, placing a hand on my knee.

"What can I do?" he asks.

"My mother is actually dead. Ha. I mean, I know she's been sick and I knew it was coming, but well—now it's real."

I expect Alex to say he's sorry, but he just nods. Then I think, why would he be sorry? Then I realize I'm not even sorry. I'm glad she's gone.

Is it bad to be relieved about something like that? Does that make me a bad person? I cover my face with my hands, feeling disorientated by how I feel. "Argh! I think I'm in shock."

For a moment, Alex just rubs my back. When he starts patting, I'm compelled to look at him and confess that I'm glad she's dead. But I don't know what I'm meant to do.

"What happens next?" I ask.

"What do you mean?" Rising to his feet, he takes my hand to draw me up and lead me back to the living room.

"I'm her only child. Am I expected to arrange something?"

"Not really,"

"But then, what will they do with her?"

"They'll cremate her. But, maybe you should go."

He offers me some water before we sit together on the couch. Slipping an arm around my shoulder, he pulls me into his chest and rubs my arm. I catch the mixture of scents from his closeness. His cologne, salt, and the body oils he's been using. Strangely, the smells conjure up the feeling of freedom.

"Shit. I really don't need this right now, but then… Maybe it would be good to get away. Problem is, I've got nothing but that credit card. Donnie has been holding out on me, and my bank balance is not looking healthy. I might need to ask Gerard for some money and I doubt that will go down well."

"Yeah, I imagine Gerard will put up a fight. Especially for someone he doesn't give a fuck about."

When I flinch, he clarifies himself. "I mean your mom."

Nodding, I get up from the couch. I need more water.

"Maybe I should just let them cremate her with all the Jane Does. I don't think I can go back there anyway."

"I think you need to go, Paige, even if it's just for the closure. Send it six foot under and let it go. I never went to my mom's funeral, and I regret it. I thought at the time if I didn't go, it wouldn't make it real." Alex rises from the couch and comes closer. "Make it real. I guarantee it will help."

I turn away to refill my glass, sip at it, and stare out at the ocean, and for the first time, I notice there is a small park a short distance down the beach on a lovely grassy patch, just off the sand. There are two mothers pushing their children on the swings. A small smile pulls at the corners of my mouth.

"I never noticed that playground before," I say

offhandedly, making Alex come to stand beside me. He takes my glass and has a drink as well.

"I wish I'd had a real childhood—you know. Even just one parent who cared." I let out a huff. "I've blocked out a lot from my past, Alex. Truthfully, I'm afraid to go back because I'll be reminded of things I'd rather keep buried."

"I hear ya." He folds his arms and leans against the counter. His small smile encourages me to shake my melancholy away.

"Thank you for the massage. You really are good, and I'm not just stroking your ego either."

"Gets me a bit of extra cash."

"Do you have any more appointments today?"

"Nope. But what did you say to my client? She tipped me nicely."

"Just told her you were worth every penny and you might give her one of your *special* massages if she spares no expense."

"Did you now?" He pushes me back against the sink and tickles me. "I almost had you screaming before."

"Tell me about it." I raise my eyebrows and give him a look. But when everything that is my life rushes at me, reminding me who I am, I moan and cover my eyes. "I just want to stay here. I don't want to go home."

"So, stay."

When my hands drop away, I latch onto the band of Alex's cargo pants. He slips an arm around my waist but looks over my head and out the window.

"What are you thinking about?" I ask, turning to see what he sees.

"Gerard's not hurting you, is he?" He looks down into my face. When I pause, he prompts me by shoving his pelvis at me.

"To be truthful. I think I'm hurting him more than he's

hurting me." I move away and lean against the opposite bench.

"What does that mean?"

"I called him a coward. He slapped my face. I realized later that I deserved it."

"Ah no. There's no excuse for abuse, Paige."

"Didn't you hear our argument at the fundraiser?" My voice raises an octave. "I said some horrible things to Gerard."

"It still doesn't give him the right to fucking hit you, Paige. Why are you putting up with his shit?"

"Maybe because he's right. I mean, I'm here with you—aren't I?" I gesture with my hands at the ludicrousness of my actions. "If I wasn't having anxiety attacks, anyone would think I enjoy this drama."

I pause a moment, questioning whether I want to worry Alex with the details. He keeps looking at me expectantly, so I fill him in on what I now consider was a panic attack or something. "It was the morning after the fundraiser. I was so anxious I exhausted myself and passed out on the kitchen floor."

Alex frowns and looks worried. "Tell me all that again."

I run through the sequence of events on that day more clearly for him. Relieved that at least Alex, takes me seriously.

"Don't you think it's strange, that who ever it was, only took the glass egg and my computer?" I ask.

"Yes and, the fact Gerard was too casual about it. Are you sure he didn't take it?"

"Why would he take it?"

"I don't know. Have you replaced your computer?"

"Gerard told me to wait and see if the police find it."

"How are you getting your work done?"

"I'm not. Thank God I don't have any assignments. Donnie's still being an ass and giving work to interns."

Alex nods then stretches his arms over his head. "I need to piss."

"Good to know."

Alex slaps my butt, breaking the tension and I let go of a giggle.

"You want lunch? I've got food in the fridge," he says over his shoulder as he goes off to the bathroom. I don't have time to answer him because my phone springs to life.

The display tells me it's Sheree. Reluctantly, I answer it, knowing she most likely just wants to pass on her condolences.

"Hey." I take a seat on the dining table, then spin so I can rest my feet on a chair.

"I'm sorry, pea. Mom sends her love too. Laura was on shift and told her."

"Thanks, but I'm fine. To me, Mom died a long time ago."

Alex comes back out and makes his way to the fridge then pulls out what looks to be leftover lasagna.

"I'm not sure how to go about putting her to rest though? Do you think if I don't come and claim her, they'll just cremate her?"

Alex throws me a scowl, then mouths 'Go.'

I wave and shoo his suggestion away. Then Sheree is on my case.

"Paige! Come on, you need to forgive her and move on."

Argh, I hate it when she says my name in that tone, drawing out the noun.

Alex puts the lasagna in the microwave but doesn't turn it on. Instead, he comes to lean on the chair. "Do you want food?" he whispers. I nod, but he doesn't move away. He's frowning. I think it's because I'm becoming agitated by Sheree.

"Look. I'm having dramas with Gerard, and I don't think he will be happy funding my mother's funeral, that's all."

"Are these dramas because you're sneaking around with Alex?"

"It's more complicated than that." I grimace at Alex.

"Paige, why are you ruining what you have? Just last month you said Alex was a mistake and now you're sneaking around making fake appointments."

Seeing my frustration. Alex lifts my legs and sits on the chair I'm using for my feet. He replaces them on his lap, and when I roll my eyes, indicating I want to get off the phone, he gives me a smile then begins massaging my feet, trying his best to distract me. Which works.

"Sorry, Ree, I've got to go, but I promise I'll call you tomorrow. We'll have a big talk then."

"Will you at least tell me how your so-called massage went? What was so urgent, and why couldn't you just call him yourself?"

"It was nothing, don't worry about it. Look, I can't really talk at the moment because I'm— actually still in the middle of my massage." I grin at Alex. "He was running late."

"Sure you're in the middle of a massage and not something else? I hope you know what you're doing, Paige."

After reassuring her and promising to call tomorrow, we disconnect.

"God almighty, talk about pressure from everywhere." I give Alex a gentle shove. "You and Sheree are a good pair. Together you're sure straightening me out."

Alex lifts a single brow then rubs my thighs in unison. His thumbs sliding wickedly close to the bottoms of my shorts.

"Are you still hungry, Princess?"

"Don't you dare start something you're not going to finish." I scoot myself back a little farther on the table to get away from him.

"Well, well, well, looks who's becoming a demanding little queen now," he says, grabbing me under the knees and sliding me close again. He takes turns kissing just inside my thighs. Working his way up slowly as my fingers comb through his hair. The electricity that ignites between us, seems to wrap me up in a cocoon, threatening to swallow me whole and into oblivion, again. Then my conscience getting the better of me.

"I could easily lose days being around you, Alex. I should go home,"

"Yeah, you should go," he says deadpan, but slides his hands under my shorts and to the top of my legs.

"Well, you'll need to move then," I say, breathy, my hands halting his fingers when he tickles my thighs. Alex pouts for a moment, then squints his eyes and smirks. Getting rougher, he inches his fingers higher until he is grazing the top of my panties, causing my heartbeat to escalate. I look around, expecting a worker to suddenly appear, being used to seeing them when I was helping Alex.

"You are so bad, Alex," I whisper when he keeps looking up at me with a cheeky grin.

He slides his hands down, keeping a firm grip on the top of my panties to draws them out, so they are taut against the crotch of my shorts and resting on the top of my thighs.

"Shame about these getting wrecked."

I look down at the stretched white lace fabric, wondering what he means, when he pulls harder on my panties, causing me to gasp. He bends forward licking and kissing me, meandering higher along my inner thigh. Embarrassed by the proximity of his face to my crotch, I push myself a little farther away. Alex growls. Then using the grip he has on my panties, he yanks me back toward him and I need to quickly steady myself, my hand landing heavily on the table.

Then with one long intake, Alex breathes in my scent and

his eyes darken with desire. My sight stays firmly fixed on him, and the hunger pooling in his eyes makes me beyond aroused. Argh he is so goddamn sexy and hard to resist.

"Fuck, you smell good. I just want to bury my face in your pussy and live there."

"Alex, you're so crude." I push on his shoulder with my free hand, but seconds later I grab hold of his chin, tilting his head, desperate for him to kiss me. I lick my lips in anticipation. "Kiss me," I beg, leaning forward and taking his face in both hands. Alex shakes my hands off, then leans into my crotch and inhales again. Then his teeth are at my lace undies. "Alex, no." I try to still his head but using fingers and teeth, he tears into the lace, then pulls them gently out and down the other leg.

My breathing becomes audible. I'm heady and trembling, and when he slides his finger in behind the crotch of my shorts and brushes against my pussy, I know in seconds I'll be sopping wet.

"Oh God, Alex, let me off the table. Let's go into your room." I push myself backward hoping he'll let me go, desperate now for him to just make love to me.

Ignoring me, he slides more fingers along the inside of my shorts, curling them into a fist around the crotch of my shorts then yanks roughly. My hands fly out behind me, snatching hold of the table tightly for fear of being swept clean off, and onto his lap.

Excited by his game, I secure my feet onto his thighs and push myself back farther on the table. But his fist, still gripping firmly to the crotch of my shorts, still won't let go. I play for a moment with my toes on his thighs then inch them slowly toward his cock, which is still trapped within his cargo pants. Going by the tension of the fabric, he must almost be blue by now.

His eyes, so hot and lusty, stay locked on me. Then he

yanks me closer again, jarring out the air in my lungs. He presses teasingly against the hot junction between my legs then glances at my heaving chest. Alex smiles, his eyes lifting slowly until he's again staring into my glazing eyes. Peeling away from me, he stands to unzip his pants then pushes them and his boxers away. His cock stands beautifully aroused and ready.

Mesmerized and waiting, I bite my bottom lip, hoping he begs me to suck him off again, but he doesn't. Instead, he takes his seat again.

I look down at his dancing member then bring my feet together to cup him. It takes all my abdominal strength to hold the position, so when he yanks me again by my knees, I slide too far and lose balance to land splayed out on the table with a giggle. The man is a goddamn expert at sexing. Even when he slides his thumb past my shorts and inside me, I'm in awe of his mastery. I don't know how it comes so easily to him, but this man knows how to arouse a woman into submission. I arch into him, wanting more.

I lay panting as Alex unbuttons then unzips my shorts, raising my hips so he can slide them off. I'm now waiting for him with such desire, I think if he were to blow his minty breath on me, I would instantly climax.

"You know what I'm going to do to you, Paige?" he asks seductively, rising out of the chair again. I shake my head, letting my exposed lower body relax, surrendering to him unabashed when he bends my legs against my chest to splay me wide. My warm desire trickles down between my crack, and when he looks down at my aroused state, he shakes his head slightly and murmurs, a grin splicing his cheeks.

"Perfect," he says, taking a finger and spreading the wetness down. "I need you nice and wet because I'm going to fuck you right here." He presses his finger to my pucker hole, causing me catch my breath and clench. Heat radiates off my face, and my heart feels like someone has taken a jackhammer to it. I shake my head gently, eyeing him.

"What? You don't want me to fuck you right here?" he asks, pressing his finger harder. He sounds so seductive, I'm becoming heady and intimidated by him. Yep that's how he does it. He's so primal and unpredictable.

"I don't know."

His eyes widen to resemble something like glee, and I think I notice his breathing deepen.

"A virgin hole maybe?" he flicks a brow.

Staying silent but widening my eyes, I leave him to assume whatever the heck he likes.

"Lucky, lucky me." He smiles, sounding exuberant.

With his finger still pressing against my anus, he pushes other fingers inside my swelling pussy. "You're so fuckin wet, Paige, you're turning my table into a swimming pool."

I make a noise like a moaning groan when he presses harder and a single finger enters my forbidden spot.

"Fuck. You have no idea how hard my cock is throbbing."

"Give it to me, Alex. I want you in my mouth," I beg. He shakes his head, withdraws his fingers a little, then pushes them in my pussy and ass again. Deeper. My legs involuntarily spread wider, and he shoots me a wicked look. I'm so wet his fingers glide in and out effortlessly. Then he's grabbing me around the legs. Sitting down he pulls me to the edge of the table and strokes the length of my slit and thumbs my clit. The second his tongue invades me, I'm singing out and lifting myself off the table.

"Christ," I wail, resisting the urge to grab his face and just start humping. He flattens his velvety tongue against me before plunging fingers inside again.

Then he's sucking on me, cupping his lips, trying to devour as much of my flesh as possible, his tongue darting in, then flicking on my sensitive spot.

Just when I'm on the brink of spilling over, Alex seems to feel it and stops. "Fuck you're wet. I need you on my cock right now." He quickly fixes on a condom that he must have gotten from the bathroom, then coaxes me closer.

Coming down off the table, I straddle him and allow him to position me on his dancing veined erection.

He is big and hard, and it hurts when he penetrates me where he wants me most. I yelp and clench and grab onto his shoulders to still him.

"Alex!" I breathe, uncertain I will fit him, but the yearning to please him is so overwhelming, I start shaking my head into submission.

His chest is pulling in and out deeply, and he reaches for my face, stilling me, then pulls me down slowly onto his shaft.

"Relax," he breathes, kissing my lips and neck while his fingers get busy unbuttoning my blouse.

Freeing my tits, he latches on and sucks gently, still slowly filling me. I'm so slick, that in seconds, the burning gives way to an explosive sensation making me quiver and hum until he fills me up entirely. I spasm around his pulsating cock which seems to thicken his girth even more. I can barely handle the pleasure and pain of him inside me as he raises me, then pulls me back down. Getting harder and faster with urgency and then, just like that, I'm shuddering around him from a long, intense orgasm. My moans of ecstasy escape involuntarily. They are deep and throaty, and don't even sound like me. I barely stop shivering when his fingers are rubbing against my clit, urging, needing to claim another orgasm from me. I wrap my arms around Alex's neck like an exhausted boxer, clinging in the hope of slowing the pace, but my orgasm has swooned him into a frenzy to enrapture me all over again.

"Fuck yeah. Slick me all over, babe," Alex moans, digging

his fingers in me, trying to locate that magic spot inside. I arch back against the table giving him the access he wants and the penetration he needs. He sounds out his appreciation then his fingers get to work again, thrilling me like nothing I've ever felt before.

"Alex, what are you doing to me?" I lean back farther, take more of him in my ass so his fingers can do whatever magical thing they're doing inside me. The intensity of my desire and the throbbing of his cock in my tight hole is soon shattering me again. Long and lasting, the waves of pleasure unite us.

Clinging to each other, I bury myself in his neck, feeling him shudder and twitch in response to my waning orgasm.

His arm encircles my waist tighter, pressing all the air out of my lungs with his powerful embrace. He catches my mouth, dragging the last of my own breath from me, giving me wild and erratic kisses, chomping and sucking on my tongue and lips. Pulling me onto him with all his might, he impales me completely to his ball and erupts with such force, I feel him explode.

"Fuckin' Christ!" Alex shouts, his eyes closing and his head falling forward so our foreheads are touching. "Oh, Paige," he murmurs, tucking my head under his chin and rocking us slightly.

I can't help it. I start crying.

"What's the matter?" Alex rubs my back, tugging free my hair that's falling out of the loose bun I put it in, making it cascade down my back. "Paige, what's the matter," he repeats, stroking my hair.

"Why am I letting you do this to me?" I murmur into his neck.

"What do you mean? Do what? Did I hurt you?" He pulls back, looking concerned.

Using his shirt as a cloth, I dry my tear-drenched face and

sit back. Unknowingly, he has fragmented me. I'm not me anymore but who the hell am I?

"No. I love you. I love you so much. Nothing has been the same since you. You're the best thing in my life, Alex." I search his eyes, his beautiful, honest eyes. Then at the expense of sounding needy, I blurt, "And as if going back to Gerard now isn't going to be hard enough, if I see you with someone else… and that's just not fair for me to think like that. I just wish… Argh," I can't finish.

Alex pulls me in again, strokes my head and shushes me.

"It'll be okay. You'll level out, you're just post-orgasmic. You've got a pile of hormones racing around, and with everything going on, it's most likely too much. You don't mean that stuff, I'm just something different." He gives a little chuckle, and I fear this is all a game to him while inside, my heart is slowly being shredded to pieces.

"You can't know what I'm feeling, Alex." I comb his hair with my fingers and smile weakly. "It's easy for you. I'm just a bit of fun, but for me, this is difficult."

Alex heaves a sigh and shakes his head like I don't get it. Still wrapped around him, he carries me to the shower, and we clean ourselves off in reflective silence. It suddenly feels awkward that neither of us knows what to say.

Alex is everything I want in a lover, in a man, in a friend. If I felt attached to him before, being with him today took it to a whole new level.

When I step out of the shower, I throw my blouse back on and instantly go to find my phone. It's nearing one thirty and I pray nothing has been waiting for me at home. I don't know how I will cover my deceit this time. This time it's for real, my feelings have solidified.

I don't bother to return to the bathroom to dress. I just find my shorts and slip back into them. Picking up the torn panties, I toss them in the bin, then find a cloth and some surface spray. I hastily give that table and chair a going-over.

In no time, Alex is back in cargos and the gray tee. He leans against the wall watching me. He has styled his hair with gel and that damn cologne seeps into every orifice I own.

"You don't have to do that. I can do it."

"It's fine," I reply, wiping harder and faster.

"Paige, come on." He comes up behind me and tries taking the cloth.

"It's fine," I say, twisting away from him and throwing the cloth into the bin with such force the lid spins all the way around, then I sigh in defeat. None of how I feel is Alex's fault. I'm the one setting myself up to be hurt.

"This is hard on me too, Paige. I have to stand back and watch you with him."

"Well, what do I do? He threatened to get you thrown back in prison." A few steps and I'm wrapping my arms around his waist, holding him for all I'm worth. "I know he's serious, but I don't know what to do about it. I know I should stay away from you, but it's so hard when we're like that together." I point at the table as though we are still making love on it, then look back to him for advice, a suggestion or admission that maybe he feels the way I do.

"I don't know either." Prizing me off, he runs a hand through his hair then shoves his hands in his pockets and walks the room looking pained.

"Alex, do you want me for real, or am I just a good time to you?"

Sunshine is pouring through the sliding doors behind him, highlighting dust particles that he is stirring from his pacing, and when he stops, his level gaze tells me he'd rather not deal with either of our feelings. Then I'm backpedaling faster than Lance Armstrong.

"I'm sorry, that came out the wrong way. I'm the complication, not you. I should get going."

His eyes narrow, but he can't help the smile that forms on his sexy face. "No, come here." He reaches out for me.

When I don't move, he lunges forward, grabbing my arm and pulling me into a hug.

"Why do women always need to get so emotional and clingy?"

"Maybe it's got something to do with how hot you are."

He huffs, looking amused and vaguely flattered.

"Listen," he tilts my face, so I'm forced to look him straight in the eye. "Just let everything unfold in its own time. Don't rush in to things. You've got a lot to sort out with Gerard, and you've got your mother's funeral to get out of the way."

I shake my head still in his hand, convinced I don't want to go.

"Yes, you're going. It'll give you time to think things over, okay? Once your gallery is set up, you might feel differently."

"I doubt it."

Alex moans. "Paige, it's not just that. I don't want the commitment either. Not to you or anyone. At least, not at the moment." He pulls back his head, trying to convey his seriousness. "I was locked up for six years. I don't even know what direction I want to go in life, let alone bringing someone else along with me. But it sure as shit ain't the lifestyle you seem to like." He shakes his head.

"What I like?" I snort, putting my face back against his chest. "Who said I like it?"

"Why are you still there then? I'm sorry, but if you're not happy with Gerard, you need to leave, but don't leave him for me, that'll only backfire at this point, and you know it." He pushes me away gently. "I'm gonna eat. Want something?"

Moving away, he goes into the kitchen area and switches

on the microwave then takes plates out. I can't work out whether he's trying to brush me off because he's afraid he's not good enough for me or because he honestly doesn't want commitment. Then I'm remembering why I came in the first place. This is not about me. I need to let him know that Jolene is lying to him.

"Do you want to eat or not?"

"Sure." I shrug one shoulder in defeat then stand by the island bench watching as he works. Because I'm quietly thinking things over, he keeps glancing at me.

"So how did the fundraiser go? Get the funds you were hoping for?" Alex asks, trying to start a conversation.

"I'm ashamed to say I barely even remember the night let alone given any thought to it since. Do you know how much my photos went for? I forgot to ask Annabel when I spoke with her."

Alex's head shoots up.

"You don't remember? You were bidding on them. Gerard was practically having a coronary watching you across the room. Twelve hundred."

I can't help feeling amused at myself for pushing up the price. Then I'm rolling my eyes and shaking my head. "So unprofessional of me. Someone should have smacked me out." I pinch a piece of tomato Alex is cutting and pop it in my mouth.

"Who was that guy you and Gerard left with? Did you know him?"

I was dreading Alex might bring up Oliver. I look to the ceiling before closing my eyes, praying a hole would appear for me to fall into. I go and sit at the table.

"Not really. Sort of. Anyway, you don't want to know."

"I do so want to know."

"No, you really don't."

Alex screws up his face. His jaw tightening.

"Alex, please don't ask. I was so drunk I hardly remember leaving. And Gerard… Well I fucked up all right. It was my mistake. I was stupid. But all I could think of was you, and Gerard not punishing you. Like that even helped anyway." I look around at the packed boxes, shaking my head and sighing.

Alex looks hurt or disappointed. When he comes closer, handing me a loaded plate but looking somber, I realize it's both.

"Here, eat. And eat it all, you're getting too skinny. And if you don't, I'll be offended. I made it myself."

"Seriously?" I huff. "And to think I always believed Gerard to be the perfect man."

"Pfft," Alex scoffs, taking a seat and tucking into his food straightaway. "I think you've just been wearing rose-fucking glasses there. The man's an asshole in disguise. Only reason I'm staying is to get the money at the end."

"You mean he hasn't been paying you?" I ask, annoyed at first that I know so little about what's going on, then hurt because I'm not the reason he might still here.

"Nope. He was with the gardening. But said he'd pay me like any contractor. Deposit then the rest on completion," he says between chewing.

"I'm sorry. I didn't know that."

"It's not your fault. It was a deal between him and me. Anyway, another month should do it, then I'll give some to Jolene, then I'm out of here." His eyes flick up to me, catching me with a forkful of food paused at my mouth, before I put it down on my plate. He goes back to eating like he hasn't noticed my surprise or disappointment.

"Where will you go?" I ask in a weak voice.

"Not sure yet." Watching me, Alex sits taller and gulps down some water from his glass.

"Alex. I need to tell you something about Jolene."

"So, you said in your text messages. Go ahead but I doubt it's anything I don't already know." He flicks his head before reclaiming his fork to resume eating, giving me a moment to ponder a tactful approach.

"I'm not sure how to say this because I don't want to disappoint you, and I guess I'm confused why she would lie to you anyway."

Alex stops eating and frowns.

"I met Jolene and Grace the other week, Alex, and they are far, far from being in need of any help."

Alex places his utensil down and elbows the table to hold his chin. "You—met them?"

I nod.

"Where?"

"At home. Gerard invited them over. Reluctantly." I pick up my fork and take a mouthful of food.

Alex scrutinizes me.

"Long story short, I told Gerard I wanted to give money to Jolene for Grace. He wanted to prove you were lying to me. I knew you wouldn't lie. Anyway, he organized a get-together. She's beautiful, I can see why she was a model. I mean she's stunning, and Grace! God, what a cute little girl. But it's obvious Grace is not his. The day was torture really. I've never felt so inadequate in my life. Did you know she works for Teen Magazine now? As an editor! I don't know why she lied to you. Saying Grace is sick... and," I wave my fork at Alex who is still nursing his chin, taking it all in while I explain through mouthfuls of delicious lasagna, "she's even moving away. If you ask me, I think he might still have feelings for her, and she clearly has feelings for him. I'd leave them to it if I knew Gerard would let me go." My fork pauses midway to my mouth and my face heats when I realize what I've said.

Alex plays an awkward smile then picks up his fork again.

"Looks like you're enjoying that lasagna, Princess. Keep eating." He jabs the silverware at my plate. He's right, I was enjoying his home cooking, but something tells me Alex's nonchalant attitude is the calm before a storm, and now, I've totally lost my appetite.

16

ALL WITHOUT YOU

I can't believe my eyes. I glance at my clenched fists gripping the steering wheel when Alex touches my hand. "Are you all right?"

"No." Loosening my grip, my hands slide down and fall into my lap allowing me to slump.

Together, Alex and I stare back out the window at the dilapidated caravan. Fortunately, we didn't have to intrude and go knocking on the rusty door for Alex to prove he wasn't lying. The pretty but worn-out looking brunette is outside, hanging washing on a feeble rack mounted to the side of the van. She's dressed in shorts and a tee shirt with sneakers on. There's no Grace in sight but Alex reassures she exists, most likely asleep in the van. And going by the few toys scattered around Jolene's unkempt patch of the park, it's evident a child lives there.

We are parked well enough away that Jolene hasn't noticed us, but I suddenly feel horrible and sad that I'm sitting in a Lexus ogling her without her knowledge. That my shoes cost more than her weekly rent. That I have pop-up sprinklers to water a lush lawn and a swimming pool I hardly use. And here's Jolene and Grace living on a twenty by twenty foot plot that's predominately dirt.

"Doesn't she have any family?"

"Jolene's parents live interstate on a small property. They visit but can't offer much help. They've still got a bunch of kids at home to look after."

"I'm so gullible." I huff, still shaking my head in disbelief, then look at Alex again. "I mean, *Christ*! Look at her. She reminds me of me, before I met Gerard."

"Yeah and just like you, she fell for his rich charm."

"I bet he didn't think I'd go telling you about her fake visit."

"I bet he was counting on you believing him and you'd go back to playing the compliant wife he wants."

I nod. "Promise me you're not lying, Alex. I can't take anymore lies. I already feel like I'm going insane."

Brushing his hand along my hair, he halts my shaking head and stares straight at me. His deep soulful eyes looking sad but deadly honest.

"I promise I'm not lying. That's Jolene." He looks toward her again.

My gaze drifts back to the young woman still hanging laundry and I believe him. I absolutely one-hundred-percent believe him.

I wait four days to tell Gerard about my mother's death. I've been spending the time trying to find the fake Jolene instead, hoping to get more concrete proof. Maybe use it in case he tries to stop me from leaving.

I'd started with Teen Magazine's list of editors, then

moved to sites promoting actors for hire. I even tried Facebook. Finally, I gave up and decided to call the police about our stolen possessions. Hoping to God they found at least my computer which would put to rest Alex's theory that Gerard might have taken it. Again, the time spent was wasted. So was searching the house.

I made inquiries about my mother's funeral, then arranged for her cremation. I let Sheree know all the details, and lastly, I booked a flight for one. All on my credit card.

When Gerard gets home around eight, a little late for a Tuesday, I'm half drunk and sitting on the couch, paging through a magazine. I have our meal waiting, the table set, and the news on. Just the way he likes it. Not me—I hate the routine, and it's only now I'm beginning to see and understand this is how we've been all along.

"Hi, I'm in here," I sing out, tossing the magazine on the table. Gerard enters the living room, his tie loosened and his gray suit jacket over one arm. He places his slim brown leather briefcase on the dresser.

"What are you doing?"

"Nothing really. But I have something to tell you. My mom died." I don't elaborate on when and I'm relieved that he doesn't ask.

"Are you all right?" He bends and kisses the top off my head as he passes, then falls into the couch next to me before pulling off his tie and unbuttoning his shirt.

"Fine, I suppose. Maybe I'm just numb."

Gerard pats my knee. "Would you mind getting me a drink, Paige? I've had a hell of a day." He reaches for the television remote and increases the volume, his eyes transfixed on the large screen.

When I don't move, he looks at me again. "What?"

"My mother died, Gerard."

"And? It's not like you were close. She's certainly no loss to me, and neither should she be to you." He rises and helps himself at the bar, placing ice in a crystal tumbler and half filling it with scotch.

"Still, she was my mother. I made plans with the funeral services today and arranged for the cremation this Sunday."

"You're not serious? No, let the county burn the bitch. You don't owe her a damn thing." His venom shocks me, and for a moment, I can't think of a response.

Taking a seat beside me again, Gerard shifts cushions to make himself more comfortable and I think of how to broach the subject again. After learning about his lie, I've realized I need to do this. To get away from him so I can think without him influencing me. Now I'm panicked he won't let me go.

"Are you saying I shouldn't have made arrangements?"

"Not with my money. No," he replies looking at me only briefly.

"Your money?"

Gerard pushes the long strands of hair out of his face and sights me squarely, his face furrowed and looking positively annoyed.

"Well, do you have a spare few thousand to waste?"

I shift in my seat and gulp down some wine.

"Well do you?"

"No. Donnie hasn't been giving me any work, not to mention I don't have a computer, remember? Anyway, I already arranged everything and charged it on the credit card."

Gerard's snaps eyes on me, then chuckles. "Well that was stupid. You'll have to cancel everything, now won't you?"

My chest tightens. He really does have all the control. When he sees my bloodless face, his expression softens.

"Your mother was a whore, Paige. She treated you

appallingly for most of your life, you told me that yourself. Now you want me to spend money on her. Wouldn't that be condoning her poor treatment of the woman I love?"

"Maybe. But... I think I need the closure." I use Alex's insight as a leverage.

"I suppose that would make sense. Let me think about it all right? Would you mind getting me another drink?"

He shoves his empty glass at me and turns his attention back on the news.

After handing back Gerard his refilled glass, I check on the meal and my phone. Secretly, I'm hoping to hear from Alex but there are no messages. I think about texting him. What do I say? Help, come get me—Gerard has me trapped, and put him in danger? Instead I lean across the island bench and scroll through my social media. Checking to see what my workmates are up to and whether Sheree has posted any more photos from her time away on Instagram. Mainly, I just don't want to be around Gerard anymore.

"Do we have time for a shower before dinner?" Gerard asks, startling me. I lock my phone.

"I've already had one, but yep sure, it's just a bolognaise sauce keeping warm. I'll put on some pasta now so it's ready."

Gerard comes closer then takes my phone from me. Laying it on the bench, he then lifts me onto the countertop. Umm, what's he doing?

"I need you to forgive me, Paige," he says, resting his hands on my hips then wedging himself between my legs. "I know that you're still angry at me about Oliver, and maybe even Jamison." We both watch his movements as his hands start sliding up and down my thighs. "I behaved stupidly. I admit that," he says. "I wasn't prepared to feel so inadequate after our experience with Alex."

"I can forgive you, Gerard, but no more kinky stuff." I

grab his hands. "I don't want to have sex with strangers. I felt dirty and disgusted in myself afterward."

He nods. "So, you're satisfied with just me then. I'm enough for you?"

The air in the kitchen gets thin. I try swallowing, but my throat is dry, too dry. I cough. Dropping my gaze, I take hold of Gerard's shirt collar and nod. Then sliding off the counter I quickly wrap arms around him and my face falls against his chest. I need to bide myself time. I need to maintain the status quo so he doesn't get suspicious. And then I hear it. His heart is racing. I stiffen in his arms. Pulling away, I search his eyes. He doesn't smile.

"Are you still in love with me, Paige?"

It becomes painful to breathe. I nod again, but I know my eyes lack conviction.

Gerard keeps staring at me. "Are you sure about that?"

"Yes."

Gerard picks up my phone and presses the screen. It lights up locked. I look from the phone to him, and see he's scrutinizing me.

"This needs charging," I say, taking the phone from him and putting it back on the counter. "Why don't you have a shower, I'll start on the pasta." I go to move away.

Gerard doesn't move. He keeps me pressed against the bench, his hands still on my hips.

"I'd like some sex first."

"What?" I let out a nervous chuckle. "Now?"

Gerard spins me around so that my back is to him and starts caressing my breasts. I push on his hands and try twisting out of his embrace.

"Gerard, not in the kitchen. Later. Go have a shower."

Ignoring me, he keeps pressing into me, folding me over the bench, getting a little rough. His hand dives down the front of my baggy track pants.

"Why are you wearing such tasteless clothes tonight?" he asks breathing into my ear then nipping my lobe.

"Oww. That hurt." I push back on him. "Because I was just relaxing."

"Well, you know I don't like it. What's the point of me buying nice clothes for you if you will not wear them?"

"Sorry, I just didn't feel like dressing up tonight." I try turning around, but Gerard is keeping me caged, breathing heavily and groping me. He pulls at my pants.

"Gerard stop it, not now. Let's have dinner first," I suggest, pulling my pants back up. His increasing strength is making me nervous. Something is off. Nice one minute and now this. I keep holding onto my pants. "Gerard," I snap.

"I need a fuck, Paige. You've been holding out on me for three weeks now. Jesus!" He lets go of me and steps back. When I turn, he's shaking his head at me, his lips puckered. "Why not?"

I sigh, feeling genuinely bad for betraying him but an excuse just falls right on out of me. "I felt violated that night with Oliver. Why did you do that to me?" I say in a quiet voice, not wanting things to escalate.

"You just said you forgave me. Besides you betrayed me first, and are you forgetting it's an 'eye for an eye' sort of thing now?" he says, reminding me of the cliché he mentioned weeks ago.

"What do you mean?"

"How was Alex today?"

"What?" I suck in my breath as if he's slapped me. "I don't know, just like I didn't know last week when you asked." It takes all my effort to not let my face flush.

"Oh, I just thought he might have dropped by to do some gardening by now," he says, clearly lying through his teeth because I now know he fired Alex.

I move around the kitchen counter to get a pot of water

on to boil, trying to put some distance between us. He's playing games. He knows something.

"Gerard, why do you keep saying an eye for an eye?"

"Just forget it. It's obvious you haven't forgiven me. Maybe I made a mistake forgiving you," Gerard mumbles, walking off toward the stairs.

When Gerard returns twenty minutes later, his cologne is the first thing I notice. Looking up from the pot of meat sauce I'm stirring, I'm surprised to find him dressed in jeans and a lightweight blue sweater. He moves straight over to the side table just inside the living room and picks up his keys. Not slowing his brisk pace through the room, he heads straight for the French doors.

"Where are you going? I'm just about to dish up dinner." I move around the counter, one hand supporting me because I suddenly feel woozy.

"Out." He pulls open the door and leaves. I dash after him catching him just as he reaches the garage.

"Gerard." I snatch hold of his sweater, halting him. "Where are you going?"

"Let me go, Paige," he replies in a calm voice, not facing me. My hand falls away.

"But where are you going? I have dinner ready. Look, I'm sorry." I place a hand on the rear of his car as if I'm capable of holding it there.

He pauses for a moment at his open door. "It's clear things are fucked up between us, Paige. I'm going out because I don't want to be around you."

"Gerard, no. Please don't leave. I'm sorry. I didn't mean no. I just meant later." I wring my hands, terrified he knows something, and he will do something to Alex.

Slowly, he turns to face me. He shakes his head as though exasperated. "I don't know how to make you happy anymore, Paige."

I can't answer him. I don't know what to say. When no response comes from me, he turns and gets in his car.

Gerard pulls the vehicle out of the garage so quickly, I'm forced to jump out of the way. In shock, I stay outside, watching until the car's taillights disappear. Then I run inside to find my phone.

17

EVERYTHING I EVER WANTED

It's around two in the morning, and I can't sleep. Every time I close my eyes it feels like I'm standing in a swamp in the pitch-black hearing my pleas that came out as whispers against a protective chest.

'Please. Don't go. I need you to stay. What if Carlos comes back?'

In the living room, I'm sitting curled up in the oversized armchair, tracing the printed wording that covers the fabric. It looks like a newspaper print, and I'm forcing myself to wonder who ever thought to decorate a chair in century-old style headlines and paragraphs instead of letting the ghosts of my past creep in. But the house is deathly silent. The only sound that penetrates my reverie is the occasional dog barking outside and then the drip coming from the laundry tap that's echoing down the hall. Its methodical tempo is making me drowsy.

Gerard has my phone. He must have grabbed it before he left for a shower and I didn't notice until I went looking for it. I wanted to warn Alex. And now, Gerard still isn't home, and every time I close my eyes, anxiety sends my mind spinning.

Desperate for sleep, my lids struggle again to the cadence dripping. *'I've loved you for such a long time, but you know that don't you? I've always loved you, but can I trust you with my love?'* The words jerk me when the ghost of a hand cups my chin. *'Make sure you cover your teeth with your lips.'* In my half-asleep state, I swipe at my chin and neck, moaning and shaking my head, trying to rid a memory that wants to surface, but it's insistent.

'My God, you're such a sweet and precious girl. Men really like this. Oh God yes, just like that. No. No, you're not a girl, with a mouth like that, you're a goddess.'

My eyes shoot open when I experience the ghost of a hand caressing my hair. My heart and head begin to thump in unison, making me groan. I sink my palms into my eye sockets and pull my legs tighter beneath me. Go away, I don't want to remember that stuff. But I have no choice. It's as if Gerard's disappearance is a trigger, allowing memories to saturate my already spongy mind.

Carlos had seen us. I bobbed down in the car, but it was too late. Then Sheree's dad slowed the car. I felt sick because I knew I was getting Sheree's dad in trouble, and I was afraid of what Carlos would do to him.

"What are you doing, please don't stop the car?" I begged.

"It's all right. I'll talk to Carlos. It wasn't your fault those boys attacked you." Sheree's dad said. I sat back up so I could look out the back window, watched as Carlos pulled up behind us. Then they were talking. Carlos came back with Sheree's dad and opened my door.

"Come on, kid. Get out the car, I'll take you home. Just need to give Richard here a talking to first. Looks a bit suspicious him and you, don't you think?" he said, confirming all my fears.

Sheree's dad nodded when he got back in the car, reassuring me I'd be okay. But he didn't know how violent Carlos was, how mean and hurtful he could be. Reluctantly, I did as I was told, walked back and got into Carlos's car while he stayed to talk to Sheree's dad, leaning in through the passenger window. I picked at my fingernails waiting, wondering what Carlos was saying and whether Sheree's dad would keep quiet about Peter and his friends. I looked down at Sheree's Broncos sweater, knowing I should have given it back, used it as an excuse to defend Sheree's dad because he had done nothing wrong. But I didn't.

When we got home, my mom looked me up and down. "What the fuck happened to you?" Then she looked past me. "Where are me drinks, Carlos?" I shrugged her pretentious hand off my shoulder, hating the sensation.

"Nothing," I snapped, annoyed because alcohol was the only thing she really cared about.

"Sure as shit don't look like nothin'."

Carlos came up from behind, giving his version of the event he wasn't even a witness to. Twisting it so it sounded like I was asking for it. I pushed past my mother to have a shower and put some clean clothes on.

"I suppose your school shirt is ruined. You shouldn't have been at that stinking dump park, anyway. What did you expect to happen hanging around those filthy Roderick kids?" she droned on, following me down the hall until I slammed the bathroom door, wedging a chair under the knob so Carlos couldn't barge in. When I came out, she had changed her clothes and her tune.

"Let's eat out tonight," Mom said excitedly. "We've got things to celebrate," she said.

Then we are all in the car. Carlos was driving, but he was swerving, making my mom laugh because they'd both been drinking. I was shivering in the back because not only was I scared but shock had set in. I should have stayed home. My lip felt sore, and I had a massive headache. Closing my eyes against the throbbing, I let my head fall back, drowning out their laughter. By the time I realized we'd been driving too long to be going to the steakhouse on the edge of town, it was too late. We'd pulled up outside the rental lake house, and it only took me a split second to understand why. Looking around, the fifteen-year-old girl I was, understood it all too clearly. There was not a soul around—who would hear my screams.

I jar to attention when the door slams shut, announcing Gerard's return. He grumbles incoherently and drops his keys. I get to my feet, flinching as my cramped knees protest.

"Gerard?" I call out, heading toward the kitchen. We meet in the hall. He is sneering at me. Swaying and clearly drunk. Then he waggles his finger at me.

"You are here to be my wife," he slurs.

"I know, and you're right. I'm sorry for taking you for granted." I take a step toward him, my hands reaching for his chest, hoping to sedate him.

"Where have you been?"

Gerard smirks. "Let's just say I've been taking care of unfinished business shall we." He humors himself with a chuckle.

Alex flashes through my mind, and I feel myself pale. Gerard wobbles. I reach out to steady him, and he seizes the opportunity to wrap his arm around my shoulder and turn me toward the stairs.

With some effort, I get him up to our bedroom as he rants half incoherently about having a superb time. That there were lots of mature women out there who love the fact he is a successful lawyer. Then he's questioning why he settled on someone so stupid and immature as me.

"They were throwing themselves at me," he taunts. "Not like you. You've turned into a sour bitch who's forgotten her place."

I try to let his hurtful words roll off me but the more he speaks, his tone becoming more menacing, the deeper it cuts. I don't doubt he's telling the truth. Women are always admiring him. And I'm a cheater.

Inside our bedroom, Gerard stands still as I help him get undressed. Opening his shirt one button at a time, I feel his eyes burning into my skull. When I look up, he is smirking.

"Now this—is more like it." He brings up an unsteady hand to smooth my hair. "My beautiful, young, adventurous wife. What are you doing to me?" he says, contradicting himself. "There were so many things I wanted to do with you. He reaches for his crotch, grabs hold, then growls in my face before lurching backward so violently, I'm forced to grab him under the armpits to stop him from falling.

"I was planning on taking you to Dubai. On a shopping spree, but you blew that didn't you? Silly, stupid girl." Gerard taps my nose with his finger playfully but he's anything but funny.

"Sit down, Gerard, you're going to fall."

Steadying himself, he reaches for his belt buckle. I take a step back, allowing him to finish off undressing, but as soon as I turn my back on him, wanting to get ready for bed myself, he grabs me.

"Uh-uh, I need help." He digs his fingers deep into my soft underarm, and when I meet his gaze, his lids are hooded, and his mouth drawn tight.

"Ow, you're hurting, Gerard. Let go." I try twisting my arm out of his grip, but he digs in deeper.

"Undress me. I want you to look after me. I damn well looked after you."

His breath is so ripe from alcohol, I can't help but recoil and my heart starts banging in my chest, causing a surge of blood that makes me dizzy. Somehow, I manage to resume the task of undressing him, peeling off his shirt and tossing it on the chair. He whips out his belt, but when I try to take it from him, he hangs on tightly. Our eyes connect, and he smiles wickedly.

"I might need this. Keep going," he instructs.

With shaking fingers, I unbutton his pants and unzip his fly. He pushes my hair back over my shoulders and runs his fingertips along my collarbone. And as his pants fall to the floor, there's a thud as he lets go of his belt. I almost allow myself to sigh in relief, but then he reaches up to wrap a hand around my throat and regards my lips, his fingers tightening, making it difficult to breathe. His gaze meanders from my mouth onto my eyes. Searching. And even though I'm close to tears, he smiles.

"Touch me," he says through clenched teeth, squeezing my throat a little tighter.

Lips trembling, I cup his package still covered by his boxers while a sob gets caught in my restricted throat. Gerard closes his eyelids and lets his head fall back with a sigh. His hand slackens slightly but he doesn't let go.

Petrified what he might do if I don't comply, I massage him gently, watching the delight of my touch relax his face until his free hand pushes with urgency on his underwear and his face contorts as he tries to set himself free.

Knowing it will work to my advantage, I take hold of the fabric with both hands and draw his boxers down, then take hold of him again, massaging him everywhere. He relaxes his grip and lets his hand slide to rest on my collarbone, finally allowing me to take a full breath. For a moment, Gerard revels in my caress, his eyes still closed, seemingly enjoying the attention. I turn my head, distracted for a moment then from nowhere he slaps my face.

Gasping, my hand flies to the rescue to cover my face as the sting radiates across my left cheek.

"Don't you ever fucking refuse me again." The chill in his voice freezes the lump of shock in my throat.

I'm so stunned, it takes a moment before the tears brim, then spill over. Then I am sobbing.

Gerard ignores me. Grabbing me roughly, he shakes me until I'm no longer rigid then pushes on my shoulders, forcing me to my knees.

"You know what to do." He grabs a hold of my loose hair, balling it into his fist making me yelp.

"Gerard. Stop. Let go you're hurting me."

He pulls tighter, forcing my face closer to his erection. "Well, you hurt me first, and you just keep hurting me."

He smells dank and musky and something more. He's been with someone, I'm certain of it. With both hands, even though I can feel my follicles ripping from my scalp, I push on his thighs.

"Please, Gerard, stop. You're drunk." I sob, relaxing from the fight knowing I can't win. "Just let me go and I'll do what you want. You're hurting me, Gerard," I plea, slumping on the floor. "Have you been with someone else, are you trying to humiliate me?" I sob at his knees.

Gerard shoves me as he lets go of my hair then marches off to the bathroom. My fingers massage my scalp before I'm getting to my feet, and I hear the tap turn on. I don't even have time to think about what to do next when he is back in the room, his proud hard-on leading the way and smelling of soap. I feel sick from the confirmation he cheated on me. Is this how he felt? I have no right judging him, but somehow, his infidelity seems worse. He's done it to punish me for rejecting him. But how can I not reject him when he's no longer in my heart? My head is thumping, and I have the strongest urge for alcohol and a cigarette.

"Come here," Gerard demands, sitting on the edge of the bed and stroking his penis. "And take off those awful clothes. I want you naked and kneeling in front of me. Just the way I like women to be." Then his eyes dart to his belt lying on the floor.

18

APOLOGIZE

When I open the French doors to outside, there's a slight dew on the lawn and the trees, now bare of leaves, are dark from moisture. It must have rained last night.

I look at the cigarette in my hand. I knew there'd come a day when I'd need one.

Stepping out into the early dawn, I pull my fleece robe around myself then sit on the steps then stand again. It's too uncomfortable. I strike the match and inhale the first drag deeply. It causes me to cough and my head to swim.

Something is wrong with me. I'm damaged, and I need help. I bite at my fingernails then catch myself. Tucking my hand under an armpit to get it out the way, I take another hit of nicotine, listening intently for Gerard's footsteps upstairs, though I doubt I'll hear them, anyway.

Was it my fault? My fault Gerard became aggressive. After last night's abuse, I'm confused as to whether I need to get away from him or that maybe I deserved it. I haven't exactly been the best wife. Taking another drag, I rub my backside, feeling the welts Gerard's belt left behind. Rolling my aching shoulders, I try to push back the sting of tears. I failed him as a wife, just like my mother failed my father.

In my head, the psychiatrist is babbling in the background somewhere behind my own thoughts. "Could you have been a better daughter?" she said. The ground beneath me swirls, and I go to sit again then think better of it, instead, I reach for the boards of the house to steady myself.

No, she should have been a better mother, but I never told the psychiatrist why. I couldn't speak of the tens of times I watched my mother sway and rant incoherently from the doorway of my bedroom while I tried to do my homework. Or the times I panicked when she'd fall face first into the wall before sliding down and sleeping on the gritty, mite-infested carpet all night.

I inhale more smoke deep into my lungs, then blow it out and study the yard. Daylight is just breaking. I catch a glimpse of a cat, which could be Delilah's friend's, as it sprints across the yard then leaps the fence and is gone.

Tired and needing sleep, I extinguish the half-smoked cigarette, stuff it beneath the soil of a potted plant, then go inside.

I find my handbag. Pop a mint in my mouth and spray myself with perfume. Then I'm meandering in an exhausted daze through to the hall. I look from the stairs to the closed double doors of the living room then back again, trying to decide which option to take.

"I could smell that disgusting cigarette in my fucking sleep, Paige," Gerard growls, on his way down the stairs. I feel the blood literally drain from my face and pool in my gut. I stand in fear-locked silence as though he is a ghost as he makes his way past me and into the dining area. "Don't just stand there, I need breakfast," he demands. But I can't seem to move.

"Paige," he yells from the kitchen.

"I'm coming."

"So's fucking Christmas. Now get in here. Please."

When I enter the room, Gerard is at the coffee machine changing the filter. "Why were you up so early?" he asks when I sidle up to him and take over making the coffee, pulling a new filter out of the plastic bag, then taking the used one off his hands.

"I—well—last night was all a bit…"

Gerard's eyes narrow, causing his brow to furrow deeply.

"I just couldn't sleep. I've been thinking about my mother and her funeral," I answer in a level tone I don't feel, thinking it's better not to stir up last night's horror. I toss the filter away, then close the cupboard door on the bin gently and avoid eye contact.

He reaches up, pulls his mug from the cupboard and places it on the countertop, then leans back, watching me. I get my own mug down and press some buttons on the machine to make it start.

Gerard folds his arms over his chest. "Why are you suddenly smoking? You know I don't like it."

"I'm sorry, I'll throw them away. It's just with my mom dying and the thought of not going back to Ponderosa…"

"I don't want your excuses, just throw them out," he cuts me off then reaches for my face. I flinch when he makes contact. Narrowing his eyes, he turns my face slightly, checking out his handiwork. "There's not much to see, but I suggest you cover that up if you go out today." He's referring to the slight blemish his slap last night left behind. "I'm sorry I hit you. I was drunk." He searches my eyes then releases his grip. "I don't consider myself an abusive man, but I feel you pushed me last night."

My mouth wants to fall open and my eyes to go wide, but I hold my passive expression. I pushed you? Not an abusive man? You're a manipulative asshole! The accusation reverberates inside my head causing stabbing pain. Moving away, Gerard heads for the French doors, presumably for the morning paper that I neglected to pick up earlier because he says I'm getting lazy in caring for him.

"I remember not so long ago you were standing right there offering me the paper every morning with a loving smile on your face. Where did my beautiful wife go? So sad and so disappointing and after everything I've done," he huffs.

Where did I go? Because the old me loved him so much, and I was happy. He was kind, and we laughed, and he was… was… everything to me. Literally. I put him above everyone and everything including myself. That is—until Alex.

"I'm sorry. Can I make you a nice breakfast? Do you have time?" I bend to get the frying pan out and dry heave. Luckily, my stomach is empty. I feel so nauseous the action would have caused me to puke on the floor.

"I need to leave for work early. Toast will do." He takes a seat at the island bench in front of me, pushing pots and plates I never got to use last night aside, and spreading out his paper. My hands are shaking as I get the loaf of bread and find the spread he likes.

"I think I enjoyed seeing Jolene the other day. I guess I should thank you for that."

My head snaps up.

"What are you jealous?" he says smugly over his paper.

"No," I reply. Turning away, I put in toast and pull a face. Ah a new angle, so I'll do whatever he asks? I can't help visibly shaking my head.

"You're not? Because you should be. She's a stunning woman."

If Alex hadn't shown me the real Jolene, I think I may have just fallen for that. Nevertheless, I play into his game.

"Well maybe a bit." I turn back around and face him, then lean against the bench and cross my arms, watching him as he pretends to read, while I wait for his toast.

Every cell in me is vibrating. All these years, Gerard has hidden this side of himself, and now, he's bringing out all his ammunition. Hanging my head, I stare at the floor, feeling the defeat wash over me. I'm at his mercy until I can figure out what to do.

"I'd like to invite them for dinner next time. Reacquaint ourselves, I think," Gerard continues. "I'm going to plan it for next week when you get back."

The toast and my head pop up together.

"When I get back?"

"Your mother's funeral, don't you want to go?"

"I do. But last night—I thought—well, I thought you didn't want me to acknowledge it."

Engrossed in his paper, Gerard pauses for far too long for me to realise he's antagonizing me deliberately.

"Gerard?" I prompt, removing the toast from the appliance.

"I didn't say you couldn't go. What sort of man am I to deny you that? I said, I wasn't going to *pay* for it. Give me your phone please."

"What, why?" I question, spreading the toast.

"I'd just like to see your phone."

"I don't know where it is. I thought—you must have taken it last night," I say, turning to frown at him.

"Why would I take it? It's most likely in the office." He folds his paper in preparation for eating and when he puts it down, he huffs out, "Ah, here it is," when he conveniently spots my phone next to the fruit bowl.

It—was not there last night.

"Why have you started locking it?" he asks, handing it to me.

"Because after the burglary I figured if anyone stole it, it would make it more difficult for them. Why—do you suddenly care?"

"Don't get smart with me, just unlock it." Gerard holds out his hand.

Knowing he might do this I had smartly deleted all my recent unanswered calls to Alex, and changed the name associated with his number to Donnie Work. I'm hoping he doesn't recognize it at a glance. I hand him his toast and my unlocked phone.

"I'm not trying to be smart, I just don't understand what you'd be looking for?" I pour coffee then hand him a mug.

"I want to know I can trust you before you go away." He scrolls as he eats his toast. "Who is Tyler?"

"A girl I met at the hospital when Annabel and I went to get photos taken for the paper. I told her I was a photographer also, we exchanged numbers."

He continues looking at my phone still munching on toast, seemingly engrossed in—I don't know what because there's hardly anything on there. After some time, while I wipe countertops that don't need wiping, Gerard seems satisfied. He hands back my phone which I plug in, before leaning against the bench to watch him eat.

"I don't want you staying at Sheree's," he says, brushing crumbs off his suit pants looking positively collected, making me question why he doesn't seem to be suffering a massive hangover. If anything, I look worse than him. Maybe he wasn't as drunk as he let on.

"I will book you in at the Caledonian Hotel. I understand Sheree will most likely turn up to the funeral, but I'd prefer it if you had as little to do with her as possible, and I hope while you've been sneaking around behind my back you've been sensible enough not to discuss our marital affairs with her. You shouldn't burden people with your own problems.

They've usually got enough of their own." Gerard takes a sip of his coffee, glances at his watch, and then looks straight at me.

"Are we agreed?"

"Yes."

"And how much will this gallivanting around cost?"

I push myself off the bench and rinse the dishcloth as if it needs it, deciding whether it's safer to tell the truth or lie. I've never had to justify my spending to Gerard before.

"I feel bad, it's actually quite a lot really," I opt for the truth.

"What's a lot?"

"Including my flights and rental car it was almost five thousand dollars."

To my relief Gerard nods. "Well, so long as you have that in your savings, you'll be fine."

My stomach twists. "Well no, I don't. I put it all on my credit card." I put the dishcloth down. "I thought when you said…"

Gerard pulls a condescending smirk. "I'm just messing with you. I'll check your credit card balance and make sure there's enough to cover the expenses, all right? Now give me a kiss and I better get going. Whatever you have planned today, put it off. I would rather you clean the house properly. Seems to be getting ahead of you doesn't it?" Getting up, he grabs his keys then picks up his briefcase.

I shoot a thousand imaginary daggers at his back as he walks away, but when he turns, looking for my response, I pull a tight smile and nod. "I know, and I'm sorry. I'll take your suits into town today for dry cleaning too. I'll get on top of things, I promise."

Gerard grabs my upper arm to pull me in for a kiss but stops short of connecting our lips. "Good, because I'd like my wife back. Last night was regrettable but necessary I think."

He arches his brows, silently challenging me before giving me a quick peck on the cheek.

Is he serious? Last night was necessary?

He lets me go and I follow him as he heads toward the door.

"Gerard, at the expense of sounding spoiled, can I look for a new computer when I'm in town today. I need it for work and I really don't think the police are going to recover mine."

He pulls the door open before turning to face me. "Well that might need to wait. I think five thousand a month spending is more than generous of me, isn't it? And this month it seems your mother's funeral is what you've chosen to spend it on. Next month." He leans forward and kisses me again. "I love you." He looks at me expectantly. I return the sentiment with a tight smile.

Gerard cocks his head and frowns. "Umm, a thank you would be nice."

Holy crap, what the fuck is happening here?

With a racing heart, sweaty palms, and a sickening, killer headache, I still manage to respond to his wishes and thank him. I feel like running and screaming from the house. Tears are right there, almost choking me to death. Who is this fucking man?

As soon as he's out of sight, I begin pacing the kitchen, thinking over all the things that need doing and the control I finally realize Gerard has over me. I'm one of those women. The ones who are stuck in a controlled relationship. He owns everything. The car, the house, the furniture... would he even allow me to leave with my clothes, my jewelry. I need to calm down. Don't blow this out of proportion. Next month, I'll get a new computer, contact more publishing houses. Save every cent. I could start selling things. Things he wouldn't notice. I stop pacing and cover my face with my hands. Who am I kidding? Gerard notices everything. I want to run away. I need to run away. But then I start second-guessing myself because he has every right to be angry at me. I've done this to us. I'm the one who cheated first, denied him things that could have saved our marriage. I owe him. Don't I?

I let my anxiety drive me as I attack the housework. I want to call Alex, I want him to take me away from this mess, but I don't go anywhere near my phone. I can't drag him or anyone else into the mess I've made. I can't keep doing that to Alex. Then I'm remembering what Gerard said last night. That he was taking care of unfinished business. Was he referring to Alex?

The house gets tidied up and the laundry gets done. I drop suits to the dry cleaners and fill my car with gasoline. I know by the look of the freshly mowed lawn when I return, that Gerard must have arranged a mowing service to stop by. The pool will now need skimming.

Distressed, I become irrational and take to the windows with a cloth and spray, trying desperately to not allow my thoughts to wander back to my mother and Ponderosa Park or Gerard and his control. My only reprieve from stressful thoughts are when I think of Alex, but that only makes me teary. I'm understanding now how naïve it was of me to think that cheating on Gerard wouldn't have consequences.

I busy myself with cooking food for Gerard while I'm away. I clean out the fridge and the cupboards, then pack for my intended trip. I keep picking up my phone to talk or text Alex, but I don't. Then I am kicking myself because I didn't. I become more agitated and nervous as the day draws to a close and Gerard's return is impending, as I haven't off-loaded my concerns or straightened the crazy thoughts in my head.

It's only when I'm done folding the laundry and putting it

away that I notice Gerard's small suitcase is missing. A quick check concludes that at least two of his suits are missing along with his favorite pair of casual shoes. Opening drawers, I look for more evidence, then sit down on our bed and stare around the room bewildered. Where would he go, and when did he take his suitcase? Was it this morning when I was outside, or has it be missing for some time and I've never noticed before?

I almost trip on my way down the stairs to get to my phone. Scrolling through recent calls, I connect with his office. Reception answers almost immediately.

"Morgan and Cartwright, this is Maureen, how may I help you?"

"Maureen, it's Paige, is Gerard there?" I don't bother with any pleasantries and I hear in Maureen's response she's a little put off by my rudeness and her reply comes painfully slow.

"Hello, Paige, how are you?"

"Fine. Is Gerard there?"

"No. He left mid-morning."

"Left! Where to?" I'm flustered that I don't even know my own husband's movements.

"Oh," she pauses, and I get the feeling she is wondering whether to divulge any more information. "He flew out to San Diego with Mr. Goodricke," she states confidently when she registers my impatient sigh. She's referring to Carter. I suspect they've gone on a business trip but why didn't he tell me he was going away though?

I ask when he is expected back, and I can imagine the smirk on Maureen's face that again, I don't seem to know about Gerard's schedule.

"Sunday, I imagine, although I can't be certain. Perhaps he and Mr. Goodricke will take time out to enjoy the sights."

I don't appreciate her smugness when I'm feeling so

vulnerable. The tone in her voice is making me paranoid because for a moment I wonder whether Gerard had spoken intimately to anyone in his office about us and news has spread. I abolish the notion straightaway. Gerard is a private man and would never discuss his sex life with work colleagues. But then I think of Jamison and cringe. Maybe it was Maureen he was with last night, or Issy? I let out an unchecked groan.

"Paige?"

"Thank you, Maureen. I'll try him on his cell." I end the conversation with a brusque goodbye.

Recent calls reveal Gerard's number and I press call. Shifting my weight from one foot to the other and picking flint off the lamp by the window, I wait anxiously for Gerard to answer. I imagine he would have long since arrived at his destination so when he finally answers after many long rings, I'm startled when his voice booms out my phone.

"What is it?"

My heart hammers in my chest and my palms get sweaty. I hadn't expected him to be so rude. Surely, he noticed it was me calling.

"Gerard it's me, Paige."

"I know who it is. What do you want? I'm in a business meeting."

I hear chatter in the background, and it sounds more like he's in a club rather than an office room. I press on nervously even though I feel he's lying.

"I'm sorry, I was just curious because I noticed your suitcase is missing. I didn't know you were going away."

"Well there's no need for me to hang around, when you're not going to be home. Is there?"

"But why didn't you say anything this morning and where are you?"

"I didn't realize I had to answer to you, but if you must

know, I'm with Carter. We're poaching for clients in San Diego. We arranged it days ago."

"And you didn't think to tell me?"

"I didn't think it mattered to you one way or the other. Now if there's nothing else, I need to go."

"Gerard why are you being like this?"

"Like what?" he says, sounding obtuse.

There's silence while I think of the right thing to say.

"You know like what. I'm freaking out here, Gerard. With what happened last night and you not telling me things, I just don't know how much more I can take."

"How much more *you* can take. Is that some sort of patronizing joke? Look, Paige, I haven't got time for this right now. I thought we settled things this morning," he says, in a hushed, firm tone then disconnects without saying goodbye.

I think I'm going crazy. Gerard keeps giving me mixed messages, and I'm wondering whether to take a drive around to Annabel's just to talk to someone about it. Just then, my phone lets out a ping and I see a message from an unrecognized number.

New message: Booked that flight yet?

Me: Who is this?

Me: Are you there?

New message: Alex, just checking you booked your tickets.

Tickets? Plural. I'm suspicious that it's Gerard pretending to be Alex on someone else's phone and blocking the number.

I type, 'How do you know about that?' Then delete it. What do I say? I walk around the kitchen staring at my phone until it times out and goes blank.

When in doubt, don't say anything. I place my phone

gingerly down like it's a delicate object. Then I get on with packing for my trip.

I've been sitting on the couch in my black jumpsuit with my heart racing for the last three hours. Just staring at the muted TV screen. I had every intention of slipping into something comfortable after my shower and relaxing but when my fingers trailed along my clothes hanging in my closet, Alex's voice came back to haunt me. His compliment on how stunning I look in the jumpsuit and how he'd never share me with another man and that he'd rather let me go. I don't want him to let me go. I don't think *I* can let him go.

I threw on the jumpsuit just to feel close to him, but then I began fantasizing about going to the beach house and my heart began racing. I've been staring into space since, reliving every moment with Alex. From the moment I first met him to just the other day. Like a movie on loop inside my mind. I feel a combination of desire and anxiety. I desperately want to see him, but my instincts are telling me things will explode, that I'm being impulsive and reckless. But the larger part of me just can't help myself. It's only when I'm around Alex, that I feel truly safe.

Alex has become a drug, and I'm getting increasingly desperate for my fix. Gerard's away, he will never know, and one full night alone with Alex is just too tempting. I can't *not* go see Alex tonight and I become driven no matter what the cost.

After slipping on my gold octopus necklace, I grab my suitcase and everything I need, hoping I can spend the night. To be held in his arms. Drink in his smell. Listen to his voice. I suddenly want to know everything about him. What his favorite color is, his birth date, what he was like growing up.

I need to know him. Soon I'm speeding down the freeway going over everything I want—no make that, what I need to know. What's his favorite food? Has he ever left the country? Did he have a nickname growing up? What happened to his father? Does he want to be a father?

Every question gives birth to another surge of butterflies and at times I'm smiling—I even spill a giggle. But the closer I get to the beach house, the more nervous I become. There is a steady stream of headlights coming at me, bedazzling and illuminating the interior of the Lexus and when I'm almost there, it begins to rain.

Large intermittent splatters that seem to insist I regain my senses. Raindrops that remind me of the day I slipped into Gerard's car, so many years ago, and for a moment my foot eases off the accelerator. What am I doing?

Alex doesn't want anything serious, he told me that himself. It will only ever be just sex. A fling. An affair. Then Gerard's words are haunting me. "He will break your goddamn heart the first chance he gets and leave you with nothing."

Car horns blast as irate drivers speed around me, water splashing over my windshield in their wake. I'm only a few miles away from Alex's place when I realize, this could be the biggest mistake I ever make. I need to pull over. I need to be responsible. Get a grip on reality.

I pull over into the next available wayside with the intention of turning around, gripping the steering wheel, regretting my decision but knowing it's for the best.

Just as I flick the indicator on to make a U-turn, my cell phone rings inside my bag, scaring the crap out of me. Ignoring the phone, I wait for a break in the traffic and the wailing ringtone to end. Just as my heart calm downs, rain starts pelting down harder. I'm relieved I'm now off the road. Vehicles start slowing to manage the onslaught, and every second I wait, I'm expecting an accident to occur. I turn the wipers on high and stare out into the wet night, then reach inside my bag for the phone to see if a message was left. It comes to life again, ringing in my hand and without thinking I swipe and answer it. Shit! It could be Gerard. He'll hear the rain and question where I am.

"Paige. What the fuck are you doing?" Alex's voice comes to life through the phone.

"Why, what do you mean?" I ask, confused.

"What are you doing pulled up on the side of the road? We just went past. I was calling. Why didn't you pick up? Are you all right?"

Ridiculously I glance out to see if I can spot Alex, as though he's somewhere out there in the rain and watching me.

"Where are you?"

"At home now. What are you doing?"

"I—I was coming to see you."

"Why, where's Gerard?"

"He's gone out of town and I thought maybe... I don't know." I let out a sigh. "I was just thinking maybe I could come around and spend the night before I go away."

"So why are you pulled over then?"

"Because I changed my mind." I switch the phone to my other ear and fiddle with my necklace. "I mean, you probably already have plans, and... I shouldn't be doing this anyway."

There is a long pause, then he clears his throat.

"I'm with a friend actually. We're going out clubbing later. We were just going to eat first."

"On a Tuesday?"

"Yeah. Why not?"

"No, it's fine. I guess. Anyway, I fly out tomorrow morning so I probably shouldn't be out anyway. Bye, Alex."

"No, don't go," Alex rushes out. "Have some dinner—

come out with us. You may as well live a little. It's not like Gerard stays home knitting fucking sweaters when you go away." My chuckle gives way to silence.

Alex waits patiently.

"Are you sure?"

"Yes, Paige. I'm abso-fucking-lutely positive."

"All right then. I'll be there in a few minutes."

19

LOVE IS A BITCH

I'm still having second thoughts when I pull up alongside our seaside house, but even through the wet air and windshield, I can smell cooking. It reminds me I haven't eaten since I don't know when, which may explain the wicked headache I'm experiencing, and the thought of eating is overwhelming. I can't not go in now. Already my mouth is salivating.

Stalling, I chew on my nails and wait for the torrential downpour to break. With high heels and folds of fabric around my ankles, it's a guarantee I'll fall flat on my face the moment I get out the car. Why didn't I just wear jeans and practical shoes? I feel ridiculously overdressed now. I shouldn't even be here. Reaching for the ignition, I'm about to press, when in a flash, Alex is at my car door with an umbrella.

"Hey." He squats in the open doorway, the shield held high. "Are you all right?"

"To be honest, I don't really know."

"What's happened?"

An eye roll, a head shake, and the exasperated sigh that

follows, tells him I really don't want to talk about it. Alex gives my thigh a squeeze.

"Umm, a heads-up about the friend I have here tonight," he says.

Surprisingly, the lump in my throat that developed the minute I pulled up doesn't choke me up and I can still speak.

"Okay."

"It's someone I've seen casually. Like in the past. When I first got out of prison. I've known her for a long time. There's nothing going on with us right now. But I just wanted to be upfront. She's nice. You'll like her."

"No. I'll just go. I really don't think I can handle seeing a girlfriend of yours. When you said you had a friend, I thought you might have meant Tony. Is—it—Brontë?"

Alex smiles.

"No, it's not Brontë. Her name is Rebecca."

I feel so stupid and childish. I'm a married woman. Alex is a free man. I'm stressing over conflicted emotions. This is just not fair, and I don't know why I'm putting either of us through the torture.

Alex stands. "Look it's up to you, but you're cool to stay."

"I'll just dampen the mood with your date."

'It's not a date, Paige. Rebecca is meeting a friend at a club later, but she didn't want to turn up alone. Come on, she's cooking a meal. Stay. You can come out with us afterward."

"Do you honestly want me here?"

"I wouldn't have asked if I didn't. Come on." Alex holds out his hand.

The clouds decide it's time to erupt again, so I don't even give myself a chance to think. Instead, I reach for Alex's hand and we run through the rain—the umbrella doing a pathetic job of sheltering us against the fierce wind.

As soon as Alex opens the door, I'm enveloped in the warm atmosphere. Soft music is playing, and the smell of something spicy is divine. Kicking off my heels, I wait as Alex shakes then closes the umbrella and sets it against the entrance wall. Smiling, he reaches for my hand then leads me through into the open space.

Alex's friend is in the kitchen, and like he'd said, cooking. She has straight shoulder-length hair and a bohemian style about her. She's petite and pretty in an elfin way.

"Hi there. It's Paige, right? I'm Bec." Rebecca calls out warmly, dimples denting her cheeks.

I manage a shy smile and a quick wave.

"Sit," Alex instructs, moving some books and a jacket off the couch. "Wine?" he asks. I give him a nod and gaze about the apartment that is still littered with packed boxes and building supplies. Alex, or maybe it was Rebecca, seems to have brought some order, because some of what was strewn around the other day is now neatly lined against one wall. There is also an overnight bag next to what I'm assuming are Rebecca's boots. Looks like someone else planned on staying the night. I reach for my necklace, trying to distract myself and avoid blushing.

Alex slips in close beside Rebecca to grab a wine glass from the overhead cupboards, causing my stomach to knot. It's painfully obvious they've had a romantic connection, and Gerard's warning screams at me even louder. Hovering over Rebecca, Alex presses himself against her. She laughs at something he says then nudges him backward.

"Just pour Paige a wine, you manwhore." She laughs softly then looks at me. "Get this man away from me, Paige. I'm trying to cook."

I smile at her even though my insides are twisting.

Alex shakes his head and winks at me. And at the island bench, he pours me a wine.

"Rebecca's a chef at the Clubhouse restaurant up the road," Alex says.

"Oh, wow."

Rebecca flicks a look in my direction. "I love cooking. My grandmother taught me when I was a kid, haven't stopped since." She shows off her dimples again then reaches for some spices from off the rack. The way she bustles about, it's obvious she's used the new kitchen before. Truth be told, she's most likely the one who set it up.

"How long have you worked there?" I ask, giving Alex an involuntary grimace before taking the wine he offers me.

"I'm going to take a shower before you dish up, Rebecca," Alex interjects squeezing my shoulder.

"Stop calling me Rebecca."

"Well, it's your name." Alex picks up some stray clothing that's lying around.

"And you know I've hated it since we were kids."

"Kids? Have you known each other that long?" I ask, taking a sip of wine.

"We went to high school together in Portland. She followed me to LA when I left."

"I did not," Rebecca says, throwing a tea towel over the counter and in his direction. "I followed Tyler, not you, you loser." The towel only makes it half the distance on its attempted journey to assault Alex. He scoops to pick it up.

"Yeah, well that was an epic fail. He was running from you." Alex chuckles.

"Shut up. Go and have a shower, will you?" Rebecca says, trying to look serious but stifling a laugh.

"I told her he was gay, but she wouldn't believe me. Girls and rose goggles, they're all around me," Alex says in a low tone and grinning. Rebecca still hears him because she shakes her head and sighs.

"I'll spike your food in a minute." She gives him the evil eye and points toward the bathroom. "Go. Shower. Now."

I listen on silently to their bantering until the room falls silent. Alex winks at me again then leaves to take a shower, his arms ladened with the garments he collect from around the room.

"Sorry, Paige. I've been working there about eighteen months now," Rebecca says, answering my earlier question. "Straight after I got back from traveling. From Greece actually. Have you been overseas?" She taps a utensil against the pot, then replaces the lid. "I hope you like curry."

I nod enthusiastically because right now I'm so hungry, I'd devour an old leather shoe.

"I've only left the States once," I say, still fidgeting with my necklace with my spare hand. I take a sip of wine.

"Really?" She pulls a face that suggests I'm out of my mind and I feel a sudden need to explain.

"I kind of went straight out of school and into wedlock." I hold my hand up and wave in sanctimonious fanfare.

"I'm never getting married," she declares, filling a jug with water.

"Oh. Why not?" I get up from the couch and join her in the kitchen. She gathers plates then hands me cutlery to put out.

"I can't stand the thought of answering to any one person. Ever! I love my freedom. Life's too short"

"I suppose," I reply, wondering if Portland is a breeding ground for the non-committal type. I'm liking Rebecca more by the minute.

"Besides, there are not many men out there who could tolerate me on a permanent basis."

"What do you mean?" I lean my butt against the table and nurse my wine in front of my chest.

When she looks back, she's wearing a mischievous expression on her tilted head.

"Maybe I'll answer that question later. I could use a hand. How are you at chopping lettuce?"

We chat on about travel and what I do, how long I've been married, and, regretfully, Alex must have told her about my recent loss because she mentions my mother. Keeping it brief, I digress and ask about her travel ventures instead. Alex is right. Rebecca is nice and easy to talk to. Then before I know it, Alex returns, looking as sexy as ever and wearing that gorgeous scent I love that overrides the heavenly aroma of curry. What I love more though, is the way Alex is looking at me, and in an instant, I feel that rush of the drug that is Alex. Inwardly I sigh. Why can't he just fall madly in love with me and whisk me away?

When Rebecca finishes getting ready she comes out of the bathroom. The transformation from bohemian to near goth shocks me. She's barely recognizable. I give her an awkward smile then use the bathroom after her. She's left makeup spread all over the vanity making herself right at home. I need to leave. This is stupid of me. When I come back through into the living area, Alex is in the kitchen cleaning up.

"I think I should get going, Alex."

He looks up from the sink, then tosses the tea towel down.

"You don't want to come out with us?"

I shake my head. "I've got an early flight, and honestly, my credit card is nearly maxed out." I gasp and my hand flies to my mouth. "Shit, I just thought of something."

Alex comes over as I'm bending to pick up my clutch, then follows me as I head toward the front door.

"I just realized Gerard will know I was here the other day. You swiped my card, and he's got access to my purchase details. Do you think he'd recognize your merchant name? Shit, shit, shit," I cuss, stopping at the door.

"I didn't use your card, and stop that," Alex says, pulling my fingers away from my mouth.

"You didn't? But you need the money."

Supporting himself with a hand on the wall, Alex pulls some hair away from my mouth and huffs.

"I'm not taking money from you, Paige. Besides, I got something better than money, honey." He flicks my nose with his finger. "Come out with us."

He smells of beer and curry, and cleanliness, and sexiness, and I need him to kiss me. My hand goes up to stroke his face. Then I look toward the hall, making sure Rebecca's not there.

"I really shouldn't." I screw up my face because it's painful to say, and Alex knows I'm trying to convince myself more than him. He grabs hold of my loose hair, pulls it over my shoulder so it cascades down my breast and the back of his hand grazes my taut nipple. The fact that Rebecca is only a few feet away in the bedroom getting changed, makes his flirting all the more intoxicating.

I groan then look to the floor. "Why do you have to be so hot? I don't know what to do, and I don't know how to feel around you."

Looking up, I catch him sizing me up. In a flash he has my ass in his hands and is pressing our pelvises together. My purse slips from my hand and lands on the floor with a thud. I reach out and press against his chest.

"Alex, what if Rebecca comes out?" I say, breathless from the jolt. Alex ignores what seems to be a redundant question.

"I think you, Miss Paige, need to trust your instincts. How do you feel right now?" He grinds himself against me, and again I look toward the bedroom door, expecting Rebecca to come out any second and catch us.

"Well?" he prompts.

"I don't know. Torn, I suppose."

"How about now?" He pauses his grinding and I feel him twitching.

I giggle nervously. "Stop it. What if Rebecca comes out, won't she be hurt?"

"No," he says matter-of-factly, then reaches farther around until his fingers can caress between my legs. I jump at his touch. "Let me tell you how you feel." His breath is directed straight into my ear. "Hot and wet. And you know how I think you feel when you're with Gerard?"

Catching the hint of menace in his tone, I lean back so I can see his eyes. His expression turns challenging, daring me to urge him on.

"Go ahead then. Tell me how I feel when I'm with Gerard, Alex."

"Insecure, lonely, and numb," he says triumphantly, as though he knows it all. "Am I right? That's why you should come out."

I can't answer him. It's too depressing that I'm so transparent.

"Lighten up and have some fun. Come out and see how the other half live."

"What's going on? Aren't you coming out with us?" Rebecca catches the last part of our conversation. She's dressed in a shiny black vinyl or latex dress that comes down over her knees, which screams sex. I admire her beautiful figure then her laced up heels. Now I'm feeling totally underdressed.

"Nice," Alex compliments, nodding his approval before pulling me in tighter.

Rebecca comes our way, her hazel eyes smiling beneath enhanced lashes, and lips made pouty in red. Instead of moving away from me, now that she has returned, I'm surprised that Alex kisses my temple, right in front of Rebecca. She doesn't seem worried at all. In fact, she comes closer and takes my hand. Smiling, she starts pleading, "Please come. It will be fun. Alex needs a date."

"She'll come. She always does," Alex states confidently, releasing me and grinning.

"For sure, big-noter," Rebecca says, dragging me toward the bathroom as I watch Alex disappear toward his room. I assume to get a jacket or shoes.

"Let's fix your makeup and then we'll get going. The club only gets interesting after ten, but I like to arrive a little earlier. I like to people watch. Pick out my prey." She giggles then closes the bathroom door.

"I really should go home," I say half-heartedly knowing I've got no business going about clubbing. I'm supposed to be sensible, dependable. But my logic slips away because the next thing I know, I'm sitting on the toilet lid with Rebecca chatting away in front of me as she redoes my makeup. I'm not even really listening to what she's saying. I'm still going over my conversation with Alex. That Gerard makes me feel insecure, lonely, and numb. He should have added scared. Another reason for me not to go out. What if he finds out somehow? I've been constantly building up a wall of lies and deceit and yet I've the audacity to question Gerard's behavior.

I'm staring at Rebecca, only inches from her face. She is a little older than me, I think. Exuberant and carefree. I feel a longing that's peppered with envy. Alex is right, I'm getting old before my time. I should be out having fun with girlfriends.

"Do you have a birthmark here," Rebecca asks, touching my left cheek. I frown at first but then remember Gerard hitting me and my smile slides away and I reach for my face, my eyes casting to the floor.

"Sorry, I didn't mean to embarrass you, I was just wondering. You've done a good job of covering it up." She takes the brush and adds more blush to my cheeks still smiling then adds, "Not that you should have to." I'm not sure why I don't correct her, tell her what Gerard did. Maybe because I'm ashamed and I don't want to be the downer, and by the time she has straightened my hair with her hot iron, another thing I've never done before, I feel excited about going out. Why spoil the good vibes. I have a young lady standing before me pampering me as though I'm her new best friend, and Alex was practically begging me to come out with them. It sure beats sitting at home licking wounds.

"There," Rebecca says, standing back. "You look stunning. Men are going to gawk at you all night. Maybe even some women." She smiles and arches her penciled in brows. "By the way, I love your necklace, is it an authentic Monica Kosann?"

Looking down, I slide it between my fingers. "It is. Gerard bought it for me."

"Well, it's beautiful. This club we're going to though, it's classy but sometimes there are some slippery fingers around. So just be careful and don't take it off."

Why would I take it off?

"What is—this club we're going to?" I ask, a little panicked by her warning.

"Alex didn't tell you?"

"No. It seems the men in my life like keeping things from me."

Rebecca grabs my hands and pulls me abruptly to my feet. Squirting some oil between her palms, she runs her hands over to smooth my hair. Her eyes are slightly glassy, her pupils large, and I'm guessing she is high on something. Then I get drawn to her lips when she snatches the bottom one between her teeth still preening me.

"It's a sex club," she discloses watching closely for my reaction. I feel a flush rise to my neck and I step out of her reach.

"Oh. I thought we'd be going to a regular night club. I can't go. I'm married!"

When Rebecca curves both eyebrows, I feel an extra flush that no doubt deepens my fair completion. Now I'm certain, Alex has told her about me and him and most likely Gerard as well. No wonder she didn't flinch when Alex kissed me. Rebecca reaches for my hands.

"Please come out with us. You don't have to do anything, in fact, a lot of people just go to watch."

"I should send my husband there. He seems to like to watch," I say sarcastically.

"Maybe he already goes."

Taking in a few deep breaths, I let go of her hands and inch toward the mirror. My newly made-up face shows Rebecca has talent, and with straightened hair, I hardly recognize myself. My green eyes are framed with smoky hues and thicker eyeliner. My brows, usually fair, have been penciled in and emphasized, something I've never felt comfortable doing. I look nothing like myself.

Rebecca puts an arm around me and studies my reflection. "You look great," she nods. "I'm going to call a taxi, but before I do," she pauses and claims something out of her bag, "would you like one of these?" She holds out a plastic container that looks like coffee sweetener.

"A sweetener?" I asked, confused.

She smiles at my ignorance then pulls off the lid. She makes me offer a palm then taps out a capsule.

"My treat. It's Molly. Have you ever tried it?"

I stare at the drug in my hand and shake my head then look up at her. "Does—Alex take these?"

"No. But I can guarantee, he'd be more than happy if you did. Go on, try it."

I've never taken drugs before, at least not the non-prescription kind, and I don't understand why my rational self isn't screaming at me to give it back. But staring at Rebecca, I realize how little I've experienced in life. Suddenly, all I want to do is escape reality. I want to see this elusive nightlife I know nothing about. And maybe finding out more about Alex is what I need. Being with him in his own environment might just dispel the fantasy Gerard insists I've created. An illusion that just last night he seemed intent on terrorizing out of me.

Rebecca nudges my hand toward my face, giving me an encouraging nod. Drawing in a deep breath, I pull an awkward smile. "Promise you'll look after me?"

"Of course, girlfriend. We won't leave your side all night, I swear."

"Well, here goes nothing." With Rebecca's reassurance, I toss back the capsule, then chase it down with water.

Book 3 FREE - THE LUMINOUS PEARL

Turn the page for a preview

FREE

THE LUMINOUS PEARL

1

HIGH ENOUGH

I've never been to a sex club before, so I'm surprised when the taxi weaves its way around an industrial estate then pulls up outside a plain concrete building. The entrance looks like a warehouse office, but unless staff are allowed impromptu parties, the red hue emanating from inside and the slight pulse of music are a dead giveaway as to what's really going on. There are no signs to say what the club is called, and I don't bother to ask Rebecca, who has been laughing and joking with Alex the whole hour it's taken to get us here, because I have no intention of ever returning.

I'd remained quiet for the most part. Opting to watch the world whirl by while we passed through suburbs then hit the highway en route to Hollywood—apparently.

It was a sobering experience, and the longer I sat in

silence listening to Rebecca during the ride in, the more foolish I felt. I have no business going clubbing when my husband is out of town, let alone with another man and his *ex-girlfriend*.

Rebecca has spent the entire time reminding Alex about their past, people they once knew, and reminiscing about their school days. She tried to include me in on their conversation, but I had nothing to contribute. My life seems so trite and uneventful in comparison. She'd ended their witty bantering with a list of things she swore to do before she dies. All of which sounded exciting and so out of my reach. Me being stuck in matrimonial bliss and all. To say I'm feeling a little envious would be an understatement.

Shifting off my tender butt cheek, to relieve the pressure on the raised flesh from where Gerard's belt had made contact last night, I retrieve my purse from beside me and get ready to exit the car. I must be a closet thrill-seeker really. What if there's someone inside that I know? But Rebecca's excitement is contagious. She giggles and flirts as she hands over her credit card to the taxi driver and pays. Suddenly, I'm feeling elated and a bunch of butterflies wreak havoc. Inside that building is a whole world of taboo that I'm just dying to see now.

Outside the taxi, I shiver and grab hold of my pant legs to keep them from soaking up the rain puddles, then dash through the drizzle before Alex is pulling open the reflective glass doors for Rebecca and me to enter. Just as I'm passing him, he grabs my arm.

"If you don't want to go in, you can wait here. I'll just hook Rebecca up with her friend. Then we can go." Alex gestures toward a leather couch in front of a red-painted brick wall covered in a variety of framed notices explaining the club's etiquette and some pop art depicting sex symbols through the ages. Ranging from the late 30s, there's a picture of Marilyn Monroe, Grace Kelly, Brigitte Bardot, and Jayne Mansfield, with Ursula Andress being the most recent. I think. All amazing likenesses, and with their names scrawled across the background it confirms I'm right in guessing who they are.

"Paige?" Alex jolts me to attention, just in time to notice Rebecca disappearing through a large black door to our left. I glance at the couch then back to Alex. Now that we're here, it's too tempting not to take look for myself.

"No, I'll come along."

Once through the door, the dull sound of music comes from behind another closed door next to a desk. This reception room is also painted red and hosts a row of lockers against one wall.

Rebecca confirms our invitation with a bald-headed guy covered in tattoos. He sizes up both Alex and me before holding out his hand for ID and asking all of us to sign some sort of waiver. When I hesitate, Alex squeezes my hand.

"We can still leave."

"No, you're not. Come on, you guys. Hang with us. It'll be fun. Besides, Paige is curious. Aren't you, Paige?" Rebecca chimes in.

I give a small shrug and look up at Alex, who has raised an eyebrow in questioning. From the look on his face, he's not bothered either way, but that just piques my interest more. Is this suddenly something he doesn't want me to see?

Without a debate, Rebecca snatches hold of my hand to tug me along as she pushes through the door and into a scene straight out of Beyoncé's music-clip, 'Haunted.' There are long red drapes hanging at intervals on either side of floor-to-ceiling wooden wall panels, around the large room. Framed mirrors are everywhere, but when my eyes settle on the one closest to me, I realize it's not a mirror but a window that looks down a hallway. I swivel my head, trying to make sense of it. But before I can grasp the illusion fully, Alex is pulling me close and blocking my view.

The club isn't loud. I expected music to be thumping, to see couples drinking, dancing wildly, and sex taking place. The only thing that meets my expectations is the dim lighting and what some guests are wearing. It feels more like an intimate costume party than a nightclub filled with strangers.

Wedged between them, I make Alex and Rebecca walk painfully slow so I can assess the scene. I imagine I must look like a meerkat because I'm twisting my head in all directions and drawing attention. But as curious as I am, I'm starting to have second thoughts about hanging around. Everyone is so uninhibited, it's scary.

Rebecca grips my hand and leans into me, momentarily resting her chin on my shoulder. "It's okay. Nobody will bite. That is unless, you want them to." She must smile because her chin digs in against my bone. I twist and catch the naughty glint in her eyes before she gives me a big grin and tugs me onward.

Everything looks opulent, but dominating the room are two skilled dancers who hold my immediate attention. Their lithe bodies look magnetized to poles anchored to both the floor and the sky-high black ceiling. Lining a backlit bar are stools that look polished and shine like expensive Italian leather. Some are vacant and others nest bums. There's only one bartender, and it seems all he is doing, is filling water jugs with ice. Ultraviolet lighting has turned everything white, bright and the seductive clothing everyone is wearing is quite captivating. Silk gowns, crisp white shirts with loose-laid ties. Stilettos and thigh-high boots seem to be the favor. There are sequins and lace and ladies wearing their hair braided or in sleek ponytails. Pleather corsets, skin-tight underwear, chains, cuffs, and latex is everywhere. Rebecca fits right in.

Alex presses his hand to the small of my back. "Just tell me when you want to leave." He reaches around further to take hold of my waist in reassurance.

"It's okay. But look what they're wearing. I think we need to go home and change," I whisper, my attention still held by a nightlife I've been selectively ignorant to.

"You don't have to dress up, but like I said the other day, I think you'd look good in latex," Alex murmurs close to my ear, letting his hand slide until he is playing with my ass.

"I see Kaitlyn. I'll get drinks," Rebecca announces, letting go off my hand and heading to the bar.

"Is this the type of place you mean when you say you go clubbing, Alex?" I ask, scared now that the haze of lust surrounding me when it comes to Alex might be similar to why I fell for Gerard. My flaw being—I fall in love with the thought of a person without seeing who they really are.

"Sometimes. Let's find a seat," he suggests, taking my hand. I'm not sure if I'm disappointed or intrigued by this new level of knowledge. I mean, it's obvious the man has experience, but the thought of Alex decked out in leather, chains, and whips just doesn't seem to gel, and I can't stop ogling everyone as he leads the way.

The people we come across blatantly size Alex and me up. Their salacious smiles turning into lustful pouts as we pass. I've never seen such a display of eroticism. Couples and groups are freely caressing each other as they talk amongst themselves, and there is a steady stream of people heading down a flight of stairs that intrigues me. Before I know it, my palm is sweating in Alex's hand. I grip him tighter and I don't let go until he slides into a vacant booth. He pulls me in and draws me close. The warmth of his body and deep steady breathing is reassuring, and then I'm aware of the effects the drug I took earlier is having on me. All my senses are heightened. Even my face feels fuzzy.

I look up from under Alex's chin then down at my hand resting on his thigh. It feels like I'm melting into his flesh and I let out a giggle from the strangeness of it all.

"Rebecca gave me Molly before we left your place. I hope I don't do anything crazy."

"Jesus, you don't need that shit."

"I know. But this is the best I've felt in months, maybe even years, or even ever. I had no idea drugs felt this good."

"Yeah, well, Rebecca shouldn't have given it to you."

"She said you'd like me high on it."

Alex rolls his eyes, then turns his attention to the crowd until he settles on Rebecca and her friend. Kaitlyn is the shorter of the two, with tanned skin and on the voluptuous side compared to Rebecca. I glance up at Alex again. He can't seem to take his eyes off them.

"Look at her. She's so fucking out there." He shakes his head. "Sometimes I think she just does it for attention."

Kaitlyn is standing on her toes, trying to reach for something over the bar, and Rebecca is using the opportunity to slide a hand along the back of Kaitlyn's thigh and push her short skirt higher to reveal a round, meaty butt cheek. Kaitlyn, unfazed, wiggles on her toes as if encouraging Rebecca. I can't tear my eyes away. Heat travels not only to my face, but everywhere.

"Are you jealous or something?" I ask, pulling away from him so I can study his expression, praying I'm not going to regret being here. It would be my worst nightmare come true —Alex crushing on someone else.

"Not at all. I just can't believe it's the same chick I grew up with. She was always straight. Not that I give a fuck. She can do whatever she wants. I just worry where she's headed."

"Oh. Well, maybe she's just putting on a show for you. Is she still in love with you, do you think?"

Alex's head snaps around, and he frowns. "No romance there, Princess. We're just friends. Nah, I think she's putting on a show for you, actually."

"Me?" I gasp, taking her in again, then flush in embarrassment when Rebecca looks our way. I quickly divert my attention back to Alex, but I'm sure she caught me gawking.

"Was Rebecca who you went to visit when we were in the city together?"

Alex nods.

I need to make a conscious effort to relax my mouth. It's not because I'm annoyed, but for some reason, I can't stop clenching my jaw, and my mouth is so parched, my tongue feels like a piece of beef jerky.

"God, I feel feverish," I comment, gripping onto the table to pull myself upright again so I can fan my jumpsuit.

Alex chuckles. "That will teach you for taking drugs."

I give him a nudge in the stomach before my attention returns to Rebecca and her friend, wondering if Alex is serious about her showing off for me. Suddenly, I'm panicked that Gerard may have tried calling. I reach into my purse for my phone to check. He hasn't called, but the guilt that I'm out with Alex makes me feel sick, and I stare absently at the screen. I'm such an untrustworthy hypocrite.

Suddenly, there's a man standing beside us. "No phones," he snaps, drawing Alex's attention to me holding my phone.

"Sorry I was…"

"No phones. Lock it and leave it in your purse. Any calls are to be taken or made out in the foyer."

"Okay, okay." I slip my phone back into my purse. It's only when I've snapped it shut and put it on the far side of the table does the security guy leave.

"Christ, that's a bit over the top. What is this place?"

"Photos can be used against someone. *Especially* in a place like this," Alex explains.

"Well, I wasn't going to take photos. I was just seeing if Gerard tried to call."

My admission puts the scowl back on Alex's face. He stiffens before his attention goes back to the girls at the bar, and the hand I place back on his thick thigh doesn't seem to register my apology because he snaps out,

"Wish she'd hurry up with those fucking drinks."

We sit quietly for some time, taking in the music which seems to meld with the scene that's at the bar. Rebecca is still caressing Kaitlyn's ass, making large circles on her bare flesh and with one boot heel poised on a barstool footrest, she sways to the music, daring and enticing Rebecca to do more. Rebecca looks our way again. I feel my embarrassment for only a split second before it gives way to a heady erotic feeling and I'm imagining myself in Kaitlyn's place, Rebecca stroking and caressing my ass. I'm there at the bar, and Alex is watching me with her. Is that something Alex would like to see? Me with another girl.

"Kiss me, Alex," I murmur, pulling myself onto his lap. "I need to feel your lips. I miss them."

"Is that right?" Uncertainty lingers in his squinting gaze, but he shifts in his seat to accommodate me. Then he's laughing. "You're high."

Relieved by the shift in tension, my mouth meets his and I let myself get lost on his lips until they're tingling and melt, and I can't discern the difference between his lips and mine. I forget everything. It's just me and Alex, our uniform breathing and the music. When he pulls back, I'm left breathless and giddy. I open my eyes slowly. Alex is watching me, searching my eyes and drinking me in.

"I love it when you do that, Alex. When you search inside for my soul."

"Is that what I'm doing, is it?"

I nod dreamily and stroke his face without an ounce of inhibition.

"You're just rolling."

"Is that what they call it? God, I'm so high, it feels amazing. I want to know everything about you, Alex. Tell me everything. I just want to hear your voice. I love the sound of your voice. Do you know how often you're on my mind?"

Alex shakes his head, still amused by me.

"All the time. Every day, even when I'm asleep, I hear your voice. I honestly can't get you out of my head. What you said earlier about how I feel around Gerard, you're right, and I don't care if you're a player. I only care that you want me around."

"I'm a player, am I?" His mouth curves downward, his head nodding slightly as though in mock agreement.

"Gerard's words, not mine." I squirm on his lap, desperate to get closer. Alex wraps his arms around me tightly to still me, then plants a kiss on my forehead.

Lingering there, he whispers against my skin. "Well, don't believe everything you hear. Anyway, I should get our drinks. Rebecca doesn't seem to be in any hurry." He sounds a little curt, like I've hurt his feelings. Not knowing what to say, I slide off his lap and stand. I look toward the bar.

Rebecca now has Kaitlyn's skirt around her waist, her ass exposed, and my eyes dart around to see if anyone else is watching. I'm siding with Alex—Rebecca seems to love the attention she's getting because she's teasing two men sitting at the bar who seem to be enjoying the salacious act.

I look at Alex again, take in his eyes, his nose, his delectable lips. I brush the back of my fingers along his stubble then weave my fingers through his hair and give his head a tug.

"Do you enjoy watching girls get it on, Alex?"

"Doesn't every guy?" My breath hitches when his hand is suddenly between my legs, feeling me. I know I must be hot to the touch because he smirks and presses harder.

"I don't know." I glance back at Rebecca and her friend. "But I suppose it looks erotic enough." I turn back and face Alex. "I've never been with a girl."

"No shock there, Princess. But it sounds like I shouldn't have brought you here. I'll turn you wicked."

"Maybe I enjoy being wicked around you, Alex," I tease, pressing against his hand still between my thighs. "This is— interesting," I say, looking around again.

"You think so?" He pulls his hand away and slaps my butt. "I think I need to get you out of here to keep you pure."

"Pfft. Bit late for that. No, I want to stay awhile. As long as I'm here with you, I feel safe."

"I'm right here, Paige." Alex reaches for me again and pulls me closer, his chin resting on my belly. "You know, you look pretty fucking sexy tonight." He drops a kiss between the opening of my jumpsuit, right below my necklace, then pulls back to take the piece of jewelry between his fingers to study it.

I could honestly push him back on the booth seat and throw myself at him right now. It's crazy how relaxed I feel around him, and all I want to do, is make him happy. I glance toward the bar again. Kaitlyn's skirt has returned to its rightful place, and both she and Rebecca are sitting on barstools talking.

"How about I go get the drinks?" I suggest, grabbing my purse and stepping away. Snatching me back, Alex pulls me onto his lap before his mouth dives onto my neck, kissing and nibbling me hungrily then cupping a hand to my breast with a growl. I giggle and look around the room, suddenly conscious that people could be watching us.

"No, I think I should take you back to the beach house and fuck you," he whispers into my ear. "But all right. We'll have one drink, then go."

I stay there in his arms for a moment, enjoying the closeness, the eagerness of him because the drug in my system seems to turn reality into a fantasy that eludes to no consequences. I know I shouldn't be behaving so uninhibited in public with him. There could be people here who know me and Gerard. Everyone is so dressed up, I'm certain I wouldn't recognize anyone, even up close. For a brief second I feel anxious and paranoid that I don't know what I'm doing, but then my feet seem to have a will of their own, and soon, I'm drifting toward the girls at the bar, faking confidence I don't own.

I'm only halfway across the length of the room before a man and woman approach me, halting me in my path. The woman tucks her fine silver blonde hair behind an ear and smiles, then starts fiddling with the top button of her short silk dress that looks authentically Asian. She nudges her partner who is bald, middle-aged, and reminds me of Vin Diesel, though not as robust. I notice the way he is holding his glass tumbler, looking slightly on the feminine side. When he speaks, it confirms my suspicions.

"Well, hello, sweetie," he playfully oozes the noun. "My name is Howie." He runs a hand down my left arm as he makes the introduction then tilts his glass toward his companion. "And this here is Carol."

"Hello." I feel awkward and throw a look back at Alex. To my horror, he is no longer sitting at the booth. I scan around quickly, trying to locate him, and as if people are becoming aware of my presence, they stop talking and look at me for a moment before resuming with their conversations.

"This must be your first time here? Because we..." Ignoring Howie for a moment, I look ahead at the bar for reassurance and see Rebecca and Kaitlyn still seated. I calm myself and draw in a deep breath then turn my attention back to Howie.

"... and we've been watching you over there with your boyfriend and just couldn't tear our eyes away. You're just gorgeous, sweetie," Vin Diesel's doppelganger says, running a finger along the edge of his glass then reaching out to touch my hair.

"Ahh, thanks, I guess."

"What he means to say is, would you'd like to join us in one of the back rooms?" Carol asks, getting straight to the point.

When my eyes go wide, Howie slaps her arm playfully and scolds, "You're meant to ease into questions like that, Carol. God," he says on an exhale. "Now look at her, she's scared."

"What? Oh, sorry, no. I'm just here with friends. I don't do..." I pull a tight apologetic smile. "Stuff—like this."

"You can bring your boyfriend along if you like," Carol suggests, looking around, I assume for Alex, and I'm betting it's the real reason they're inviting me to join them.

"I don't think so. Sorry, I should go. I'm on drink duty."

"Well, if you change your mind, just come looking for us," Howie says, taking a sip from his straw and eyeing me seductively.

Ignoring them, I wander over to Rebecca and when I reach the girls, they are already studying my expression.

"Oh, my God. Did you see that couple trying to hit on me?" I laugh, then take a seat next to Rebecca.

"Well, duh, that's why we're all here," Kaitlyn says, cutting me down sarcastically.

Rebecca slaps her thigh. "Get down bitch, be humble."

Rebecca turns back to me, an apologetic grimace clouding her features. "Don't mind Kaitlyn here, she's possessed by the devil himself."

"Ha, she should hook up with Gerard," I mumble under my breath, putting my purse down and looking for the bartender.

"However." Rebecca keeps speaking. "Paige, Kaitlyn. Kaitlyn, Paige."

"Hello. Nice to meet you." I hold out my hand for Kaitlyn. She takes it then pulls firmly so I'm stretched out over the bar in front of Rebecca, then puts her lips around one of my fingers. I snatch my hand back and fall onto my stool. Rebecca laughs, then slaps Kaitlyn again.

"Stop it, you're frightening her."

In an instant, beads of sweat are dampening my brow and I'm swiveling on my stool looking for Alex. Thankfully, he has returned and is watching us from the shadows of the booth. I give him a little wave. He gestures in return by rocking his wrist in front of his face, encouraging me to get our drinks.

"Kaitlyn is just playing around. Aren't you, babe?"

"I am. It's nice to meet you, Paige," Kaitlyn says. I reward her with a friendlier smile. "Bec tells me you've only just met."

"We had dinner. Rebecca cooked. And—it was excellent."

Rebecca growls and rolls her eyes. "Call me Bec."

"Sorry, Bec it is."

"Bartender," Kaitlyn hollers, clicking her fingers to get the bare-chested male attendant's attention. "We ladies are getting a little dry over here, sir."

Waltzing over as he polishes a glass, the guy looks like he stepped off the edge of a calendar page. "Well, there's two ways I can fix that, ladies," he suggests, winking then placing the glass and towel on the bar. "One, I could serve you drinks, or two, I could take each one of you out the back and fuck you until you come."

We all burst out laughing. Me from shock.

"You know I'm serious." He elbows the wooden surface the drills his eyes into Rebecca.

Kaitlyn rises on her stool and leans over the bar, intercepting his gaze. He twists his head attempting to stare her down.

"Maybe we don't like cock," she says coyly.

Rebecca twists her stool slightly, so she has access to Kaitlyn's ass again, and I watch in disbelief as she runs her hand between her friend's thighs.

"Girlfriend," she says sweetly, catching the bartender's eye. "You're not dry at all." With Rebecca's hand hidden under her friend's skirt and Kaitlyn gyrating her hips, I can only imagine what Rebecca is doing under there. I'm embarrassed to admit it's all very arousing.

"Well then, I guess I only need to service your mouths then." The bartender concludes standing straight. "What'll you have?"

We order our drinks sending the bartender on his way. Then I'm reaching for the pitcher of iced water to pour a glass then drink it down in one go. "I'm so thirsty, it ridiculous."

Rebecca leans into me. "That's the Molly," she whispers, placing a hand on my thigh. "What do you think of the place, is it how you imagined?" She licks her lips, drawing my attention to the shape of her pretty face.

"A little. I can see I've lived a slightly sheltered life though. At least… the latter part." I glance around the room, letting my voice trail off. Rebecca squeezes my leg. She has lost her smile, and her eyes cloud over.

She nods knowingly. "Tough childhood?"

I pull an awkward smile because I really don't want to get into it. Not here, not now. In fact, not ever if I can help it.

"Me too. But we can't let that shit weigh us down." Rebecca lifts a shoulder and tilts her chin, exuding confidence that's hard not to admire. "Just party harder, is my motto."

I cover her hand with mine and squeeze, but when Kaitlyn notices my gesture, she hisses. Abruptly, I remove my hand. Rebecca's quick to respond by slapping Kaitlyn forcefully on the thigh.

"Stop being a bitch, it's not funny anymore. I'll need to punish you if you keep it up." She giggles and makes a joke, which lightens the mood somewhat. At least I think she's joking.

"Promises, promises," Kaitlyn says, dispelling the doubt which has my mind going in all directions.

"I'm going to look downstairs. Want to come with me, Paige? It's interesting," Rebecca asks, taking hold of the drink the bartender places down in front of us.

"No. I'll stay with Alex." I stand, then pick up the Budweiser I ordered for Alex. "Do you want to come to sit with us, Kaitlyn?" I offer hesitantly, knowing I'm not winning her over because Rebecca seems to pay me way too much attention.

"No, I'm good. I like it at the bar." She takes hold of her glass, but she seems to be sulking. I'm about to turn away when Rebecca presses herself behind me, pushing me up against the bar. Kaitlyn looks out the corner of her eyes and rolls her shoulders over her drink.

"I like you, Paige. You're cute but way too innocent," Rebecca whispers, her breath tickling my ear. I sense Kaitlyn's not happy about Rebecca's flirtatious remark by the way she's squeezing her glass.

"I—should go. Alex is waiting."

"Alex is waiting all right, but it's not for his drink," Rebecca purrs, sliding her hands around my waist, her mouth coming closer to my ear again. "You know, he can't stop talking about you, Paige?"

"Really?" I pull back and stare at her, then glance at Alex again.

"But you know what you're doing to him is cruel, right?"

Her remarks hit its target. Suddenly I'm finding something interesting about the floor and rubbing my forehead.

"Hey!" Rebecca lifts my chin with a finger. "I'm just saying. Alex is one of the good ones, you know. He's like a brother to me, and I don't want to see him get hurt. I know you care about him and everything. But I mean, what's with this guy you're married to? Is he an asshole or what?"

"What do you mean?"

Rebecca gives me a look that tells me she's not naïve about what's going on.

I glance over at Alex, who seems to watch us intently, wondering if he asked Rebecca to have a word with me, why he asked me to come out.

Rebecca shrugs and takes another sip, then smiles at Kaitlyn. "Let me guess something?" she says, turning her attention back to me, her eyes roaming over my face, her head tilting from side to side like she's trying to figure something out. "I bet you're a Gemini."

"Libra."

"Hah, so is Kaitlyn. I wonder if you kiss the same." Taking a finger and thumb, she pinches my chin and licks her fiery lips. I can feel Kaitlyn watching and try to look, but Rebecca keeps my face directed at her, gently swiveling me so my back is to Kaitlyn, and I'm now looking at Alex instead. He's watching intently but flicks his gaze across the room. Rebecca taps my chin to get my attention back.

I don't know if it's because I'm rolling, as Alex put it, but I find Rebecca both alluring and intoxicating. She's mysterious yet transparent. Calm but exciting. She's like Alex. A contradiction. The longer she gazes at me, the heavier I'm breathing.

"Let me take you on a tour of this place."

"What?" I murmur in a daze.

"I want to show you what you've been missing since you've been tangled up in matrimonial bullshit."

Then her lips are coming closer, and I do nothing to stop her. When her lips reach mine, she teases, nipping gently, then runs a tongue between my lips. I pull back, shocked by her forward gesture.

"You taste like coconut," she whispers. "I like it. What could you taste?" She searches my eyes.

"Um… Bubble—gum. I think." I'm shocked that I let her kiss me. I stare at her lips, mesmerized by the memory. How they tasted and how soft they felt.

Rebecca is a canvas of lust. Licking then rubbing her lips, satisfied. I look nervously in Alex's direction. Even though Rebecca made the advance, it feels like a betrayal, nevertheless. I twist around and catch Kaitlyn chuckling and wonder what's so funny.

"Sorry," Rebecca apologizes. "It's the Molly. It makes me just love everybody." She rubs my arms. "Kaitlyn, can you take Paige's purse and our drinks to the table, please? I'm taking her on a tour of the place. Can you let Alex know where we're going?"

"What—fucking—ever. Maybe I'll suck his cock while we're waiting."

I hope she's not serious. Would Alex let her? Not giving me a chance to see if Kaitlyn even goes over to Alex, Rebecca takes my hand firmly and leads me away. When we're out of earshot she says, "Seriously, that woman drives me crazy sometimes. We aren't even dating, and she's possessive as all hell."

I don't comment, and I'm sure I look like the newbie I am as I'm taken along a darkened hallway and past the toilet block, because everyone we pass smiles and wiggles their eyebrows. Then we're turning left onto some stairs.

"Now. Don't freak out. We are just looking, okay?" Rebecca says over her shoulder.

"O—kay."

"You've got to keep in mind, people come here willingly," she says, navigating down the stairs in her heeled boots and gripping her spare hand on the rail.

The walls, painted a deep pink musk color, are dotted with framed black and white erotic photos of people clad in leather and chains, bound and gagged. Holy crap, this place is totally a bondage and discipline club. I jerk on Rebecca's hand.

"Ah… Bec. I really don't think this is my thing."

"I'm not saying it is. I just want to show you something. I promise I won't let anything happen to you." She pulls me a few reluctant steps down. I'm feeling ill. What the heck am I even doing here? Is she trying to tell me Alex is into this kinky stuff? Maybe Gerard knew and has been trying to protect me from this, always insisting Alex is a player. Is this what he means? I come to an abrupt halt and jerk my hand out of Rebecca's.

"Come on, don't be such a baby. Everyone here is a consenting adult." Rebecca grabs my hand again. When she sees my concerned face, she lets go. "What's wrong?"

"Does—Alex do this kind of thing? I mean, was this the kind of thing him and you were into when you were dating?"

"Dating? We've never dated. More like fuck buddies, and I don't know. Maybe you need to ask him. You can go back upstairs, but I'm going to see what's happening in the viewing rooms."

Viewing rooms? Christ, maybe Gerard does come here.

Rebecca moves on without me. Interested to know about Alex and viewing rooms and people jumping bones with strangers, and now that the pressure is off, I follow her slowly down the stairs until we're standing in another long hallway. The passageway itself is dimly lit, illuminated solely by a series of windows to the left. Along the right wall are nothing but doors and more artwork. If that's what you can call it. Old iron chains and things that look like ancient torture devices, and more erotic photos adorn black walls. Thinking of Oliver, I try to spot a signature but don't find one. But I'm certain these are the type of photos he'd shoot.

The closest window to us is only a few feet away. Rebecca marches toward it and peers in. I assume there is nothing going on behind the glass because she quickly moves onto the next window. and then the next. Finally, she stops at the last window and coaxes me to join her.

I want to look, but I don't want to see. Once I've seen it, I know I cannot unsee it. I'm terrified that it will taint how I regard Alex. But with curiosity getting the better of me, I step forward, my eyes focusing on Rebecca as she stares longingly in the window. She checks to make sure I'm coming, and as I pass the first window, I glance in expecting it to be empty, but it's not.

Stopping dead in my tracks, I'm embarrassed that I've caught a couple in the throes of lovemaking. Afraid they have seen me, I retrace my steps, my stomach doing a flip-flop. What if I see someone I know? I'll never be able to look at them again. I should turnaround, go back upstairs and ask Alex to take me home, but I'm too intrigued now, especially when Rebecca turns with a big grin plastered across her face.

"They can't see or hear you, Paige, go ahead, watch."

After a moment of hesitation, I move in front of the window again and see a masked gentleman with his partner lying face down on the bed. Her ass is in the air and he's fucking into her. His eyes are locked on his reflection in a large mirror on the right-hand wall, and the woman is gripping the bedsheets as though for dear life. When the man pulls out of her, I can understand why. His appendage is massive. My face contorts. Can she really be enjoying that?

Intrigued and slightly aroused, I stay to watch when he rounds the bed, his companion waiting for his next move. She's still on all fours, her fists still knotted. Slowly, the man kneels on the bed in front of her. Then a door next to the mirror opens and I guess it's someone who may have been in the next room watching through the mirror. This man is not wearing a mask. He is bigger in stature but his cock not as ridiculously large. The two men exchange words that I can't hear, but the woman on the bed looks up and smiles at the intruder. Still in position, the woman looks ahead and reaches for the first man's erection. He feeds himself into her mouth before the second man moves around to the other side of the bed and takes hold of her ankles. The first man quickly removes his cock just in time, so the woman doesn't scrape him with her teeth as the second man flips her over and jerks her roughly toward his awaiting penis.

Even though he's so rough and demanding, I'm shocked by how my body reacts. Anxiousness and excitement coalesce and then I'm tingling everywhere. I can't imagine why Rebecca moved on past them—this alone is enough, my racing heart and damp panties being a clear indicator.

Not quite as intimidated now, I skim past the other rooms, barely looking in. Rebecca turns as I approach, a broad, lush smile still on her face. Her eyes are wide with fervor, her pupils large and hungry to see more by the way she turns back in an instant, leaving me to sidle up shyly beside her. I peer into the room. What's going on behind the glass is so confronting, I gasp. Then in an almost infantile manner, I reach for Rebecca's hand and grip tightly, then move until I'm standing slightly behind her, as though for protection.

"I know, right," she says, twisting her face to look at me. "How dirty, hot is that?"

BUY BOOK 3
NOW

To discover more books by Ariana Keddie and be notified of new releases, deals and specials, visit:
arianakeddie.com

ACKNOWLEDGMENTS

I have so many people to thank for helping me get the Bound by Infidelity trilogy published, even those who indulged me without judgment when I began with, "Yeah, so I'm writing a book," and I can assure you, there were plenty of unsuspecting ears, too many to name. But to all those who listened and didn't roll their eyes, thank you. Your interest and encouraging smiles helped me to believe in myself.

Firstly, I'd like to thank my husband Mick. Wow, what a journey you took me on to get me where I am today. Thank you for all your support and encouragement. For believing in my talent regardless of the lack of evidence to support the fact I have any. You have come through for me in so many ways.

Jay-Jay, you brave, patient, indulgent little girl of ours. Thank you for giving me the space to find my writer's voice. Those red flowers truly were a gift from beyond this realm. Without you handing them to me, I wouldn't have persevered to live this, my passion, my dream. A big shout out must also go to you for compiling the playlist. Songs that evoke the true essence of my story. It was a huge task and your selections and ear for music is to be commended. The list can be found on Spotify.

Mare, I will never forget you. I dedicated the first book to you because you gave so much to me when I really needed the shove. Not just knowledge, praise, and encouragement but you also shared the pain of real-life tragedies that made me realize these stories need to be told and told in a way that brings empowerment to those who read them. While the topic of my story I know is too close to your bones to read, I hope I have done you proud. I feel honored that you shared so much with me even though we've never met face to face. I love you Mare, for making me forgive myself, for believing in myself, and most of all, for loving myself.

Kira, against your initial reluctance to read your mother's cringe-worthy erotic words, you sucked it up as my first reader. Thank you for being honest and then later, proud. It means so much to now have your admiration and constant encouragement.

To my beta readers that followed. Terrianne, Joy and Timma, thank you. Your feedback gave me more purpose, and my writing got better because I drew from all the experiences we women collectively share.

To developmental editor Cate Hogan. Thank you so much for pointing me in the right direction when assessing my first chapter. Your advice was paramount in crafting this novel to have readers wanting more.

Amber, thank you for beta reading and proofreading draft copies along the way. You did a great job daughter, and thanks for the deadly truth, "No mother. Never, ever use the word moist. EVER!"

To all my family members, thank you for your enthusiasm and undying encouragement. Tyson, my son, for taking me seriously and putting me onto a talented author by the name of Harry Colfer. While Harry's work is not in the same genre as mine, I drew inspiration from his talent then later got to know him which made the world of published authors not so intimidating. Not to mention he also loaned me his grammar guru wife to go over my work.

A massive big thank you to second editor Marni MacRae. Not only is Marni a published author herself, but a fantastic resource who goes above and beyond. I'm so glad I found you Marni. Getting praise and help from another author is truly a gift.

Thank you to those of you who received an ARC and said they loved it. I appreciate your interest and for reading my debut work.

Thank you, author Gerard Byrne for allowing me the use of an excerpt from his novel, © Nemesis Publishing Limited / Gerard Byrne - *No Man's Audience.* You can purchase his interesting and well written book here.

Thank you to all those authors, song writers, bloggers, platforms and writing aids that help writers become published authors. Your advice and online services have been a godsend and truly invaluable.

And finally, the biggest thanks need to go to you, dear reader. Thank you from the bottom of my very humble heart for buying my novel. I hope you enjoyed the fictitious representation of true-life drama as much as I enjoyed bringing it to life.

If you enjoyed LURED - The Unrivaled Serpent, please visit Goodreads and write a review.
By leaving a review, you help authors get noticed for their work so they can bring more exciting stories for your enjoyment.
Thanks again for purchasing my book.

♥ Ariana

ABOUT THE AUTHOR

Ariana Keddie is the author of suspenseful, sexy, intriguing fiction. Growing up addicted to romance novels, it seemed a natural progression to hone her passion for writing to become a junkie of the craft. Spending most of her spare time researching the art of storytelling, Ariana hopes to resonate with an audience via her writer's voice. A voice she found while struggling with personal demons which became the inspiration behind her debut work, *Lured - The Unrivaled Serpent.*

In quick succession *Bound - The Catalytic Rose* was published followed by *Free -The Luminous Pearl* to complete the *Bound by Infidelity* trilogy.

A lover of animals, fine wine, and Byron Bay, when Ariana isn't behind her laptop, she spends her time helping her cowboy husband on their Queensland properties and creating memories with their family.

To find out more about Ariana Keddie visit
arianakeddie.com